The Slaves of Tenebrae

**** * ** *** **** * *** * * ***

R.J. Jewell

Published by Caelum Archives

For information contact CaelumArchives@gmail.com

Edited by Katrina L. Hayrynen

Cover art and design by Brooke Hayrynen

First Edition

ISBN 979-8-9884450-0-5 (paperback)

ISBN 979-8-9884450-2-9 (ebook)

ISBN 979-8-9884450-1-2 (hardcover)

All referenced scripture is in the public domain

...that seeing they may see, and not perceive;
and hearing they may hear, and not understand;
lest haply they should turn again, and it should be forgiven them...

To my dearest Charity,

As I sit to write, I find myself laughing over your last letter once again. You certainly are your mother's daughter! Nothing gives me more satisfaction than to hear that the ones I care most about are happy and thriving. Please know that you are greatly loved, my dear girl, and give your little siblings and your parents my love as well.

I must confess, it was with great interest that this grey-whiskered historian received your request about the documents in my keeping. You see, the thought has also been growing in my own mind that these significant records should be shared. That being so, my beloved granddaughter, I have written a detailed account for you. Compiled from various sources including my father's letters, state documents, recorded interviews, and also much of my mother's diary, this account concerns the great battles and momentous events of their time so that these histories may be remembered in the ages to come.

For we know the golden age of man, as foretold, will span the length of many years. Therefore, it seemed fitting to me to satisfy your wish of furnishing a record for succeeding generations—in hopes that the lessons gleaned in times of trouble might not be wholly forgotten in the coming days of prosperity and long-lasting peace.

Your adoring grandpa,
Able Stalwart Crux

The Slaves of Tenebrae

**** * ** *** **** * *** * * ***

Being the first installment of

The Assorted Archives and Histories of the Kingdom of Caelum

Including excerpts from both the ancient and modern eras

**** * ** *** **** * *** * * ***

Compiled by Able S. Crux

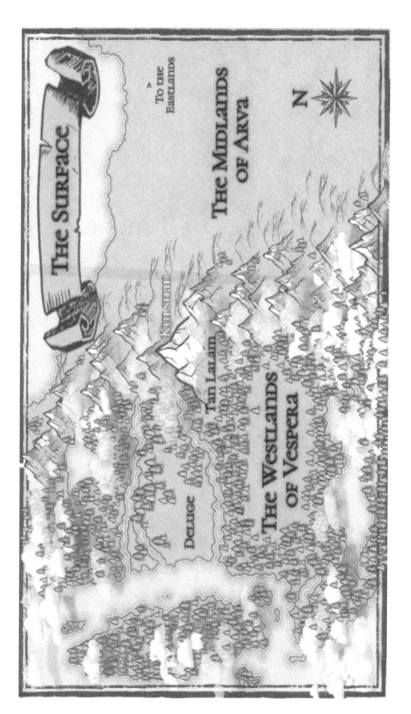

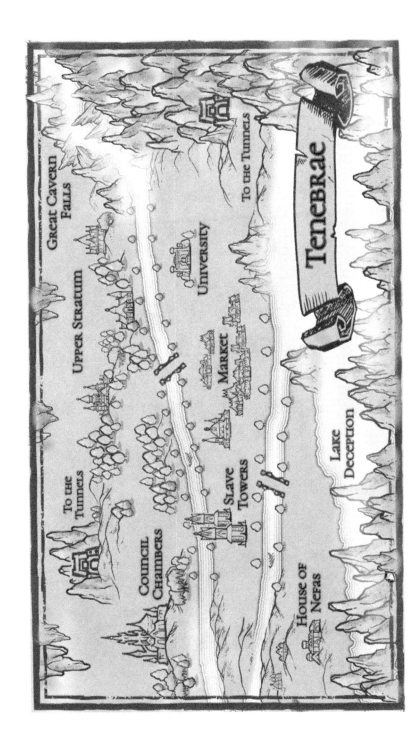

Contents

Chapter 1

The City of Darkness

T here was once a city, miles below ground, where children were told fairy tales at bedtime about something called the sun. It was a very advanced civilization—if you call inventing many magical machines, and many terrible ways to treat people, civilized.

This city's name was Tenebrae. It had an opulent, levitating train so magnificently swift that it raced the light as it glided above the city boulevards. There were avenues lined with flowering, sweet-scented trees and alluring canals full of dark, teeming water. And, when anyone became ill, there were advanced machines that the people of Tenebrae would lie in to make them well.

In the heart of this city lived a girl named Stella. Stella was a slave. She had lived and served, for as long as she could remember, in the home of a couple who were very advanced in age. They were not a sweet, old couple, treating her as the daughter they never had; instead, they treated her in the way people do when they want to make themselves feel bigger, by making others feel small. But they were the only family that Stella knew, and she was happy in her way, not knowing anything different.

The old man eventually died, and a month later, the old lady succumbed as well. The estate agent had come, and Stella found herself being priced and sold with the rest of the old couple's possessions. She was taken to the Tenebrae slave towers, and there, by chance (if chance you would call it), she was purchased by the household of a great scientist of the city. He was called Dr. Nefas.

Dr. Nefas was famous for performing many experiments that the people of Tenebrae loved (and his slaves dreaded)—like the one where he had a slave boy walk across a busy avenue blindfolded or the experiment where he sent a slave girl over the Great Cavern Waterfall on a big rubber duck. Dr. Nefas had many ideas and many slaves to try them out on.

He also had a very large and very messy laboratory with all sorts of inventions scattered about. Some of them were finished, but many were not. One machine that Dr. Nefas had built was an enormous atom race track that moved particles around at incredible speeds. He found that if he made them move fast enough and then smashed them into each other, they made enough energy for all sorts of delightful weapons. He discovered that it could also be useful in sending and receiving messages from other places—places that average people didn't even know existed. He thought very highly of himself for this discovery.

Another one of his impressive inventions looked like an oval table that had arching arms over the top. With it, using very complex mathematical equations and massive amounts of data, he could tell the probability of an outcome in any situation—that is just another way of saying it could predict the future. He called it the looking glass. For years, it was his favorite invention. He spent countless hours poring over and experimenting with this machine, manipulating future events to his heart's desire. This was how he had been able to increase his wealth and fame exponentially and out-maneuver all his enemies.

But not anymore. Something had changed. It started predicting something he didn't like (he would never say what exactly). No matter what he tried, he couldn't change it. Eventually, when he got tired of it not predicting what he wanted, he just turned it off. It was now pushed into a neglected corner, covered with a blanket of dust.

The looking glass had been powered by something called the yellow book. Above all of the devices in the doctor's laboratory, this strange object had the most mysterious origin. Nobody knew exactly how or when he had found it, and there were all sorts of strange stories told about where it had come from and what it was for. Dr. Nefas didn't even really understand how it worked or how dangerous it could be, but that never stopped him from experimenting with it (he always had his slaves do all the dangerous parts). In the last few months, he had built a mechanical mirror and powered it with the mysterious book. The Tenebrae mirror was what he was experimenting with now.

'I have recently discovered that this device,' he would explain to his slaves, using his best authoritative voice, 'when handled in a particular manner and when exposed to certain external and internal stimuli, will cause the most amazing and extraordinary reaction.' This was his way of saying that it did something odd, but he didn't know why. Dr. Nefas did not like to use simple and direct language. On the contrary, he enjoyed using language that complicated things whenever possible. The people of Tenebrae asked fewer questions that way, and he did not like to be questioned.

When his slaves weren't helping Dr. Nefas with his experiments, their time was spent working in the kitchens and cleaning his house. Since Dr. Nefas was a very messy person—most scientists are, you know—and his house was very large, his slaves never ran out of work to do.

Stella, being a tier-one slave (the lowest of all), was given the jobs that no one else wanted and the chores the other slaves were too busy to do. One day, she was told to go to the market and buy some things that were needed; so Stella put on her shoes and set out. Along the way, she crossed over a bridge and stopped for a moment to look at the beautiful gondolas passing by in the water below her.

There was, without a doubt, a bewitching beauty to the city of Tenebrae. Its extravagance was magnificent, but just as breathtaking, Stella knew first-hand, was the dark, heartless cruelty beneath.

She turned her face up to the soft glow, high above Tenebrae, that spanned across the city. During the day, the lofty cavern roof was lit up in brilliant tones of blues and violets; and at night, its distant surface sparkled with precious gems and countless shimmering stalagmites. While she lingered, her ears heard the familiar gentle hum of the levitating trains that followed their gleaming paths in a lightning-fast, choreographed dance, carrying the stratas wherever they wanted to go.

The stratas were the rulers of Tenebrae. These were who Tenebrae was built for. Living lives of luxurious pleasure, they were relatively few in number and never married outside of their circle. Those who did were cast out of their ranks.

As a result, over the countless years, the social and physical traits of the stratas had diverged noticeably from the rest of Tenebrae. When they grew past childhood, their skin took on a translucent, almost deathly shade. The lifespan of the privileged few was also greatly extended beyond that of the general Tenebrae population— almost threefold—seeming proof that their rule was firmly established beyond the influence of mere men and ordained by the gods. All of Tenebrae existed to serve these few masters. All were owned either by the stratas or the corporations that were owned by them.

Stella's eyes scanned out over the water past the levitating trains' grand terminal, beyond the buzzing, upscale market in the business district, and onto Odhrán's Bridge afar off. It was a wide, stone bridge that stretched across the deep, churning rapids of the great canal and led into the section of the city called Upper Stratum. Carved into its sides was the image of a grotesque, writhing sea serpent.

That part of the city, as its name suggested, was not for all stratas. It was where the most powerful, highest stratas—the elite of the elite—resided and did their entertaining. The road there abruptly transitioned from the common, rough concrete of Tenebrae to smooth-polished, white marble paving stones. There were many great houses with ornately carved moldings, casements, and pillars whose properties were lined with flower-laden trees and gardens, most echoing the theme of water serpents. Every house was a masterful work: each larger and statelier than the one before. There was more green vegetation in that part of the city than anywhere else in Tenebrae. It was very beautiful, even from where Stella stood distantly gazing.

After a few moments, as she was turning to go, Stella caught movement out of the corner of her eye. There was a boy nearby. He was about her age. He was leaning precariously over the edge of the bridge, reaching for a tree branch that angled out over the water, where a large orange was hanging.

'Boy, aren't you afraid you'll fall in?' Stella asked him.

'No,' he replied, looking at her. 'Why should I be afraid?'

'Because you might fall,' she repeated matter-of-factly.

He glanced down. 'It isn't too far. Anyway, it's worth a shot.'

He stretched farther and grazed the orange with his fingers. She watched him doubtingly and then looked at the orange. She never ate such food at home. Slaves rarely had fruit in their rations. It was an impractical food: much too sweet and lacking in calories. But it *did* look very good.

He suddenly caught the edge of the branch between his fingers and pulled it toward himself. With his other hand, he reached out and plucked the orange from the branch.

'You did it!' Stella chimed happily.

He hopped down off the ledge and grinned at her. 'I'm Abon. What's your name?'

'I'm—' she paused, hesitating. It was foolish to tell a stranger who she was. Instantly she felt shy. 'I'm . . . I'm on my way to the market,' she said remembering her errand. 'I'd better go, or I'll be late.'

'I'll go with you,' he offered.

'Won't your owner be angry?' she asked.

'I don't have an owner,' he replied. 'I escaped.'

Stella's eyes grew big. 'Aren't you afraid they will find you and beat you?' she asked breathless.

Abon laughed. 'He would beat me anyway if I was still there.' His eyes flashed. 'I would like to see him try now.'

They talked as they walked along the avenue. Abon peeled his orange and offered half to her.

'But it's yours. You don't have to share,' Stella said surprised.

'But that's just it. I didn't grow the tree. I just picked the orange.' Abon paused, thinking. 'Somebody else planted the tree and takes care of it, right? We just get to enjoy it. There was a time,' he said

5

lost in thought, 'when I was so focused on my own misery, I didn't even notice that these were fruit trees.' His arm swept through the air in a wide arc towards the long, solemn lines of trees.

'What happened?' Stella asked curiously.

He glanced back at her. 'I learned the truth,' he said simply.

Stella got the impression that he was implying more.

'Anyway, this is a big orange,' he grinned. 'There's enough for both of us.'

Stella smiled and took the half he offered. She ate it thinking that it was the best thing she had ever tasted—like water from a fresh spring blended with sweet spices. As they walked, they talked about many things.

'How did you escape?' she asked Abon when she had worked up enough courage.

He looked at her, contemplating for a moment, and then began, 'I wasn't born in Tenebrae. I was stolen from my home, but a group of travelers saved me. They took care of me and set me free. Now, I help them in their work.'

'What do you do?' she asked, intrigued.

He looked at Stella intensely. 'We rescue children from Tenebrae.'

* * *

Stella couldn't get the boy from the bridge out of her head. They had met now several times, but still she hadn't told him her name. Though he had asked more than once, she had never found the courage to tell him; she was too afraid. What if he came to her house asking for her? He seemed to have no fear, but Stella shuddered at the thought of what could happen. He was so different than anyone she had ever met.

She volunteered for every errand possible, just to meet with Abon and hear more about his many adventures. His life seemed so strange and exciting to Stella. Now on the days when she was sent for supplies, instead of walking to the city center, Stella would run. And, when she reached the market, she would look anxiously around, hoping to see her one friend in the world. Most days he was there waiting, and it soon felt unnatural for Stella to not have Abon strolling by her side as she shopped. He told her about the people who had helped him and about their leader, whom they called high commander. He explained that the commander served a great king who lived far away.

'Do you mean the Creature of Mare?' Stella asked puzzled. She had been taught, like all Tenebraean children, that the ultimate ruler was a terrible sea serpent. He was savage and strong, having taken for himself the power of the gods.

'No,' Abon replied, 'the high commander serves a different king—a wise king who is more powerful than even the monster of the sea.'

Many stories had been told about the terrible things that the Creature of Mare had done to people. Stella decided that the great ruler sounded spiteful and cruel next to Abon's king. He told her that, with the help of the high commander, they had rescued many children from the city.

'Rescued them from what?' Stella asked confused.

'In my country,' Abon explained, 'children are not slaves. They are not bought or sold. They are not experimented on or sent down waterfalls or lava vents. They are free.'

Stella paused, trying to understand. *Was that true? Could there be a place where children lived differently? Free?* Stella wasn't sure what it meant to be free, but she thought it sounded very nice.

One afternoon, Abon grew quiet as Stella finished her shopping. He watched her take the automated receipt from the door as they left.

As they stepped onto the market street, Stella turned to him. 'I'll come back as soon as I can, but it will probably be a few days at least. Good-bye, Abon,' she said and turned to go.

'Wait,' Abon said, stopping her, 'there's something I need to tell you.' Regret was written on his face.

'What is it?' Stella asked.

'I . . . I will be leaving soon,' he said, shoving his hands into his pockets. 'I'm leaving Tenebrae. They are taking me back to my home—the place that I was taken from. It's very far away. They tell me we're going to leave soon.' He frowned. 'This is the last time I'll be able to see you.'

Stella stood in shock, unsure of what to say. She felt betrayed by him but wasn't even sure why. *It's not like he has a choice; why shouldn't he go home?* She bit her lip. She should feel happy for him, but instead, she only felt hurt. He was looking at her, gauging her expression. She forced herself to give him the answer that she knew he deserved.

'That's great, Abon. You'll get to see your family again.' She tried to smile.

He saw her effort, and his eyes softened. 'I will miss you.'

'I'll miss you too,' Stella told him in a choked voice. She didn't want him to see her cry. 'Good-bye, Abon.' She turned suddenly and dashed away, leaving Abon in the road staring after her.

'Good-bye,' he said quietly to himself as she disappeared from his sight.

One of Abon's companions, who had been watching the exchange from across the water, approached in haste. Having caught a glimpse of Stella, he hurried to Abon with alarm. 'Abon, who was that girl you were speaking with?'

'It was the girl that I told you about, Malachi,' Abon replied sadly. 'The one I met on the bridge.'

Malachi was still looking for her in the crowded market street. It was no use; she was gone. 'What is her name?'

'She never told me,' Abon answered.

'Do you know where she lives?' he asked with urgency.

'No,' he said shaking his head, looking at his friend questioningly.

'We'll have to find her,' he said frowning, his eyes still scanning the city.

'Why, Malachi? What's wrong?' Abon asked him.

The man turned his eyes to the boy. 'I recognized her the moment I saw her, even at a great distance. The commander has been looking everywhere for her.'

The men delayed their departure from Tenebrae for some time, searching diligently for any trace of the girl. Abon waited for many long hours each day, hoping for Stella to return to the market where they had last met. But she never did.

* * *

Stella had been so upset by Abon's news that she had run without knowing or caring where she was going until she was too tired to go on. By the time she had come to herself, she saw that she was in quite a distant part of the city. She immediately realized her folly and turned, making her way back as fast as she could, but the journey took her much longer than normal.

By this time, the slave manager, Atrox, had become suspicious of the girl and decided that she needed to be taught a lesson. He was waiting for her when she finally approached. Atrox was a large man with a massive head. His sleeves were rolled up over his great biceps, and Stella could see the house crest clearly on his forearm: a great horned owl clutching a sprig of holly in one claw and an ivy leaf in the other. It was the symbol of her new master's estate: the house of Nefas. Outlined by two thin lines, it indicated that the imposing man was manager class. Below the symbol were five black strokes: tier five. Stella's forearm had been etched with the same crest on the day she arrived here but with only one thin outline and one solitary stroke beneath, for she was the lowest of all slaves: tier one.

He stepped directly in front of her. 'You, girl!' he snarled.

Stella's eyes grew wide. She hadn't spoken to the manager since moving here but had seen enough to want to avoid him at all costs. *What could he want with her? Did he know what she had been doing?* Her heart pounded in fear.

'Where have you been?' he asked her sharply.

'To the market, sir,' Stella responded, feeling a knot forming in her stomach.

'And what did you buy, girl?' he asked her, his deep voice growing menacingly quiet.

With her trembling hand, Stella held out the basket of disheveled groceries for him to examine. His eyes narrowed, and he nodded slowly, silently observing her. Stella felt beads of moisture form on her forehead. Still, he watched her in silence for what seemed like hours. Finally, he spoke.

'You belong to Dr. Nefas,' he said, 'but you answer to me, tier-one. I've noticed that your little trips to the market take much too long. Every slave in this house gets a proper reception sooner or later to remind them of one thing: to do as they're told. Today is your lucky day.'

He put a firm hand around the back of her neck. 'Those who don't listen, live to regret it,' he said, his eyes laughing at the rising terror in her own. He pulled her forcefully into the house.

In a guard room off the service entrance, two Tenebrae soldiers were waiting. Atrox called to them as he entered. 'The tier-one is finally here. Give her a low, first level penalty.'

He shoved her towards them, and they took hold of her. 'Just a light, *facile* beating, mind you,' the manager added, eyeing her closer. 'I need her able to work first thing in the morning, and she doesn't look very promising.'

Although, by law, Stella belonged to this new house, her true slave master was fear and that tyrant had long held her in his cruel grasp, widely amplifying all her suffering. The soldiers began to strike her, and she cried out, but her cries only encouraged the soldiers. They took turns hitting her, light-heartedly and jovially counting aloud the required number of hits, until she fell, and then they struck and kicked her on the ground.

Before their count was over, the first guard put out his hand, 'Stop, Leger!' he said, restraining the other guard. 'She's had enough.'

Leger looked down, observing her. To his surprise, Stella lay unconscious, her head still loosely covered by her arms. He immediately halted; the law forbade the lowest level penalty to continue if the offender lost consciousness.

Disappointed, the guards backed off as the manager approached. 'She really is weaker than most, isn't she?' Leger commented with a laugh. 'Nefas isn't getting his money's worth out of this one. Next time, give us a challenge, Atrox. I'm sick of going easy,' he grumbled.

'Go to the front then, Leger. You can kill all the foreigners you want there,' Atrox said sharply. 'Until then, I have no more slaves to spare for you. The science program is taking all the excess I have.'

'Rumor has it that Nefas has an invention that will win the war,' the first guard commented.

'Maybe he does; maybe he doesn't,' Atrox hedged non-committally.

'Well, he'd best get one if he doesn't have one already,' the guard said, eyeing him closely. 'The council is expecting it.'

Atrox said nothing. They all knew what the council was capable of if angered. There was no use in talking about it.

As the guards left, Atrox called over a male slave. 'Take the tier-one to her bunk,' he ordered, motioning to the girl.

He watched as the man lifted Stella's limp form. The girl had only been here a few months, but she was already a disappointment, Atrox concluded, shaking his head. She was too weak. What was he thinking, accepting that timid, scarecrow of a girl from the towers? He should have refused her and sent her back the moment he laid eyes on her. She was never going to amount to much. He needed his slaves to be hearty and strong enough to pull their weight. He had seen enough slaves to know this child most certainly wouldn't survive—a pity.

Atrox shrugged. Sometimes he won, and sometimes he lost. If she didn't keep up, he would use her as compensation with the Tenebrae soldiers. He needed their protection, and an occasional tier-one was an easy way to keep them pacified. It wasn't a matter of importance; there were plenty more to take her place. Who cared if one meager slave lived or died?

Chapter 2

The Chasm Dwellers

The gorgeously arrayed former knight of Caelum arrived in all his splendor, a handful of followers pouring into the throne room after him. He no longer wore the uniform of Caelum; in its stead, he wore a rich garment of shimmering, golden cloth. A haughty look was in his eye, and rebellion was on his brow.

Miguel and his soldiers barred the way as he tried to advance toward the great dais. 'No farther, Oran,' Miguel commanded. 'You have been banished by order of the King. Return to wherever you've come from.'

'You know where I have been, Miguel,' the former knight answered pointedly, 'but why not say it in front of the whole court?' He turned his resplendent form away from the throne and toward the hosts of Caelum, gathered together in the court of the mighty King. All had been summoned and were present; not one was missing.

'I have come from a great journey, and I have discovered for myself the truth about what the King has been doing. I have seen it with my own eyes. And what of our domains, those very empires that we nurtured and protected for untold years? He is giving them away. Already, the dominion of our great people is diminished. Even on Terra and Mare, the King has granted full stewardship into foreign hands: debased and weaker than our own.

'Why has our leader done this—instead of choosing one of the mighty and deserving among you for this great honor? How else are we to interpret this act but as a grave insult? By this, what is the High One telling us?' Oran looked around with deliberateness, cleverly crafting his narrative in their minds.

Slowly, with significance, he pointed accusingly to the magnificent throne. 'Our great leader of old is displaying to us that he is great no longer. The wisdom of age has finally passed into the age of infirmity. Once rich in counsel, now he has given reign to foolishness and abandoned dominion for weakness. The old is passing away. The security and strength of the realm of Caelum can endure no longer under such a leader!'

The court was held entranced by the clever words of Oran. His beauty and the spell of his voice were powerful enough to cast doubt in the minds of even the great Caelum knights. The multitude stood harkening to his poisonous speech until the Lord of the realm stood. Oran's smooth words then faltered as, suddenly, all eyes turned to the King.

The vast beauty, power, and glory of the Caelum host shone in that place, but all paled in comparison to the gloriousness of the King. He was clothed in power and goodness. Light radiated from him and, like a rainbow, seemed to surround him. He was very old—beyond reckoning. His silver hair glimmered beneath a golden, gem-filled crown, and yet age had not diminished him. He still had the appearance and bearing of a warrior in the zenith of his strength. Deep wisdom was in his glance, and might was in his right hand.

He looked down from his great throne to where Oran stood, and the ground trembled at his voice. 'Enough, Oran,' he said with authority, truth slicing through the web that Oran had woven. 'You would enslave multitudes in your desire for power. Do you think that you can hide your heart from me? In truth, you seek your own glory and revenge for your banishment—not Caelum's security nor her greatness.

'What right have you to question what I do? I made you the greatest of my knights. And that is what you became, before you, in your lust for your own greatness, turned against your King and your country. Have I not called your name Oran? Light and song no longer follow you. I now call your name Odhrán. You have proven yourself unworthy, and for that, you were stripped of your titles and banished.'

Odhrán felt rage and a deep hatred well up inside himself but deemed it unwise to answer the King. Instead, he turned to the court where the minds of the multitude might still be swayed by his cunning words.

'He is mocking us! Do not be deceived by his caring tone towards you or his generous condescension; he cares not for any of you! Great and shining army of Caelum, will you suffer to be insulted in your servitude to a tyrannical fool while the realms fall to ruin around you?'

His persuasive voice painted a vivid picture in each of their minds. They imagined themselves breaking free of their bonds to save the drowning realms from utter destruction and, in doing so, ruling all-powerfully in the King's stead.

Odhrán's eyes shone with enticement and unparalleled charm. 'Join with me, all you mighty ones! Together we will create a new realm in Caelum. Our time has now come. We will finally overcome the Old One, and we will rule now. Throw off his yoke and fight with me!'

Now, it had come to pass that among the great hosts of Caelum were some who, growing unsatisfied over the span of their unending years, had bent their ear to the whisperings of deceit. Through the slow corruption of their hearts over the long ages, a number of these mighty ones had been induced to pledge allegiance to the King's enemies in secret. Watching for his signal, at his command they now unexpectedly sprang, their hidden weapons suddenly unveiled, and savagely attacked the knights who guarded the throne.

At the revelation of this new betrayal, the hosts of Caelum were plunged into chaos. A tremendous struggle erupted, as nearly one-third in their midst chose to believe the deceptive words of Odhrán and rebelled, joining the insurgents. While the guards at the foot of the throne struggled to fend off the well-planned attack, the Duke of Esen swiftly called his men and took upon himself the defense of the King. He and his troops formed a tight wall between the throne and the King's enemies, thwarting their advance.

Wave upon wave, Odhrán's men broke upon the duke's forces

like water. Each time they were repulsed; but, alas, the pride of Odhrán would accept no defeat. Soldier contended against soldier, battalion against battalion: a countless surge of warriors seizing each other and grappling for mastery with astounding power. The immense battle raged and spread furiously throughout the great realm like billowing flames—each subject of Caelum making his choice of allegiance—one that would follow him into the edges of eternity.

While the duke's men hedged in the King, Miguel and Cebrail, knights of Caelum, rallied to the high commander along with the remaining host. Miguel, himself, strove against Odhrán. The glint and fire from the clashing of their weapons was seen upon the great heights for many miles until, with tremendous effort, Miguel prevailed, throwing Odhrán down violently from the precipice.

Together, at last, the King's host triumphed over their attackers, slaying many and driving the rest with force to the borders of Caelum and, at the high commander's order, casting them out. The great battle for the realm of Caelum had come to an end.

* * *

The meadow rolled gently, unfurling out in every direction, cheerful wildflowers dotting the landscape here and there in a thick carpet of lush green as far as the eye could see. As Stella sat, an intense and pleasant warmth enveloped her, and she basked contentedly with her face in the light, gazing at the wide horizon. She felt the fresh-scented breeze stirring tendrils of her hair and softly caressing her cheek. An unexplainable feeling engulfed her. She gazed around, drinking in her surroundings deeply and eagerly, like one who, after suffering of thirst in the desert, comes upon a hidden fount and euphorically consumes the life-giving drops. This place—it held the answer to the question she didn't even know her heart had been asking, aching for. Here she knew, beyond any doubt . . . peace. It was peace!

A perfect peace beyond what she thought was possible. She felt the presence of something and turned. Next to her, very close at hand, a small lamb was grazing. She smiled in recognition and reached out, running her hand gently down its back and through its soft, milky-hued fleece. As she touched the animal's wool, something inside of her, parched and dying, gasped and breathed anew. The animal glanced up at her; its large, gentle, brown eyes held her entranced, and she was unable to take her own gaze away. She heard a voice in her mind. *Estellah.*

'Stella?'

Stella opened her eyes and looked around, pain flooding her senses in a nauseating wave as she moved her head. She was lying on a hard bunk in a pungent, over-crowded slave dormitory. A girl was sitting next to her on the bed, watching her.

It had been a dream—*the* dream—the same reoccurring phantom scene that had been haunting her for as long as she could remember, taunting her: as a tropical island on the edge of sight taunts a tempest-tossed raft, buoying up hope yet mockingly smashing it on the jagged and deadly outcroppings of an utterly impassible reef. Why could she never get away from it?

'Thank goodness, you're awake, finally. Your name's Stella, right?'

Stella looked at her. She thought she remembered seeing the girl once or twice in passing. She was a year or two older than Stella, with long, dark hair and raven eyes that smiled. Stella slowly nodded and sat up painfully.

'I'm Raya. I'm in the bunk two rows that way.' She pointed down a long row of beds. There was concern in her eyes. 'They really did a number on you yesterday. I've been trying to wake you for twenty minutes. Can you move everything alright?' she asked in a gentle voice.

Stella looked down at herself, trying each limb carefully. Her body ached miserably, but nothing was broken. The soldiers had done their job well.

'I was told to get you ready. I don't know what you did, but they're not happy with you—that's for sure. You've been re-assigned to the kitchens,' Raya told her, knitting her brow. 'We have to get going, or we'll be late. Can you stand? I'll help you.'

Lending her aid, she began to dress Stella in the new kitchen uniform. It was charcoal grey, augmented with crisp-white accents, a typical lower-slave's dress: calf length with a collar and long sleeves that buttoned at the wrist but could be rolled up and secured at the elbow when needed. As she put it on, she noted that it fit her well, and the quality was good. All the uniforms in the house of Nefas seemed to be a more modern style than in her last house.

'Report to Chef Rowen in the large kitchen,' Raya told her as she hastily put Stella's old uniform in the small chest of drawers at the foot of her bunk. 'And mind that you listen to him. He's manager class—a tier-four. Turn left at the bottom of the stairs and go straight. You can't miss it. Now I'd better go. I'll see you at dinner.' She gave Stella an encouraging smile and turned, hurrying off.

Stella watched her go and, taking a deep breath, left to find the kitchen. Raya was right; she couldn't miss it. She could hear the chef before she saw him, and he sounded angry. Stella hesitated at the doorway, wondering what she would find on the other side.

She held her breath and walked into the room. It was the largest kitchen she had ever seen; the walls were stark white, graced with light walnut cabinets on every side, except for a row of coal-colored ranges that filled a wall and a large collection of ink-black cast iron pans occupying the long shelves opposite. The room was teeming with life and commotion; fires were lit, and a dozen slaves were busy weaving through each other to complete their tasks in a dizzying pattern. Stella slowly worked her way through the room to where she could both see and hear the head chef dressing down some unfortunate slave.

'…alter my recipe! What were you thinking?' The chef was purple with rage. He vented his frustration, spewing insults and profanities at the young man. Finally, he paused for a moment, taking a breath. 'You're dismissed.'

The miserable boy hurried away like a whipped dog with its tail between its legs. The chef turned and saw Stella, timidly hovering on the outskirts of his view.

'Who are you?' he barked.

Stella swallowed hard. 'I'm Stella, th-the new kitchen help,' she stammered.

'You're late. Come here out of the shadows, and let me see you,' he said impatiently.

Stella came forward, and he looked her over. He swore angrily. 'What is the manager playing at? How am I supposed to run a kitchen when he keeps sending me incompetent children? Have you worked in a kitchen before?'

'No, sir,' Stella answered in a low voice, afraid.

'I didn't think so,' he answered. He swore again under his breath and scrutinized her once more. 'You look like your last job was as a punching bag, and I'd wager you couldn't lift twenty pounds. What am I supposed to do with you?' he demanded.

Knowing full well that her life hung by a thread without the acceptance of the head chef, Stella took a quick, tight breath and knelt humbly in a smooth Tenebrae curtsey, as she had been carefully taught. 'May the warmth of Terra be yours, as it fills me at our meeting, Chef Rowan,' she said in the traditional greeting. Lifting her bowed head, she continued, 'I know I don't look like much, but I'm a fast learner. If you give me a chance, I won't let you down.'

He looked at her, and through his bristly exterior, she saw his mouth twitch. 'See that you don't,' he said after contemplating her a moment longer.

Turning, he called over a nearby girl. 'This is Codi. She'll be training you. She is one of the best. Watch carefully and learn from her. And stay out of the way. You're dismissed.'

As Stella rose and turned to follow Codi, the chef called after her, 'Oh, and Stella,' his gruffness cracking for a moment, 'may the warmth of Terra be yours as well.'

Codi led Stella across the crowded kitchen into a storeroom. She had flax-colored hair, shaved on the sides with the rest tied back out of the way, and sad, sober blue eyes. She was in her twenties, tall, and slim. She took a bleached-white apron from a crisply folded pile and handed it to Stella. 'This is for you. You'll get a fresh one daily.'

It was industrial quality: well-made and large. It went over her neck and covered almost the full length of her grey dress.

Codi watched as Stella put it on and adjusted it. 'I've got to tell you, that's a first,' she remarked. 'You certainly made an impression with Chef. I've never seen that before,' she laughed. 'I've never heard him be so polite with another slave. When he returned the Tenebrae greeting, I almost fell over. I don't know how you did that,' she said astounded. Shaking her head, she turned to the business at hand, 'Do you know much about food prep, Stella?'

'No, not much,' she answered honestly.

Codi raised her eyebrows, 'Well, you're going to have a steep learning curve then. I don't have time to babysit. You'll just have to figure out a way to keep up.'

Stella nodded meekly.

'Let's get started then. Follow me.'

Codi led her through the other storerooms and began rattling off a long list of chores and ingredient prep work for which she would be responsible. Stella was determined to do well and excel in her new position, but Codi was true to her word; she moved so fast that Stella struggled to keep up. She was hopelessly left behind and scrambling to remember all that she was supposed to do.

She fell into her bunk every night, exhausted and spent. It was truly grueling work. She was now completely restricted to the house; and, indeed, from this period, she was rarely allowed to leave the kitchens at all, except to sleep. But she didn't care. Even if she could go to the market again, she wouldn't volunteer to go. Why should she? There would be no Abon waiting there to greet her. She focused instead on her new position. The weeks and months began to blend together and flowed by in a rapid stream until, with perseverance, Stella slowly began to learn her tasks well.

With the passage of time, the kitchen and its furnishings remained much unchanged; however, the young girl bustling about the stoves and cupboards was a different story. She slowly grew in strength and sprang up in height, and one afternoon, several years later, Chef Rowan noted to himself with satisfaction that Stella worked with the speed and skill of the best in his kitchens, rivalling even Codi herself.

It was during this period that the kitchen was swelling with excitement for the upcoming annual dinner that their master was hosting. It was going to be big. Several of the city's councilmembers would be in attendance, along with many famous artists, musicians, and scientists of Tenebrae.

But this year would be something for the record books; Chancellor Tallis, Tenebrae's supreme leader and the head of the council, would be in attendance with his family. The chancellor rarely attended private events, and nobody seemed to know how Doctor Nefas had been able to secure the honor of the distinguished guest's RSVP. It was a certainty that he was coming, however, and Stella was kept awash in preparations as the event approached. Many new and exotic foods began to arrive for Chef's special menu, and new slaves were rented specifically to help with the event.

The morning of the banquet arrived. It started early. The excitement in the house was palpable—each slave thinking of the famous people that would be under the same roof and wishing beyond hope for a chance of just a glimpse of someone they admired. The science team arrived early and began to set up their inventions on the stage in the auditorium.

'Stella, have you seen the upper slaves that came with the science team from the university?' Raya asked, sweeping into the kitchen in exhilaration, her eyes dancing. 'They're all tier-nines! Their uniforms are so beautiful! I couldn't take my eyes off them,' Raya sighed and lifted her eyes to the ceiling. 'And the upper-slave boys. Just. Wow. The taller guy is to die for—with eyes from Caelum!' she said longingly.

'What is Caelum?' Stella asked curiously, the word stirring something inside her strangely.

'You're such a ninny, Stella. You've really never heard of Caelum? Sometimes I think you must have lived under a rock before you came here.' She laughed and then explained, 'It's the beautiful fairytale place far from Terra. A strong, terrible tyrant named Ander took it over a long time ago and locked everyone out.'

Another server, overhearing, came over and added in a sing-song voice, 'All good Tenebrae children hope that the tyrant will be overthrown one day, and then they'll take back their home.'

'It's just a story for the stratas, anyway,' Raya rolled her eyes and continued, 'and, even if it *was* true, I'm sure us slaves wouldn't be allowed there.'

The other girl nodded in agreement. 'I don't care whether they overthrow the tyrant either. I'm just waiting for Oan,' she said with a laugh.

Just the mention of the tale of the dreaded highwayman was enough to chill the very hearts of the stratas. According to legend, the outlaw Oan snuck past the city's defenses in the deep of night, wreaking havoc—robbing the wealthy elite of Tenebrae, burning their houses with fire, and letting loose their slaves.

The girls giggled merrily at the thought of the highwayman until Chef Rowan poked his head into the room with a scowl, putting an abrupt end to the conversation. Stella quickly turned back to her work and sighed to herself wistfully. An outlaw hero coming to save the slaves? That would be the day.

Chapter 3

The Mirror of Tenebrae

R aya was one of the coveted servers who was chosen to be in the dining room that evening. 'Don't worry, Stella,' Raya assured her, 'I'll tell you about everything I see, and I'll recount every juicy detail that happens.'

Stella had been up several hours earlier than normal and was still pressed to get all her work completed. She rushed through the morning prep as fast as her limbs would go. As she moved on to her late morning chores, she saw that she had somehow neglected the trash cans, and now the bins were overflowing. Chef hated full trash bins. She ran quickly to take them out before he noticed.

As she was hauling the cans through the doors out to the back, she became aware of a large group of slaves gathered outside, not far from her. She saw that Raya was there with several other household servers, talking and laughing with four newcomers. Stella knew that they must be the upper slaves; they were creating quite a stir.

A group of lower slaves had assembled and were watching them admiringly. The two young men wore the telltale, stylish tier-nine tunic and breeches, in blue and black, while the girls wore the flattering, floor-length dress design in the same colors and styling as the young men. All four of the young people were singularly good-looking. Only the most talented, attractive, and indispensable slaves ever became tier-nines. They were also the only level of slaves allowed to purchase their own freedom, with the permission of their owners.

One of the young men saw her struggling to get the large bin out of the door and, stepping over, held the door for her. It was a gentle and good-natured act, simple as it was, but the kindness felt like balm to Stella's starved heart. She thanked him.

'Stella!' Raya called to her. 'Come and meet the upper slaves who are presenting tonight.'

The upper-slave girl standing closest to Raya was tall and stunning, with glossy, golden hair and smooth, unblemished skin. She glanced at Raya dismissively and then turned to Stella with a barely concealed sneer. 'I'm surprised they let you out of the kitchen,' she said. 'Most kitchen help is not fit to be seen.' Her eye lingered pointedly on Stella's dirty apron and traveled slowly over the plain lines of her lower-slave dress, finally coming to rest on the dark circles under Stella's tired eyes.

Stella felt little and sensed herself shrinking further under the girl's critical gaze. She shrugged it off with an effort, however, and lifting her chin, answered in challenge, 'Yes, they try not to let us out—but sometimes we have to deal with the trash.'

The girl's mouth fell open, and the others burst out laughing. Stella turned and walked away, continuing across the yard to throw the bags in the compactor. Why in Terra did she say that? What was she thinking? Stella was mortified. The girl was a tier-nine. She was able to cause all kinds of trouble for a tier-one if she felt inclined to. Stella heard the girl demanding loudly that they knock it off, which caused them to laugh all the more.

As Stella returned, she glimpsed the girl storming away into the house, the others still laughing uncontrollably. She chided herself—now she'd done it.

Stella would have walked by them, back to the kitchen, but the young man stopped her. 'I hope you're not offended,' he said, calming himself and wiping his eyes. 'Anuka's a bit of a snob, but she's not that bad once you get to know her.'

'Stella, this is Abon,' Raya said, introducing them and giving Stella a playfully significant look. 'And this is Rafiya and Imus,' she continued, gesturing to each of the upper slaves in turn. 'And you already met Anuka.'

Stella started when Raya pronounced Abon's name. Was it possible that he could be the same Abon? She looked intently at him, searching for any resemblance to her childhood friend. The name was common enough in Tenebrae, she reminded herself, and if it was him, he certainly didn't remember her. He smiled at her, but there was no recognition in his gaze.

'Abon, I haven't seen Anuka that angry since you knocked her from first place in mentoring!' said Imus, who was still laughing.

Abon shot a guilty, lopsided grin at Stella, and at the sight of his startling, bright eyes smiling at her, her heart did a little flip. Whoever he was, he was handsome—very handsome, lean, and athletic, with dark hair and light-filled grey eyes, unlike any she had ever seen. The emotion caught her off guard, and she felt the color rise in her cheeks. She dropped her eyes shyly, hoping no one would notice, and tried to scold herself back to sense. The other girl, Rafiya, was talking.

'It's about time someone put her in her place. She gets too high and mighty with people. I would pay to see her reaction again,' she giggled. 'Are you free later for another go, Stella?' she asked playfully.

'I think once is enough for me, thanks,' Stella said with a quiet laugh, recovering her composure in time.

She was envious of the way Raya seemed to be able to converse with them naturally, like it was nothing. Tier-nines usually didn't talk to lower slaves at all; and these were practically celebrities, well-known for their work with famous scientists. On top of that, Stella had rarely spoken to men at all in her life and certainly not young, attractive ones. The kitchens were filled mostly with women, and the men that she knew there were old enough to be her father or, indeed, grandfather. She wished that she felt more at ease, but she couldn't seem to shake off her timidness. In desperation, she decided to excuse herself before she did anything embarrassing. Plus, she knew Chef would be angry if she delayed any longer.

'I wish I could stay,' she said shyly, 'but I really do need to be getting back. I'm glad we met. May the warmth of Terra be yours, as it fills me at our meeting.' She swept to her knee in a low Tenebraean curtsey. The upper slaves were pleasantly surprised and returned the traditional greeting with grace.

Reentering the kitchens, Stella at once felt a conflict in her mind. She needed to focus on the mammoth task at hand, but stray thoughts continued to push in. Could the upper slave somehow be the same Abon she remembered? The young man was very different, but something made her hesitate. *He would be about the same age. And there was something about him. Was there any possibility that it was him?* She realized that she needed to concentrate; the dinner was approaching, and she required all the wits she had for her tasks. With effort, she took hold of the reigns of her mind turning it once again to the banquet.

The menu was a complex affair with ten full courses—several had dry ice in their ingredients and presentations which required perfect execution in timing. It was the most involved meal she had ever seen. Even the menu card was edible.

Stella worked feverishly with the chef and kitchen staff as they painstakingly created the dishes and carefully and artfully laid out each plate for the servers to present before their guests—earnestly aspiring to please, but above all, desiring the approval of their master, Dr. Nefas. As the hors d'oeuvre went out, a tense hush fell over the kitchen, and all talk was suspended. Every slave waited with bated breath for the response.

After a few minutes, Raya peeped her head in the door. 'The master likes it!' A corporate sigh of relief swelled over the kitchen as they prepared for the soup to go out next and the appetizer after that.

When the salad was going out, Raya stole a moment to whisper to Stella, 'Everything's been a hit so far. I heard Councilman Jolon's daughter say it was better than the food at their own dinner last spring! And the music is top notch! Nine of the best music groups in the city are here, but my favorite, Scotia, is on the other side of the room,' she pouted. 'Each group is performing during one course. During the last course, the presentation from the science team will happen, and that's what everyone seems to be waiting for. It's supposed to be something new and exciting!' Her eyes sparkled with anticipation as she expertly lifted the large platters and glided out of the room.

Whether from the skilled planning and execution of the chef or the diligent work of the slaves, the meal continued without hitch or setback. As they sent out the last dish, the mignardise, the kitchen staff fell into a celebratory mood.

The chef clapped his sous-chef on the back and threw his hat on the table. 'We will have to wait and see what the master and his guests have to say. But,' he said with a relieved smile, 'to my taste and eye, it was well done! All of you, take a well-earned fifteen minutes, and then we'll start clean up.'

Amid the slaves congratulating each other, Raya came in and, weaving through the crowded kitchen, pulled Stella aside. 'Quickly! You can catch the last of the presentations. Follow me.'

Surprised, Stella followed her to the dimly lit observation room on the second level. There were several slaves seated at a long instrument board, running the lights and sound for the banquet. Through the glass they had a commanding view of the dining room and stage.

She had seen stratas only a handful of times in her life, but now, a room full of them spread out before her eyes. It seemed to her that the room below was awash in a sea of the fashionable black and gold robes that only the stratas were allowed to wear. On each aristocratic head perched a strange headdress—whether formed of precious gems or glistening scales, Stella couldn't say—but each was enhanced with an upright disk held between a pair of curved, black horns.

Looking to the stage, Stella saw the invention that the science team had brought earlier: an upright mechanical mirror. It was set up on center stage; it had an aluminum frame entwined around jet-black glass. Downstage from it, the four upper slaves she had met stood in a row.

'This is the best view in the house,' Raya whispered, handing Stella a set of headphones. 'You'll hear everything through these.'

Stella put them on and listened as Dr. Nefas spoke from the stage.

'. . . our respected dignitaries and revered councilmembers of Tenebrae! Tonight, you have seen the best Tenebrae has to offer in music and song. Now, as you enjoy the remainder of an exquisite meal . . .' Applause broke out, and he paused and bowed low in Tenebrae fashion.

Then he continued, 'Without further ado, let me present the best the whole of Terra has to offer in ingenuity and innovation. Last year, the brightest minds in Tenebrae discovered a way to travel that goes far beyond any capabilities we formerly possessed—a form of travel that will transform Tenebrae and, indeed, Terra forever.

'This chasm stabilizer, called the Tenebrae mirror, has allowed us to make this form of travel safe for our skilled contenders to demonstrate to you tonight. We have searched Tenebrae diligently for those who, due to an anomaly that we don't yet fully understand, possess a unique ability to harness the chasm stabilizer's energy and use it to open a door to other worlds. They will travel almost instantly to faraway places and, indeed, other realms—places so distant that they cannot possibly be reached in a lifetime by any other means.'

The crowd murmured with excitement. The scientist signaled to the science team. They immediately obeyed and powered up the chasm stabilizer. The mirror started to hum, and an ink-colored, smoke-like mist appeared and began to cover the dark surface of the stabilizer.

'Anuka will be the first chasm jumper,' the doctor announced.

Anuka took a deep breath and walked to the upright ring. She held out her elegant hands and extended them into the mist. She seemed to be straining against the glass. She pushed harder, and her arms sunk into the swirling tendrils of fog. One more push and, all at once, she disappeared. The mist cleared, and the room gasped. She was gone! Stella couldn't believe her eyes.

The science team was monitoring Anuka's vital signs, calling out numbers. Suddenly, the dark mist appeared once again over the surface of the glass, and Anuka fell through, collapsing onto the platform. The science team hurried to her as the audience gasped and applauded. They helped her to her feet, and she stood unsteadily, curtsying low to the head table where the councilmembers sat. They nodded and applauded her as she was led away.

'Abon is our next chasm jumper,' Dr. Nefas announced.

Abon walked confidently to the chasm stabilizer, and as Anuka had done, he put his hands through the mist and onto the dark mirror. He pushed hard and began to sink in. One more hard push and he disappeared, covered by the mist. The haze cleared, and the dark mirror came into view.

The science team called out his vital sign readings to each other as the seconds passed. Ten seconds . . . fifteen . . . twenty . . . and still Abon didn't return. The scientist's eyes began to dart to his team questioningly. Thirty seconds had now passed, and the crowd began to murmur and fidget impatiently. Dr. Nefas moved towards the science team, and they collaborated in low tones.

Abruptly, the mist began to appear again. Abon's left arm emerged through the mirror, shaking violently, followed by his head and torso. Then, passing through, Abon fell onto his hands and knees on the stage, gasping for breath. In his right hand, he clutched a large bouquet of freshly picked flowers—wild, bright, and exotic looking—unlike any that Stella had ever seen in the hothouse stores. Indeed, they were unlike any flower that had ever grown in Terra.

The team rushed to Abon; but he stood, shaking them gently off, and descended the stage steps, stumbling determinedly to the head table where the councilmembers sat. He bowed low before the head of the council, Chancellor Tallis, and his lady. Then he reached out and humbly presented her with the stunning flowers.

Lady Tallis flushed with pleasure and, rising, took the color-drenched bouquet from him, smiling brightly. The room burst forth in surprised and enthusiastic applause. Abon bowed low again and, with help from the science team, regained the stage.

'This is but the beginning,' Dr. Nefas spoke proudly to the admiring crowd. When the tumult finally settled, he continued, 'This is the start of an exciting new age of exploration and discovery. Imagine the new worlds just waiting to be discovered.' He paused for effect. 'Thanks to the ingenuity of our team and your generous support,' he gestured grandly across the room to the head table, 'the future of Tenebrae has never been more promising.'

The room broke out once again in applause as the scientist and his team, to the delight of the crowd, knelt together with a flourish in Tenebrae fashion.

Stella was stunned; new ideas flowed in fast succession across her mind. She had rarely wondered about the other cities in Terra, outside of Tenebrae, let alone worlds beyond them.

Raya looked at her with enthusiasm in her eyes. 'Can you imagine going someplace like that? Another realm? It's so amazing!' She put a cold hand on her forehead to cool it. 'And did you see what Abon did? As if he wasn't perfect enough!' She sighed and then gave Stella a mischievous smile. 'You sure made an impression on him earlier. He must have asked me a dozen questions about you when you left.' She saw the pink rise to Stella's cheeks and laughed at her. 'I think you surprised them. They were all stunned when you gave them a perfect Tenebrae greeting—one fit for a councilmember.' Raya looked at her friend with pride. 'Where did you learn to do that so well?'

Stella winced. The old lady, years ago, had used every chance to punish her until Stella's Tenebraean manner had become flawless—but at the cost of deep scars that would never heal.

Raya noticed her discomfort and gently changed the subject without waiting for an answer. 'We'd better get back before we're missed,' she said, returning the headsets and turning to the door.

Stella followed Raya back to the kitchen in silence, her mind too full for small talk. The cleanup was just commencing. Looking around at the mess, Stella rolled up her sleeves. It would be a long night.

As they worked, Stella listened to the servants discussing the events of the night and the people they saw. There had never been a dinner like it. The slaves would be talking about it for months, if not years, but the pinnacle of the night had been, without a doubt, the chasm jumpers. Every slave was eager to meet them and find out what it was like to pass through the Tenebrae mirror. They wanted to ask them where they had been and what kind of other worlds they had seen. They laughed and talked as they worked, the excitement of the night making the time pass pleasantly.

Abruptly, Chef Rowen came into the kitchen and ordered them to halt the cleanup. 'All of you,' he said tersely, 'form a line and come out into the dining room. Quickly now.'

They looked at one another in confusion and did as they were told. Stella dried her arms on her apron and got in line with the others, wondering what was happening. As they filed slowly into the large room, she could see that the guests had all gone and the cleanup had been underway in the large auditorium; but it was suspended as the rest of the household servants were forming lines at the front of the dining room, by the stage.

The master was there along with the science team and the chasm jumpers. Dr. Nefas was speaking to his science team, '—run them a third time. Something is throwing off the readings.'

As their line approached the platform, the machine unexpectedly came to life. The large dark glass swirled angrily with thick, black smoke, and a loud, humming sound began emanating from the chasm stabilizer.

The scientist's head snapped up, and he came over to them. 'I'm certain there is one here! It's someone in this group. All the rest of you stand aside. You slaves,' he said motioning to the kitchen girls, 'walk one at a time to the chasm stabilizer, and lay your hands on the glass.'

'They're just lowly kitchen wenches—all tier-ones—there's nothing special there,' Stella heard one of the gathering slaves whisper, complaining to another.

The first girl in line, when she understood what she was being told to do, walked up the steps and timidly touched the Tenebrae mirror. Nothing happened.

'Next!' Dr. Nefas called impatiently.

As they went through the line, each one pressing a hand against the glass, the machine's humming seemed to grow, but there was no response when any of the slaves touched it. The chasm jumpers had moved closer and were watching intently.

Stella was near the back of the line and could see Anuka on the stage watching the lower slaves with disdain. Abon stood alert next to her, observing each slave in turn with his intelligent eyes. There was definitely something different about him, Stella thought as she watched him from where she stood below. He held himself, not with pride nor with the patronizing humility of most slaves, but with a simple, humble confidence that was irrepressible. His face held a clearness that spoke of a freedom from all sense of injustice and bitterness—unusual for anyone in Tenebrae, slave or free. And a light shone in his eyes: guarded and determined but bright and hopeful, nonetheless. He had the appearance of someone that, although in the midst of trouble, is confident that the outcome is going to fall in his favor. She had never seen anyone remotely like him—except, perhaps, for that strange, brave boy she had met as a child.

Stella slowly advanced in the line, until her turn came. She hesitated, afraid, at the base of the stairs.

'Hurry up, girl!' Dr. Nefas called to her with impatience.

She held her breath and started to climb. The stabilizer's noise began to grow until it reached a feverish pitch, and then it suddenly flashed and shot out rays of blinding light. She shielded her eyes and, at the same time, felt the strange sensation of it pulling her in. There was no mistaking it—the mirror was drawing her toward itself! As she set foot on the stage, she began to slide like she was on a sheet of ice. Desperately, she tried to grab something to keep from getting pulled into the mirror. She barely caught the edge of the top step with her fingers and stopped herself.

The mirror's pitch screamed in response. It flared up wildly with energy; tables and chairs began to drag across the floor, vacuumed towards it. One table lifted up and flew, tumbling past Stella and disappearing into the chasm stabilizer. There were screams of terror as the slaves crouched to the ground, grabbed hold of each other, and anchored themselves to whatever fixed object was near them. The mirror was pulling the room into itself!

Stella couldn't hold on for much longer; her body was lifted by the force, feet first, and the stair slipped from her grasp. She felt herself being sucked through the air towards the Tenebrae mirror. The black mist emerged from it to receive her; but, before she was pulled in, a hand caught her wrist. She looked up. It was Abon. He was holding tightly to her and clutching the stair railing with his other hand.

'Hold on!' he yelled to her as debris flew past them violently.

She clung to his straining arm with all her strength. After what seemed like an eternity, someone cut the power to the stabilizer. The noise of the machine died slowly as it powered down, and Stella and Abon dropped to the stage with a hollow thud. All in the room remained cowering and stunned, trying to make sense of what had just happened.

After a pause of several long seconds, everyone began talking at once, and the scientist and his team approached Stella, staring at her, wide-eyed. She looked down at herself. She was enveloped in a shadow. Her hands and arms were faded, like in the gloom of dusk. She held her hand up. Even her fingers were dim and hard to see. After a few moments, the shadows began to dance on her skin and then evaporated into the light.

She looked at Abon. He was staring back at her in disbelief. He still had a painfully tight grip on her arm. Suddenly realizing the intensity of his grasp, he gently let her go.

'What happened?' she asked him.

'I'm not sure,' he answered quietly. 'I've never seen anything like it.'

Dr. Nefas approached and, in an exhilarated voice, began speaking to his team, 'We will run diagnostics on her immediately. She's the most powerful conductor I've ever seen.' He turned to her, 'What is your name, girl?'

'Stella,' she answered timidly.

'As of now, Stella, you are no longer a kitchen slave. You will begin training immediately as a contender in the chasm-jumping program. You will start in the morning.'

The scientist then abruptly turned, dismissing the room with a quick command. He hurried away, giving orders to the science team. A murmur arose as the slaves all turned to go, and Abon held a hand out to Stella, helping her to her feet.

'Are you alright?' he asked.

'I think so,' she answered shyly, looking down to reassure herself that the strange, moving shadows had passed.

'Welcome to the chasm-jumping program, Stella,' he said smiling at her irresistibly.

Stella didn't know what to say. When Abon had grabbed her, the veil had fallen from her eyes, and she had finally recognized him as the boy on the bridge from so long ago. He had changed, but still he retained the same grin and the same spirit that she had admired with wonder all those years before. It was him. Stella dropped her eyes shyly. He tugged at her heart in a way that she couldn't understand, and in that moment, she realized that he had captured something inside of her—effortlessly and ignorantly, it seemed—with his confident, brave kindness, bright eyes, and heart-rending, crooked smile.

Chapter 4

Vie Eternelle

From the mighty heights, Odhrán had plummeted, struck down by the knight in a storm of energy and blinding light. As he descended, his beautiful form had suddenly begun to change. His once captivating shape transformed into something abominable and hideous; his luminescent and flawless skin was covered with seeping, viridescent slime, and many scales began to form within it. Odhrán screamed in bewilderment and rage and fled.

Erelong, he found himself alone in a deep, underwater cavern in the distant realm of Terra and Mare, spewing curses against Caelum, its laws, and, above all, its King. In the cold darkness, time passed unheeded as his form twisted and further devolved. His mind festered, scheming—plotting his revenge against the ancient one.

He knew that he had lost forever his chance to challenge the King in his own domain. The King had been utterly unassailable, surrounded by his glorious armies, together with the Duke of Esen's powerful militia and the high commander's well-trained forces. There had been too many. Not enough of the host of Caelum had joined him. *Curse them,* he spat in his malice and hate. No outright attack would ever prevail now. It would be useless.

He would have to use other, more subtle means to get what he wanted. The hope of luring Esen into defecting was futile, he mused; but, perhaps, he could still tempt the commander in some way. If all else failed, he would bend his will toward making everything the King held dear burn to char and ash. He would start with the parasitic creatures in this forsaken realm. He perceived that the King valued them; that was enough to earn his hatred and venom. He would savor destroying as many of them as he could—one at a time, if necessary—even if it took millennia.

His cunning mind continued to work long and treacherously in the deep. Finally, with his plan perfected, he stirred—his mind intent on winning the revenge he thirsted for. He would gather the others to himself and achieve his much-cherished desire.

The luminous, hate-charged eyes of sea green unclosed—their large, slitted pupils adjusting slowly in the blackness and peering out into the depths. The grotesque form of the fallen creature then emerged from the darkness, writhing and churning the seas around himself.

Leviathan had come forth.

* * *

The contenders waited in anticipation while the announcer cleared his throat. Stella fidgeted in her chair, glancing across the aisle at Abon. He sat facing ahead, appearing calm. This would be it; she was sure. One of them would be chosen. He caught Stella looking at him and gave her a quick wink and grin.

The announcer's deep voice reported, 'No new chasm jumps this week. That's all for today. You may go.'

A disappointed murmur rippled through the ranks as the contenders rose and began to file out of the auditorium. Stella let out a relieved sigh. Another week at least before she would have to go near the mirror.

Abon sauntered over. 'Better luck next week.'

'I hope not,' she answered under her breath.

Abon cracked a smile. 'How about a game of kings after lunch?'

'I can't. I've got mentoring today,' Stella said, shaking her head.

'Are you sure you're trying to stay out of the chasm? Because, with all the extra mentoring, it seems like you're trying to make me look bad,' he teased.

'No, you do that all on your own,' she said with a mischievous raise of her brow.

'Ouch! Hey, now,' Abon laughed, his bright eyes smiling at Stella. Giving her a playful nudge, they crossed the courtyard of the dormitory wing and headed towards the cafeteria.

Stella had been at the university for several weeks but, thankfully, had not seen the Tenebrae mirror since the night of the banquet. It surprised her. She had assumed that they would force her into it at the first opportunity. What were they waiting for? Stella had undergone battery after battery of intrusive tests. She was spending all her time in training and other classes. But she had not seen Dr. Nefas again since that night. She was growing impatient to know what was going on, but the mentors continued to tell her that she wasn't ready.

At first, she was content with that; the thought of being near the gaping darkness of the Tenebrae mirror was terrifying. But, as the days passed, she was surprised to find herself growing curious as well. What if they were able to control it so it worked like it had for Abon? She felt a thrill course through her at that thought. To be a chasm jumper was synonymous with adventure. Stella felt the dueling nature of her thoughts toward the chasm as she continued to press forward with her training and studies, learning as much about the chasm as she could while she had the chance.

As they entered the cafeteria, many heads turned in their direction, and Stella once more had the uncomfortable sensation of being on a stage. The fame of her experience with the chasm had yet to wear off, apparently.

Abon laughed. 'You'll have to get used to it sooner or later, Stella. Everyone here knows who you are now. Every last one of them would give anything to be the next big chasm jumper.'

'Well, I haven't chasm jumped yet so I wish they'd stop looking at me,' she said miserably.

Abon saw her discomfort. 'It'll wear off eventually. You'll see,' he consoled. 'In the meantime, let's get you something to eat.'

He took her arm and guided her to where Anuka and Rafiya were getting in line, and they fell in behind them. At the casual touch of his hand, Stella felt the pink rise to her cheeks, and she trained her eyes down. She still hadn't worked up the courage to ask him if he was the boy from the market. Each time she had taken a breath to do it, her throat had tightened and no sound had come out. Why did he still make her so nervous?

'Another week, at least, before anyone jumps. Unbelievable,' Anuka said, turning to them with a scowl.

'I really thought there would be something this week,' Rafiya added, disappointed. 'That makes—what is it now—three weeks since anyone's been in the chasm.'

'Ever since the Nefas dinner,' Anuka said, looking hard at Stella who was still studying the floor. 'It's like they've shut it down since the mirror went haywire.'

To everyone's surprise, Anuka had been mostly civil to Stella since she had been given upper-slave status and joined the university.

Stella's fingers strayed to her sleeve-covered forearm. Those little marks made a world of difference, but she still felt strange and foreign here. Only upper slaves were allowed to attend the university—tiers seven, eight, or nine. In consequence, Dr. Nefas had requested and received fast-tracked permission from the council to advance Stella's tier: an almost unheard-of occurrence. Contrary to convention, the morning after the banquet, the symbol on her arm had received embellishment from the council's tier-branding official. Two more thin outlines surrounding the crest had been skillfully added—three outlines in total—delineating that Stella was now an upper-tier slave. And, underneath the crest, seven black marks were now etched: tier seven. Stella still had trouble believing it.

They took their lunch. It was the typical Tenebrae slave fare: enriched gruel, a rasher of dried meat, and toast spread with a thin layer of oil. They were also given a glass of boire: the common drink of Tenebrae, consisting of sweetened water flavored with anise. With trays in hand, they all headed to the tables.

'Do you think Stella's the reason they've stopped the jumps?' Rafiya asked them as they joined Imus where he sat. Not surprisingly, he had his food and was already eating.

'Bravo, genius,' Imus replied, glancing up at her between bites as they took their seats. 'Why else would they have stopped all of a sudden?'

'I don't know. Maybe the war ended, and they forgot to tell us,' Rafiya shot back.

'They'd shut the whole program down if that were the case,' Abon commented. 'It's got to be connected to what happened with Stella. It must have scared them.'

'Like, they're afraid it might happen again if someone jumps?' Anuka asked him curiously.

Abon shrugged.

'We don't even know *what* happened,' Rafiya commented.

'Do they? Does Dr. Nefas even know?' Imus interjected with a full mouth.

'They must know something,' Abon answered him, contemplating, 'but I don't think they know fully. That's why they've spent three weeks running every test on Stella that they can think of and why they haven't let us jump yet. Stella probably understands what happened as well as anyone.'

Stella glanced up and saw that they were all looking at her. 'I don't know anything,' she said, looking around in bewilderment. 'I'm the last one you should be asking.'

'You must have some idea of what happened,' Rafiya coaxed. 'Something that you might have done to cause the chasm to react the way it did.'

'No,' Stella told her, irritated. 'I didn't DO anything. It just . . . happened.'

'Maybe if we all think back . . . we were all there.' Rafiya pressed further, 'If we go over how it all unfolded together, we might find a clue—'

'I've already been over this in my mind a thousand times,' Stella interrupted in exasperation. 'I've answered all the mentors' questions—hours upon hours of intense questioning. I just can't do it anymore.'

'This affects more than just you, you know, Stella,' said Anuka sharply. She paused for a moment and then went on, her cold voice slowly rising as she did, 'This is because of *you*, and it affects *all* of *us*—Rafiya, Abon, Imus—this whole school. Every moment that we are not in the chasm, learning and being useful, we become dead weight. Do you understand that?' Her eyes narrowed and became threatening, 'So I don't care if you think you can't do it. You'd better find a way to do it, and then do it some more, and then some more after that, until we find out what in Terra is happening— before something worse happens or they shut us down for good.'

Stella was unprepared for Anuka's raw emotion. She looked ready for a fight. Stella relented. 'I'll do what I can. I'm not giving up, if that's what you think, Anuka.' As she rose to leave, she added, 'I'm going to keep searching for answers.'

'Then why are you running away?' Anuka asked in challenge.

'I'm not,' she answered calmly.

Anuka crossed her arms, and her expression grew dark. They watched wordlessly as Stella returned her tray and left. None of them saw the extra hours that the mentors were working her. They didn't know about the grueling nights and punishingly early mornings. Every muscle and sinew in Stella's body ached from the daily physical training that she was enduring, and the mental strain was even worse. She tried to clear her head as she crossed the campus toward the mentoring wing. Focus training was bad enough without Anuka's words echoing in her thoughts.

The next morning, after yet another hard session, Stella stumbled to her room to get ready. She adjusted her dress and tried to hurry her sluggish limbs. It had taken every ounce of will that she possessed to get through training today, and still they pushed her. How much longer could she keep going? She felt like she had nothing left to give. She glanced around at the empty room and felt even more alone. She missed Raya's laugh and her witty gossip. Stella had never in her life had a room to herself, and she didn't like it. The silence felt eerie.

A loud bell rang suddenly, making Stella jump. It was time for class. She glanced at her desk, her bed, and the dresser at its foot, checking that everything was in order and then left for the mentoring wing.

On the way, she ran into Rafiya. 'Hi, Stella,' she said cheerfully, coming over and walking with her. 'You missed an epic game of kings yesterday after lunch,' she said smiling.

'Why? What happened?' Stella asked curiously. 'Who won?'

'Well, Imus and Abon were winning, as usual,' Rafiya rolled her eyes, 'but then they cornered each other, and while they were busy attacking each other relentlessly, I swept in and throttled them both.' She swung her arm dramatically and then laughed, 'It's the first time I've won against Abon in months.' She held her head proudly.

Just then, a set of soundproof doors next to them swung open, and the girls had to move quickly to get out of the way. A fully loaded cart of boxes issued out in front of them, pushed through by two male slaves in white medical coats. Stella and Rafiya stood to one side to let them by. As the load passed her, Stella saw that each package was carefully labelled:

Vie Eternelle

Nefas Laboratory

Ready for export

'What's in there?' Stella asked.

Rafiya wrinkled her brow, 'In the packages? I don't know.' She waited until the men had gone and then leaned in close to Stella, lowering her voice to a whisper, 'I don't know for sure, but there are plenty of rumors about it. Through there,' she said, pointing to the double doors that were slowly re-closing, 'is supposedly some sort of medical wing, but it's off-limits for us. They bring in young slaves; I've even seen them take children in there.'

Stella looked and caught a glimpse of a very long, sterile-white hallway before the doors closed. No one was in sight. 'What happens to them?' Stella asked.

Rafiya shook her head. 'I don't know. There must be another exit somewhere. Only packages come out of these doors, and they're all marked exactly the same. But you didn't hear any of this from me,' she spoke in a low voice and shuddered. 'Let's keep moving. Those doors give me the creeps.'

The other students were thickly filtering into the lecture hall and steadily filling the auditorium seats by the time the girls arrived.

'Hello, Stella,' said a voice from behind her, and she turned. It was Anuka. She looked strikingly beautiful today; her gold-kissed tresses waved in long, elegant cascades over the slave dress that seemed especially designed to augment her frame. 'I apologize if I came across harshly yesterday. I hope you haven't been too overwhelmed with the way things are done here,' she said sounding concerned. 'I keep forgetting that it must be so different from the kitchens.'

Stella raised an eyebrow. Something in her voice was starting to sound more like the old Anuka. Stella kept her expression steady, however, and answered in a de-escalating manner. 'Things are difficult,' she admitted, 'but I'm sure I'll catch on.'

Anuka shrugged. 'I'm sure you will,' she said smiling patronizingly, 'but if you don't, remember that it's just as easy for them to demote slaves as it is to promote them. But then, you're used to the kitchens so it wouldn't bother you a bit.'

There it was. The old Anuka was definitely back. Stella caught the thinly veiled threat but said nothing as Anuka turned away briskly to greet someone who was approaching. Stella glanced over. It was Abon.

'Hey, Stella,' he said, addressing her in an upbeat tone as he joined their group. 'Hope you were able to get some rest yesterday.'

'Thanks, Abon,' she responded shyly, glancing down when she felt his eyes studying her. Why did she feel so awkward around him at times? What was wrong with her? Sometimes it was so natural between them and she acted like a normal person, but then he would do something small, and she would suddenly become tongue-tied and flustered.

'Abon,' Anuka interjected, smiling sweetly at him, 'I had a hard time understanding the last lesson. Do you think you could help me today? I'm afraid I'm lost.'

'Sure, Anuka,' he said in surprise, smiling back at her, 'no problem. Once you understand the concept, it's easy.'

'Thanks, you're a lifesaver,' she said, looping her arm through his and shooting Stella a significant look. 'We'd better take our seats; class is about to start. Are you coming, Rafiya?' Anuka asked her pointedly.

'I think I'll stay with Stella,' she quietly responded.

'Suit yourself,' Anuka responded coolly. 'I have a hard time seeing from the tier-seven section,' she said, turning to go. The universally acknowledged rule was that slaves could sit where they liked, as long as they never sat above their tier.

'We'll see you at lunch. Good luck today, Stella,' Abon told her amiably as he turned and walked away.

Rafiya watched them leave. 'She is something else,' she said, shaking her head in disgust.

'That's one way to put it,' Stella smiled. The girls laughed and chatted while they took their seats in the very back of the auditorium, in the tier-seven section.

Another bell rang, and a quiet hush immediately fell over the room. A door was heard closing, and a man walked onto the platform from behind stage. He walked downstage center and scanned them leisurely in silence. After a few moments, he began.

'For those of you who don't know me, I'm Archer, head of the science team for the chasm-jumping program. I believe some of you have formed the mistaken idea that you have somehow earned your place in this program—that you are owed something for being here,' he paused, his eyes scanning the auditorium.

'The high council is depending on this program to find a way to achieve its directive and quickly. Our country is depending on us. This is not a game; we are at war with foreigners who want to destroy us and our way of life.' He beheld them gravely. 'The hope of our very survival rests on the success of this program. And we cannot allow the weakest of you to slow down the progress of the chasm-jumping program. I have new orders from the council. You will be pushed harder in the coming weeks than ever before. Those who cannot keep up will be eliminated. Those underperforming contenders winnowed out will be moved to the auxiliary science programs in other departments.'

A horrified gasp permeated the room. He looked sternly across all the contenders and chasm jumpers who filled the auditorium. 'Now, I suggest you get to work. Tier-sevens will go to mentoring; tier-eights will stay here for advanced physics; tier-nines, head to physical training. You have five minutes. Dismissed.'

A loud buzz swiftly rose as the contenders stood and separated. Each slave understood that to be sent to the auxiliary programs was a sentence worse than death; those departments were at the forefront of new discoveries, technology, and experimentation. Everyone knew that the road to all their greatest achievements and tremendous advancements was paved with the very lifeblood of a multitude of slaves. It was accepted as the cost of progress in Tenebrae. Everyone just hoped that that multitude wouldn't include them.

'Archer's not playing around,' Rafiya whispered, frowning. 'I'll see you at lunch, Stella.' She quickly left with her group.

Stella stood and filed out with the other tier-sevens, following them to the mentoring room. As they settled into their seats, Archer entered, and the students sat up attentively. It was unusual for the science lead to deal directly with tier-sevens. He strode to the head of the class and turned to them.

'You may have heard many different rumors circulating in the last few weeks. I am not at liberty to discuss them with you now. All I can tell you is that I will personally oversee this group for the next few weeks, working one-on-one with students.' He glanced at Stella. 'We will also be revisiting the basics of jumping. Let's brush up-—from the beginning.'

He turned to a girl seated near the front. 'Mal, tell me what a jumper sees when they first enter the chasm.'

'They see the inner chasm. Each jumper's experience of the inner chasm is different. Some see vast regions of lakes and mountains; others return with reports of volcanic fields and ash-covered wastelands.'

'Good. And what do these reports all have in common?'

'Each chasm jumper returns every time to the same strange place. Like they are somehow individually drawn by some unknown force. Each place is theirs alone, and no other can follow.'

'What else? Ardu?' he pointed to a boy sitting near the back of the room.

'In each location, there is always a door.'

'And what do we know about the doors?'

'They are always locked.'

'Good. And where does the door lead? Haine?'

The girl sitting next to Stella answered, 'To the outer chasm.'

'Are there different outer chasms?' Archer asked, raising an eyebrow.

Laughter rippled through the classroom.

'Juvo?' He pointed to a dark-haired boy near the front.

'No, every door leads to the same black, outer chasm,' the boy answered with a smile.

Archer nodded. 'And what about time in the chasm? Is it linear? Moche?' he asked, pointing to a boy behind Stella.

'No.'

'How do we know?'

'Jump 107.'

'Right. What happened in that jump?' He glanced around the room and called on a boy with chestnut hair sitting on the left side. 'Bucher?'

'When he entered, the chasm jumper had observed a piece of torn fabric, similar to his uniform, on a branch near the chasm-stabilizer. However, looking his uniform over carefully, he saw it was intact. He searched but found no sign of anyone else in the chasm. He kept the piece of material for the science team to analyze further. When he was finished taking observations in the chasm, he returned to the stabilizer. Just as he was pulled into it, his arm caught a branch, and it ripped a piece of fabric from his uniform. When he emerged from the chasm, he took out the piece of material that he had found. It fit the missing portion of his uniform as perfectly as a puzzle piece.'

Rafiya met Stella at the door of the mentoring room when her class dismissed for lunch, and the girls discussed the morning's events in hushed tones on their way to the cafeteria. The contenders could think of nothing besides Archer's words at the opening of the day; the threat of being purged from the program hung heavy over them all. Rafiya sat by Stella's side, quiet and gloomy.

Abon alone seemed undaunted. 'You have nothing to worry about, any of you,' he told them reassuringly. 'If they start purging, they will do it from the tier-seven group, and after her interaction with the chasm, Stella will be the very last to go out of all of us.'

Anuka's eyes darted from Abon to Stella and grew black. She didn't seem overly encouraged by his words.

'What are the other auxiliary programs that slaves would transfer to?' Stella asked.

'It's hard to say. There are dozens of programs the university runs that I know about and probably dozens that I don't know about,' Abon shrugged.

'Would any of them go to the Vie Eternelle program?' asked Stella.

A thick silence seemed to suddenly encapsulate them, and Stella glanced around nervously. *What had she said?* The nearby tables had grown pale and grave, and several slaves looked at Stella darkly.

After a lengthy pause, Abon spoke in a low voice, his eyes hot as embers, 'Stella, you can't speak that name again. Understand?'

Stella nodded wordlessly. The cloud seemed to pass, and the room slowly regained much of its former flow. But Stella sat deep in thought, confused and wondering more about the mysterious medical wing they were forbidden to discuss.

Anuka was watching her closely from across the table. Stella had made it clear yesterday that she was not interested in being a team player. That made her dangerous. A plan began to take shape in Anuka's mind. If Stella wanted to know more about the secret program, then by all means—Anuka pursed her lips, thinking to herself—someone should help her find out more. A lot more.

Chapter 5

The Forging of Iudicium

The glowing, amber-toned blade slowly began to take shape under the blacksmith's masterful hammer. The King watched in silence as the bronze was struck skillfully, again and again, on the anvil. This was the tool upon which his plan rested. Only he knew what hope and doom hinged on the perfect forging of this weapon. It would be fashioned with keen skill to have the deadly strength required to pierce his enemy: a power that no other blade in all the realms possessed.

There was a quick tap on the door, and the high commander entered the forge. 'I've brought a suitable piece for the hilt, at your request, Sire. It was not easily found.'

He carried a fine length of hardwood and handed it to the King. The King took it and laid it on the table, turning it over and inspecting it. It was a flawless specimen of acacia, fully displaying the wood's natural qualities: hard, strong, and dense; resistant to pestilence and decay; and a distinctive, stunningly beautiful grain.

Finally, he nodded. 'Excellent. This will do well for the task. Well done, Liam.'

The commander nodded, 'Thank you, my Lord.'

He turned to the forge, and with interest, Liam watched as the smith's hammer fell on the blazing metal, ringing loudly. 'Is it proceeding how you had hoped, Your Majesty?'

'I believe so. The weapon must be perfect, but much also rides on the execution of the plan. We cannot afford to put a foot wrong.'

'Does the enemy know what's coming?' Liam asked with a wry smile.

The King raised an eyebrow. 'As long as we play our part well, it won't matter. He won't be able to stop it.'

When the acacia hilt was fashioned and the blade assembled and balanced, the craftsmen brought it to the King. He slowly drew the sword from its bronze scabbard and looked long on the polished blade. It was made to kill and fashioned for a single purpose: to strike the final, lasting blow of defeat to the enemy of the King.

The high commander, who stood at the King's side, spoke, 'It is a fearsome weapon, my Lord. What is its name?'

'You look upon Iudicium, my son. The ultimate destruction of evil, forever.'

* * *

After a short lunch, Stella and the others had returned to their training for the better part of the afternoon. Archer quizzed Stella's group on the principles of jumping and the chasm and only released them to a late dinner. Stella sat through the meal, tired and overloaded, while the others laughed and talked. She would nod and smile, but try as she might, she caught only a portion of the conversation.

'Hello? Stella, are you home?' Rafiya sung in her ear, finally pulling Stella out of her gloom. 'A penny for your thoughts?' she inquired, laughing.

'I'm sorry, you guys,' Stella said, shaking her head. 'I don't know what's wrong with me. I can't focus. I think I'd better head to bed.'

'But Abon and Imus want a re-match, and you, partner, are my secret weapon,' Rafiya said playfully.

'Ha! You can run circles around me in kings, and you know it,' Stella laughed half-heartedly. 'You're on your own.' Then she stood and said, 'I'll see you all tomorrow.'

As she left, Anuka smirked. 'You heard her yourselves. We're on our own.'

'That's not what she meant, Anuka,' Rafiya told her.

'Then what did she mean?' Anuka's expression darkened. 'She's made it obvious that she's not interested in working together.'

'You didn't exactly make a great first impression at the house of Nefas, Anuka,' Imus reminded her.

'That was before. How was I supposed to know that she was the one who we were trying to find?' Anuka shot back. 'She didn't exactly fit the description.'

'No, she didn't,' Abon said with a smirk, 'but she sure does now.'

'I don't get it, Abon,' Imus said, puzzled. 'It might not be her. Traps have been set for us before this. And, even so, how can we trust her?'

'It is her,' Abon responded. 'I'm almost positive. I didn't recognize her at first; it's been years, and she's changed so much. But it's her. Trust me.' His eyes grew intent. 'She's the one we're looking for.'

'We can't hang everything on a gut feeling, Abon,' Anuka said, shaking her head. 'You have no proof.'

'Regardless, we should continue with the plan until we know for sure or until she proves that we can't trust her,' Abon reasoned.

'She's already proven it, Abon. You're just too blind to see it,' Anuka retorted heatedly. 'We can't trust her. I'm telling you, she will betray us. Don't say I didn't warn you.'

She pushed herself away from the table angrily and rose.

'We will continue to monitor her, Anuka, and nothing more,' said Abon, grabbing her by the arm and speaking firmly in her ear. 'Until we get new orders, you will be friendly to Stella, and you won't do anything rash or stupid. Is that clear?'

Anuka glared at him. 'Crystal.'

'Good,' Abon let out a breath, 'then I suggest we follow Stella's example and get some rest. We'll need it for what's coming.'

Anuka said nothing but returned her tray with the others. If Abon thought he could make her sit by idly while Stella handed power to their enemies, he was ridiculously mistaken. She had given everything for this and had risked her life enough times to know what was at stake. Stella must be stopped at all costs—before it was too late.

And, if Anuka was the only one who realized that, then so be it.

Stella had been in bed for several hours when she awoke to a quick tap on her door. She lifted her head in time to see an envelope slide underneath it and to hear footsteps hurrying down the corridor. She groggily rolled out of bed and took up the sealed letter.

The envelope was addressed to her in the long strokes of the Tenebrae script, in what looked like a man's hand. Seized with sudden curiosity, she quickly tore open the envelope. Inside was a single, one-sided sheet of paper written in the same firm hand. It read thus:

Stella,

It was too dangerous to say anything earlier today in answer to your honest questions. If you want to know the truth, meet me inside the Vie Eternelle wing in fifteen minutes. We will have half an hour before the patrol returns on his rounds. I will be there waiting for you. There's something there I need you to see.

Abon

Stella frowned in thought. He wanted her to go *inside* the Vie Eternelle wing? Why would Abon caution her so intensely today and then ask her to go into the actual medical wing in the night? It didn't add up. Was it possible that his harsh response had been an act?

Something was off, but Stella couldn't make out what it was. She didn't want to go, but what if Abon was there waiting for her? The minutes ticked by as she thought. She glanced at her clock, considering. She was running out of time. She would never know unless she went. That decided it for her. She would go and see. She quickly dressed and headed out the door, down the dark corridor, and directly towards the medical wing.

As she approached, she saw the door had been narrowly propped open with a small stone. *Abon must actually be in there.* She looked around; the hall was empty.

She gently pulled the door open farther and glanced inside. No one was in sight. She took a breath and entered, being careful to prop the door with the rock once more. She slowly moved up the deserted dark hall, glancing in each door as she passed. They all appeared to be examining rooms of some type.

She heard something behind her and turned back just in time to see the door click shut. She gasped and hurried back to open it. It was locked. Like a mouse in a trap, she was caught. Panic rose inside of her, but she forced it down. *Think, Stella!*

She turned and began trying all the doors down the long hallway, one by one, progressing slowly and silently down the corridor. After a few minutes, there was another noise at the main door behind her. She looked back and saw a Tenebrae patrol officer unlocking the door to enter the corridor. Desperate to hide herself before it was too late, she quickly sprinted and ducked into a nearby alcove, hoping that she made it in time.

Hiding around the corner, she held her breath and listened to him advance. She glanced around. She was next to a stairwell that held a dark, descending staircase. She could hear the guard getting closer. In fear, Stella descended as quickly and as quietly as she could, all the while wondering what she had gotten herself into.

A flight down, she peered around the corner into the lower hall. It was a long, curved hall lined with narrow cells. Stella looked both ways. No guards were there, but she knew what this place was. Like everyone else in Terra, Stella had heard the rumors about the terrible experiments that the doctors performed on slaves. But seeing the cells with her own eyes effectively tore a piece off the thick callus that lay over her hardened heart and darkened mind.

She felt sick as she proceeded down the length of the hall, resisting the urge to wretch as she looked inside the first cell. It was worse than she had been told. *Poor soul.* She pried her eyes away trying not to think about what each cell door represented. The hall kept stretching on in a wide curve until she came full circle and found herself once again at the same stairwell as before.

Finding no other way out, she descended to the level below. It was the same as above. Each room was occupied with victims of

Tenebrae's intelligent torture.

She descended level after level into the pit of depravity—all the while wondering how many more levels existed under her feet. How many more dwelt below in this dungeon of science? How was she going to get out of this place?

Several flights down, Stella heard a woman's laugh and carefully peered around the corner. There was some kind of warden station, with a matronly looking overseer sitting at the desk, watching entertainment on a screen. Stella could hear children crying on this level, but the woman gave no indication of hearing or caring.

There was a door directly across the hall from where Stella stood; it was slightly ajar. A way out! Hope swelled in her chest. Stella thought that it might be a direct way to the laundry. Perhaps she could make it to the door unseen and figure out some way of escape through to the laundry wing—or at least find a better place to hide.

She just had to avoid being seen by the overseer, who was, at that moment, turned the other way and distracted. She could think of no better option. She had to try.

Stella took a breath, but just before she darted out into the hall, a hand of iron clamped over her mouth from behind and strong arms grabbed her, dragging her deep into the stairwell shadows.

Suddenly, a guard strode past in the hall and greeted the warden. Stella's eyes opened wide. She had almost sprung out, right into the arms of an approaching Tenebrae soldier.

She turned to see who held her. It was Abon. Signaling silence, he slowly let her go. Sharply glancing around, he motioned for her to follow. They retraced Stella's steps to the first story, and Abon carefully peered out into the hallway. A man in a lab coat was approaching. Abon motioned for Stella to be still. They waited in silence, and for a brief time Stella was afraid the man would turn into the stairwell, but he passed on, continuing down the hallway and disappearing around the corner.

After waiting a moment, Abon beckoned for her to follow once more. She stayed close at his heels. He led her to the main door, and taking a mechanism out of his pocket, he attached it to the lock. She heard a click, and he pushed it open!

As they passed through, Abon took the mechanism back off the lock and let the door close softly behind them. They quickly headed in the direction of her dorm room.

'What were you thinking, Stella?' he whispered to her, aghast. 'What were you doing in there?' He sounded angry.

'I don't know what I was thinking,' she said, shaken. Why had she ever gone near that place? Then remembering the message she asked, 'Didn't you slide that letter under my door?'

'What letter?' he asked with a frown.

They were approaching Stella's room, and she produced the folded note from her pocket and handed it to him.

Abon took it and studied it carefully and gravely. After several minutes he looked up at her, 'I didn't write this Stella.'

'I think I began to realize that . . . just a little too late,' she said sheepishly.

Abon shook his head in wonder. 'One thing can be said about you: you have some guts—either that or just no common sense.'

'Definitely the latter,' she conceded.

'Can I keep this?' he asked, holding up the note. 'I'd like to figure out where it came from.'

She nodded. He turned to go, but she stopped him. 'Abon, how did you know I was there if you didn't know about the letter?'

He paused, but after a moment, he answered, 'I just happened to see you go in.'

'Well, I'm really glad you did,' Stella said with a relieved sigh.

'Stella, you don't understand how close you came to . . . I don't want to contemplate what might have happened if they had gotten to you first.'

'I know,' Stella's words held a nervous edge. 'It was too close,' she replied, turning her eyes gratefully up to his. 'Thanks for saving me, Abon.'

'Please, just don't go in there again.'

'Don't worry,' Stella assured him, 'I don't have the smallest desire to.'

He nodded and then turned away, slowly fading into the dark hall towards his own quarters.

Stella entered her room and, leaning against her door, let out a breath. That could have been bad. Really bad. She had been saved from disaster only by Abon's quick actions.

She thought about what he had told her, but then she frowned. Something still didn't satisfy her. He said he had seen her by chance, but Stella could have sworn the hall was deserted. Why would have Abon been wandering the halls in the night anyway? Something was still not adding up in Stella's mind. After a moment, she shook her head, scattering her thoughts. She had already gotten herself into enough trouble for one night. She was going to bed.

The next morning came early. Stella was still trying to clear her drowsy head as the contenders gathered in the auditorium for the morning's announcements.

Rafiya came over. 'Hi, Stella. Mind if I join you again?' she asked.

Stella smiled. 'Not at all. You can keep me awake,' she said with a yawn.

'Late night?'

'You could say that.'

Anuka came in and, looking around, walked to Rafiya, glancing dismissively at Stella. 'I was wondering if you wouldn't mind lending me your eye treatment later today, Rafiya,' she said in a friendly and warm manner. 'I didn't sleep a wink, and my eyes are paying the price today.'

Rafiya raised an eyebrow. 'Stella had trouble sleeping too,' she commented. 'I don't mind at all. Come and get it from me after class.'

The girls saw Abon enter and head in their direction. He looked relaxed and even cheerful. 'Good morning,' he said to them with a grin. 'Everyone sleep well?' he asked, his glance resting on Stella.

'Good morning, Abon,' Anuka said in a honey-laced tone. 'I thought about what you said yesterday, and you were right. Oh, and thank you so much for your help in class—it made such a difference. I understand the concepts now after you explained them so well.'

Abon glanced at her coolly. 'I'm glad to hear it, Anuka,' he said with a penetrating look. 'Next, we'll work on impersonating people. You could use improvement there.'

Stella's eyes shot over to Anuka in surprise, wondering what part she had played.

Anuka gave Abon a self-conscious look before quickly replying, 'I don't know what you're talking about.'

'Don't you?' said Abon quietly, holding her gaze.

'No, I don't. Why don't you explain,' she answered in challenge, tossing her head.

'Alright. Next time you should pick a better person to help you. Imus was a poor choice.'

He turned to Stella and Rafiya, 'Class is about to start. Is there room for one more in your section?'

'Sure,' Rafiya said quickly. She tried to keep a serious face, but the sides of her mouth betrayed her enjoyment of the situation. 'Follow me.'

'But, Abon,' Anuka shot after him desperately, 'our seats are in the front.'

He turned around with a surprised and disappointed glance. 'Do you think this is a game? You could have gotten Stella killed, Anuka. Let that sink in a bit.'

As they wound their way to the back of the room, Stella glanced behind her and saw Anuka viewing them silently, her eyes black with anger, wholly without remorse. With that one glance, Stella knew that Anuka would make her pay a hundred times over for any humiliation she had suffered. This was far from over.

When they dismissed for lunch, Stella, Rafiya, and Abon headed to the cafeteria in the center of campus and got in line.

Rafiya confided, 'I told Anuka I would meet her in the dorms right after I grabbed my food.' She glanced at Abon. 'I've known her a long time, and I've never seen her like this before, Abon. Are you sure you know what you're doing?' she asked him nervously, getting herself a spoon. 'At times, she can be like a stick of dynamite; one that blows herself up just to take everyone else out with her.'

Abon glanced at her thoughtfully as the machine dispensed into her bowl her portion of thick, perfectly enriched, and perfectly tasteless gruel. 'We'll just have to make sure she can't get her hands on a match,' he answered quietly.

'I hope you know what you're doing, is all. I'll see you both later,' she said, taking her food and heading toward the dorms.

Stella got her own portion and waited as Abon filled his bowl. They headed to a quiet corner where they could talk unhindered.

'Mystery solved,' she said to him as they sat, 'but how did you get a confession from Imus?'

'At first, he denied it, but it didn't take long to persuade the coward to talk,' Abon said, shaking his head. 'He deserved more than I gave him for the part he played.' His eyes grew flinty. 'He was the one who closed you into that accursed place.'

Stella went cold. She remembered well the feeling of panic that had flooded her body when the door closed behind her, locking her in.

'Why did he do it?' she asked, dismayed.

'Imus has been struggling to keep up in his classes. Archer's threat yesterday really shook him, and Anuka knew it. She offered to help him if he did what she wanted.'

Stella sat dumfounded. Anuka had bribed or perhaps threatened another student in hopes of hurting Stella or worse. What had she done to earn such hatred in Anuka's heart?

Abon was observing her. 'You're going to have to watch your back, Stella. There's no knowing what she's capable of or what she might do next.' He frowned. 'She's become a loose cannon.'

Stella nodded. She would have to do better than that to protect herself from someone like Anuka. She could never let her out of her sight.

The week passed slowly, Stella keeping aware of the movements of both Anuka and Imus. Imus spent a portion of every day trying to show his remorse to Stella and make it up to her. Anuka talked less than usual. In class she was even more competitive than before, if that was possible, but beyond that, a sense of normalcy seemed to return.

The next week, things seemed almost forgotten. This was most likely due, not to any relenting on Anuka's part, but rather to something more basic: the program had become more demanding than ever. Archer was doing his best to push each of them to the utter end of their limits, and the contenders had very little time or thought for anything else. It had become a punishing routine for them all.

Stella was working harder than she ever had, but still she had not been brought near the chasm stabilizer since the night of the banquet. She was simply told that she wasn't ready. She labored to understand and master the many skills she lacked, determined to be prepared when another trial with the mirror was finally attempted.

Meanwhile, Anuka watched everything that Stella did, and, the more she saw, the more threatened she became. How could she stop her? Stella was advancing far faster than she should—far beyond what had been deemed possible. Skills that should take months or years were being mastered by Stella in mere days and weeks.

Anuka could see that Stella held the potential to become the most powerful weapon Tenebrae could ever wield. And Abon still thought Stella would be able to control it. He was a fool—deaf and blind to her warnings.

Time was short. She had to prevent Stella from delivering the weapon to the council that would destroy them all. Few knew the hearts and desires of the council like Anuka did. And none desired their destruction more. Whatever it took, whatever the sacrifice, Stella must be stopped—and soon.

Anuka knew her window to act would not remain open much longer. She clenched her fists. The time had come to do what, only four short weeks ago, she swore she would never do: she would have to cause enough destruction to shut the entire program down.

Late one night, after a particularly hard day, Stella was in her room studying when the lights dimmed and emitted an intense humming sound. Then, suddenly—an explosion!

The shock wave rocked the floor; Stella stumbled against the wall as a thunder-like peal resounded and throbbed through the halls. The force shook the rafters, and the lights went out.

Stella thought it had come from the direction of the mentoring wing. She leapt to her feet and groped her way towards the door. After several minutes of trying to pry it open, the generators hummed to life and the emergency auxiliary power turned on. The automatic door then opened easily, and she quickly went out.

Many other students were also coming out of their rooms. Everyone was confused and talking in low voices.

Stella wasted no time and silently headed to the mentoring wing. She knew there was only one thing that had the power to cause a surge of that magnitude.

Turning down the hall towards where the chasm stabilizer was held, she saw many people gathering at the door of the room. As she approached, the burnt smell of electrical wiring filled her nostrils. She saw Abon come out of the room, looking stunned and ashen. Their eyes met, and he came towards her as in a daze.

Stella ran to him. 'What's happened, Abon?'

'It's Rafiya,' he responded, his face twisted in anguish.

'What about her?' Stella asked, suddenly afraid. 'Where is she?'

Abon leaned an arm against the wall as if to steady himself, laying his head against the cool cement. After a moment he roused himself and, straightening up, turned to her.

'She's gone, Stella,' he said slowly, looking at her with pain-filled eyes. 'She's . . . she's dead.'

Chapter 6

Chasm Jump

T he tormented multitude were gathering in the vast, black expanse of the outer chasm. They had been summoned and had come—compelled by a will stronger than their own. Their thoughts and fears wrestled in the darkness, each vying to subjugate the other beings to their own will for their own loathsome ends.

Suddenly, quaking in fear and anguish, their distorted and mutilated forms trembled as they sensed the approach of their pitiless master. They heeded him with unchecked hate and malice, seething and chaffing at their servitude to him but too weak to throw off the shackles of his power.

He advanced, the innumerable crowd giving way to him, drawing back at the appearance of his vile and terrible form. His arrogant eye fell on them with contempt. He knew they feared him, but his plans for them required more.

The grotesque creature summoned the immense power he possessed to deceive the multitudes. Calling it forth, he bent his thought and, as the wretched creatures watched in disbelief, their eyes saw him transform himself with his own might.

The slime and scales receded, and a glimpse of his former shell could be seen reviving a recollection of its former glory. Light channeled around them and slowly encompassed their leader, clothing him in an orb of intense brightness.

Then they gasped, momentarily forgetting their own misery—for the glorious knight of Caelum seemed to stand before them again in all his splendor. Their adoration and reverence belonged to him once more, and he basked in the knowledge of it.

Then, as had been done before, long ago, in the distant great halls of Caelum, their leader—with a grip soft as fur yet hard as steel—slowly bowed and shaped their collective, crooked will to his own, against the very purpose and intent of their original nature. Odhrán smiled to himself in malevolent pleasure. Yes, they were his to mold and command as he wanted. He would install his own great kingdom, with the help of this banished army, in the realm that he had chosen for his throne.

The time was quickly approaching. The human creature had served her purpose. She had perished but not before relaying his message perfectly. He had enjoyed her suffering. He smiled knowing he would soon crush them all like the vermin they were.

These mortal creatures would play into his hands marvelously. It wouldn't be long now before the one he wanted came to him, seeking him and handing him the key. His kingdom now awaited him—just on the other side of the chasm door.

* * *

Anuka quickly shoved the last few things into her bag, glancing around her dorm room before hurriedly closing the zipper with trembling hands. How could it have gone so wrong? She had painstakingly thought everything through. And all had gone according to plan until . . . the creature in the chasm.

Leviathan.

She would never in a million years forget the fear in Rafiya's eyes as she described the creature. Anuka didn't have to ask herself what the creature was. She already knew. But, unlike any of the beings that she had seen in the chasm before, this one had breathtaking power, beyond anything she had ever encountered. He bent the chasm to his will and even seemed able to enter their thoughts. Anuka shuddered.

She had persuaded Rafiya to help her, convincing her that they had to disable the Tenebrae mirror for good.

And now Rafiya was dead.

What they attempted should have worked with enough energy,

but in the end, there hadn't been enough. The yellow book, its source of power, had surged. Overwhelmed with excess energy, the grid had failed.

Then the beings in the chasm had come. The monster in the deep had laughed at their attempt and, grabbing hold of Rafiya, crushed her in his awful and mighty grip, whispering dark words into her mind.

Anuka had been monitoring her from the mentoring room and, at the creature's sudden arrival, had been shaken and struck with fear, unable to rise to try to help Rafiya or even move while the creature remained. She was only able to watch the monitor in hopeless terror.

He had unleashed a dark, perilous, haunting laugh—so full of malice that Anuka had stopped her ears. Then he had flung Rafiya out of the chasm as easily as batting an insect; she was thrown against the wall in the mentoring room. Anuka had run to her, but just as she touched Rafiya's battered frame and spoke her name, she heard others coming. She had hidden herself just in time. Those who had flown into the room in haste found Rafiya alone.

Archer came, with Abon at his back. Kneeling next to her, they tried to make sense of what had happened. She spoke of the creatures in the chasm—on the other side of the door—fearful, twisted creatures that tormented her just for sport. She had repeated the same cryptic things, over and over. Her mind was broken. She said they told her that she wasn't the one they were waiting for. They were waiting for another.

'He orders the council,' Rafiya had choked. 'He says to send her.'

Archer had fallen silent and seemed to instantly grasp the message's meaning. But Abon had continued to press her, undaunted, 'Who, Rafiya? Who says to send her?'

Rafiya's eyes had grown wide. 'Leviathan,' she whispered in fear. It was the last thing she said.

Now, taking a deep breath, Anuka noticed that her hands had stopped shaking. She slung the bag over her shoulder and opened her door, glancing down the hall, first one way and then the other.

No one was in sight. She had been able to escape unnoticed out of a side door in the mentoring room, but she didn't have much time. In all likelihood, they were on their way now to arrest her—but not if she could help it.

She slipped silently out of the door and disappeared down the dark dormitory hall.

* * *

Stella opened her eyes and focused on the smooth, gray metal beams above her head. She was back in her university dorm room, stretched out on the bed.

The grogginess cleared from her brain, and she suddenly remembered what had happened. She moaned in pain and slowly sat up, feeling her bandaged head. The lab session had been a disaster. Clearly, she wasn't ready.

After Rafiya's death and Anuka's disappearance, rumors had sprouted up like bindweed and spread swiftly through the terrified ranks of the contenders. Many thought that the program would be terminated. But their fears were unfounded.

Instead, a new directive had come to the mentors from the council. Chasm jumps were to be immediately reestablished, and the program, which for the last month had laid almost dormant, had burst once again with activity.

Abon was sent in shortly after the accident to examine the chasm and hunt for any clues that would help explain Rafiya's death. He found nothing to report.

The next day, in mentoring, Archer had broken the news to Stella that the council was happy with her progress; it was time for lab work. Terrified, she followed the team to the lab and waited while they connected her to the network. She knew that she was risking the same fate as Rafiya—not that she was going to jump right away, but she was a step closer.

Archer told her he needed to test her response to the tech for calibration. She had glanced uneasily around the lab, observing. The Tenebrae mirror was there, on the far side of the room.

Archer directed Stella as they worked. 'Once the team finishes getting the sensors on you, go ahead and touch the glass so we can calibrate. We just need to take your readings.'

'Don't worry,' he said, when she flashed him a look of dread, 'everything is powered down. What happened last time won't happen now.'

Stella nodded, relieved. With the sensors attached, she approached the stabilizer. It was dark and dormant. Not a sound was coming from it. She laid the palm of her hand against the glass. It felt hard, cold, and smooth, but then it seemed to change, growing soft and pliable beneath her palms.

She sensed once again, a pulling sensation coming from the dark depths. She gasped, feeling her hand sink into it. She couldn't pull herself out.

'Stella, what are you doing?' Archer called to her. 'These readings don't make any sense.'

'I don't know!' she called back, panicked.

A dark mist appeared in the center of the mirror and quickly expanded and encompassed her in its coiled grasp. Feeling herself pulled farther in, she struggled and looked desperately at Archer.

Their eyes locked, and then he saw what was happening.

'Stella, don't move!' he yelled and began urgently shouting commands to his team, just as she felt herself completely drawn into the chasm.

All at once, she was inside of it, the dark mist clinging to her.

Archer swore under his breath as he reached the stabilizer. He put his hand through the mist, but the chasm had solidified again. It was as hard as steel, and Stella was gone.

Stella was enveloped by the mist, and then she felt a shock reverberate through her senses, like a sudden plunge into ice water. She tried to cry out but couldn't breathe. She struggled in slow motion, suspended. She was completely immersed in utter darkness and bitter cold. It was how Stella imagined death might feel: painful nothingness. She could feel her panic rising. Time was suspended as she hung helpless. None of her training had prepared her for this.

Finally, the mist began to dissipate. She saw she was in a field and collapsed on the grass. She heard an animal bleating. Was this a dream? She was unable to raise her exhausted frame, but she felt the warmth and comfort of something lying down beside her. She stopped shivering and fell asleep.

When she awoke, she sat up slowly and looked around. She was in a light-drenched glade, brimming with wildflowers. She gazed up at the wide, blue expanse above her. Was she still dreaming?

She recognized this place. She had been here before. It was just like the glade from her dream, but now it felt solid somehow, crisp and un-dreamlike.

She looked around. There was a lone, majestic, spreading oak tree in the middle of the field. Beyond it, she could see a gently rising hill. At the top of the hill was a wooden door, set in a low stone wall.

Turning, she glanced behind her. The chasm stabilizer was there, but no black mist hovered in the ring. She got up and went to it, putting her palm against it. It was hard and cold. Once she felt it, she removed her hand quickly. Maybe she was stuck here for eternity now. Her heart buoyed with happiness at the thought.

She heard something rustle and turned towards the sound. Several feet away, a lamb was grazing. It lifted its head and looked at her a moment with clear eyes before continuing to graze. She started when she first saw it but then smiled as she watched the lamb. It felt somehow natural and right that it was here; it seemed to belong to the glade more than even the dancing grass, or the great, spreading oak, or the blue, arching sky above.

After a few minutes, she surveyed the hill in the distance and studied the door from where she stood. All contenders learned about the door. She had been taught that it was the last separation between her and all else.

Only the chasm jumper could open the door, but once it was opened, there was no telling what could happen. There were many stories and strange rumors of catastrophes that had occurred when doors were opened. The chasm was an unknown and mostly unexplored realm, full of peril. The objective of the chasm jumper program, however, was to find a way to forge communications between the creatures that lived in the chasm and Tenebrae.

Stella began to walk across the wide glade toward the door. The lamb lifted its head, watching her intently as she walked away. If Stella had thought to look back, she might have noticed the expression of deep sadness in the lamb's eyes as he watched her. But Stella didn't turn around. In fact, she had already forgotten that the lamb was there at all. She was too busy with the work she had to do.

She crossed the meadow and climbed toward the crest of the hill until she was standing before the door. She examined it. The door was very old and set in a low stone wall that stretched out from the door in either direction. It had an iron knob and keyhole; and resting inside the keyhole was an ancient-looking key.

Stella reached out and slowly turned the key. It grated against the metal keyhole as it turned. At that moment, a deep, swelling rumble rose around her, and the ground started to shift. She braced herself against the door and tried the knob. It wouldn't budge. Nothing. Was it rusted shut? The tremors grew more violent, rocking Stella hard and throwing her to her knees.

What was happening to the chasm? She couldn't get back on her feet. The noise and quakes terrified her. She suddenly remembered the lamb. She looked back down the hill to the place where she had seen him last. But he was not there.

Then she felt something soft and warm brush against her hand—the lamb had already followed her up the hill and was there, standing beside Stella as she knelt. He seemed to understand what was happening and breathed a calm that settled on the trembling hill. All became still. She looked with surprise into the lamb's steady brown eyes and felt the trembling inside her cease as well.

The lamb looked at her, as if commanding her to follow, and, turning, trotted away down the hill. Stella's eyes followed the lamb and then shot back to the door. Quickly taking the key from the door and putting it in her pocket, she followed him.

The lamb was steering her toward the great oak in the field. As they approached and worked their way around the tree's knotted trunk, Stella could see a freshwater spring. It must have been hidden by the great oak. It bubbled out of the ground near the base of the tree and meandered away in a deep stream. For the first time, she realized how thirsty she was. She knelt at the source and cupped the clear water to her mouth. It was satisfyingly cool and refreshing, and Stella drank long.

Then she rested in the soft grass next to the brook, in the shade of the wide arching branches. She felt the presence of the lamb nearby and was comforted. She had never felt this kind of peace in her life. She wasn't sure how long she stayed there; she had no desire to be anywhere else. She felt overwhelmed with sudden thankfulness that the evasive dream had finally become a reality. Nothing else seemed to matter. She was quiet and still, listening to the breeze gently stirring the tall grasses.

She must have slept because she awoke, but the sun-drenched meadow was the same—as if no time had passed. She looked and saw that the lamb was still near. Stella was content.

 From where she lay, Stella had a wide view of the field. As she looked out, she could see the Tenebrae mirror. She began to think that she saw black mist forming on the glass. She blinked her eyes. Was she imagining it?

Then, as she watched, she saw someone come through the chasm stabilizer. It was a girl. She collapsed in the grass just as Stella had.

Stella started, momentarily paralyzed by surprise, then sprung up and raced to her. The girl was lying face down, completely still. As Stella approached, she saw that the girl's arms and legs were covered in painful looking gashes: scars and wounds of many kinds, all in different stages of healing. Her clothing was torn, and she was covered in a layer of dust, blood, and mire. Stella gently turned her over—and then she froze, looking at the girl in disbelief and horror. Stella was staring into her own face!

The girl roused, and their eyes met. There was panic and despair in the girl's eyes, but she didn't seem surprised to see Stella. She got to her feet and looked around with eyes that seemed almost maniacal. Her gaze fell on the lamb that had come up behind Stella. Her expression hardened.

Then the girl focused her eyes on Stella with piercing hatred.

'Give me the key!' she demanded.

Stella backed away wide eyed, shaking her head. What was going on? At the same time, the ground began to shake again violently, throwing both girls off their balance. Stella gasped. The knowledge of what was happening finally dawned in her mind: the chasm was starting to collapse.

She had no time to react as the girl sprang at her, attacking Stella with skill and animal ferocity—her disheveled hair and wild eyes making her seem less than human. Stella desperately tried to defend herself. The girl was stronger than her, landing a hit that knocked Stella off her feet. She fell hard but quickly got up on her hands and knees. She tried to flee but couldn't get up off the shaking ground.

The girl rose behind Stella and hit her in the back several times. 'Give me the key!' she screeched between punches.

Nothing good would come of the girl opening the door, Stella realized. 'Not a chance!' she cried through ground teeth.

'Stupid girl,' the girl fired back, 'you don't know anything! I have to save Jared.' The girl savagely ground her knee into Stella's spine and, pinning her down, reached into Stella's pocket and drew out the key.

Stella cried out loudly and rolled over, trying to knock her down, but the girl reached for a large rock laying nearby and, grasping it in her hand, struck Stella hard in the head. She fell back, seeing stars and fighting unconsciousness. The girl raised the rock to strike Stella again, but the lamb stood over her. The girl lowered the rock and slowly backed away, looking wildly at him and around the field, like she was searching for something.

The lamb turned to Stella and looked at her intently. She understood somehow that he was leaving. He was telling her good-bye. She could feel the lamb's warm breath on her face, and then all sensation began to fade. She cried out, but as she did, she felt herself being carried far away, and everything went dark.

She had awoken on her bed in her dorm.

Now, sitting in her room, she tried to think beyond the throbbing in her head. She heard the door chime.

'Enter,' she responded in a gravelly voice. The automatic door glided open, and she watched Abon walk in pensively. 'What happened?' she asked weakly. She had never felt so drained in her entire life.

'You almost terminated. That's what happened. You're an idiot. Why did you try to open the door on your first attempt?'

She studied him. There were deep lines in his forehead, and his eyes seemed worried and tired. 'You look terrible,' she told him.

He cracked a slight smile. 'You don't look great yourself.'

'How long was I asleep?'

'Since yesterday. You were in the medical wing until an hour ago. What happened in there?'

'I don't know. It was different than I expected . . . than what we were told. Why was the lamb there? Where did my deranged twin come from? And why did she attack me?' She looked at him.

He had an incredulous expression on his face. 'You need to tell me everything from the beginning.' He looked at her with serious and piercing eyes.

She related the events to him in order, giving as much detail as she could remember: the door and the key, the field with the lamb, the girl, who looked just like her, and the subsequent attack.

He listened with an expression of alarm, observing her carefully. When she finished, he sat contemplating for a full ten minutes before he spoke. As he did, he studied her intently with his dark eyes. 'How much are you going to tell Archer?'

'I was going to tell him everything. Why?'

'Don't.'

'What? Why not? Are you insane?' She looked at him, but his expression was unreadable. 'They already know everything. You know that. They see everything with the machine. *Everything!*'

Abon sighed and knelt down in front of her, speaking quietly but intensely.

'Listen carefully, Stella. They *can't* see everything. They see *a lot* of things. But not everything. Do NOT tell them about the girl or the lamb. Don't tell them that the key was in the door.'

She laughed in disbelief. 'How am I supposed to explain my wounds?'

'You tell them that you don't remember . . . that you must have gotten injured during the chasm jump. They'll probably just assume that. Tell them you found the key laying somewhere on the ground.'

He had a strange intensity in his eyes that she had never seen before. He rose and glanced at the door. 'Don't even tell them that I spoke with you. I'll say I came, but you were sleeping. I can't tell you everything now. There's no time. Please, just trust me, Stel.' He stood and strode back to the door. He looked at her once more and left.

He was gone. She sat unconvinced and unsure of what to do. Trying to understand Abon was an impossibility.

After a few minutes, she shrugged her shoulders. 'One thing I do know,' she told herself, 'I am a chasm jumper now.'

Chapter 7

Escape

An hour later, she was lying in the medical wing under the watchful eye of the lead physician as he examined her. Archer and the medical team looked on, discussing something in hushed tones.

'One more treatment after this and you'll be ready for jumping again,' the doctor said with a smile, opening the lid and helping her out.

Most of the doctors liked working on contenders. Upper slaves were less broken, in general, and their wounds were usually less gruesome. Most other ranks of slaves were another story.

Archer walked over. 'Time for your debriefing. We'll go to the mentoring room. Feel strong enough to walk there?'

'I think so.'

'Good.' He shook his head, smiling. 'How in Terra did you get your hands on a key?'

'I uh . . .' she thought of Abon as she hesitated, 'I found it.'

'What do you mean, you found it? That's impossible.' He looked at her skeptically.

She would need to try a lot harder if she was going to pull this off. 'On the ground—I found it on the ground,' she said, meeting his gaze. 'It was just lying there.'

He looked at her for a minute, and she could see him contemplating. 'I don't see how that's possible. That doesn't happen.'

'Where are the keys normally found?'

'They are not found. We have to fabricate them. It takes many jumps to get it right. When a key does exist, it's well hidden and can only be found with a map. That almost never happens, and when it does, it only happens to the most agile and experienced jumpers.' Archer looked at her. 'What happened to you is unexplainable. Maybe the chasm was so unstable that the key was thrown from its hidden place, but I don't know. You'll have to do a lot of focus training before we attempt another jump.'

Stella thought about the lamb and the girl who was clearly unhinged. She had to be stopped. Who knows what she might do. Stella wanted nothing more than to drive the girl from the meadow and then … never leave it. Now that she knew it was real—that it actually existed—she had the overwhelming urge to go back forever.

She stopped and turned to face him. 'I want to go in again. Give me another chance.'

Archer glanced up, surprised. 'You weren't yet authorized to make that jump. I still can't figure out how it turned on. We were simply calibrating you to the machine, and you almost didn't make it out. The team couldn't extract you, and when they finally did, we thought you had terminated. Stella, you had to be resuscitated.' He shook his head. 'I don't even know how you did it—getting to the glade on your first attempt—without the machine calibrated. None of it makes sense.'

'How often do people make it as far as I did on their first attempt?'

'Aren't you listening? NEVER. I have never seen someone get as far as you did on their first jump. And we almost lost you. You need more training, Stella.'

She saw that he was adamant, and she felt her shoulders drop slightly as they stopped at the doorway of the mentoring room.

'Fine,' she said firmly, 'let's start now.'

Archer raised his eyebrows. 'Something tells me I can't change your mind.'

She shook her head.

'Well then, after you,' he said, motioning to the classroom.

That night, as she lay in bed, Stella heard the automatic waterers turn on in the gardens outside her window and knew it must be two hours past midnight. It was impossible to sleep. All she could think about was the peace that she craved: the feeling of completeness that she had felt in the meadow.

She had pushed harder than ever in mentoring. Archer said he wasn't sure why the chasm had collapsed on her since her focus was so strong. He'd told her that he would check the machine readings for clues. She almost mentioned something about the girl but had stopped herself just in time. She was getting nervous. Withholding information from the mentors had serious consequences. How did she let Abon put her in this predicament? What was she thinking?

Just then she heard a muffled noise at her door. She sat up and looked towards it in the dark. Was it opening? Her pulse quickened. She stared hard—there was no mistaking it—the door was slowly sliding open. She saw an arm appear and quietly force the door open, until finally she could see someone in black squeezing through. She thought she recognized the shape. Abon?

She breathed a sigh of relief and put down the vase she had picked up for defense. 'What are you doi—' she began to ask, but Abon clapped his hand over her mouth and signaled for quiet.

He gently let her go and silently disconnected several devices in her room. She watched him, baffled. When he was done, he looked at her and beckoned. She approached uneasily and sat down with him on the floor.

'Sorry things have to be so confusing for you, Stel,' he said in a low, soft voice.

'They wouldn't be if you'd explain yourself,' she retorted.

'That's why I'm here, but I can only give you the short answer. There's just too much. What I'm going to tell you will be hard to believe, but,' he paused and looked at her contemplatively, 'I think you can handle it. You'll have to—there's no other choice; we are out of time. So here it goes. I'll try to start at the beginning.'

He hesitated, thinking of how to begin. After a moment, he spoke in a low but urgent voice, 'Years ago, I met a young girl in the market of Tenebrae. We became friends. I trusted her and told her many things about myself and my history.'

He searched her eyes for recognition before continuing. 'I could be wrong, but I think there's a chance that girl was you.' He leaned towards her, studying her face. 'Do you remember meeting a boy in the market several years ago?'

His eyes fixed on her, and she saw in them a mixture of fear and hope.

'No,' Stella said, shaking her head.

Abon didn't respond, but his face fell noticeably at her denial.

'I never met a boy in the market,' she continued, keeping her expression serious for a moment, but then her eyes grew mischievous. 'It wasn't in the market. How could you forget, Abon? You were on the bridge reaching for that silly orange.'

His eyes snapped to hers, and he shook his head, a grin slowly spreading across his features.

'It is you! I knew it!' He felt like shouting. 'I knew it had to be you!'

'I didn't think you remembered me,' she told him shyly, 'or I would have said something. You didn't seem to recognize me at all.'

'In the very beginning, it's true,' he admitted, 'I didn't recognize you. But I could never forget you—not in a thousand years,' he said exultantly. 'Letting you run away that day was one of the worst mistakes of my life. I've been hunting for you ever since.'

Stella felt herself flush at his words.

He continued, 'You remember that I told you I came from . . . from another place, right?'

'Yes, of course,' she nodded.

'Well, the travelers brought me home to my country before returning to their own land, as they promised they would.'

'Did you ever find your family?'

'Yes, I did,' he said, hesitating. 'It was good to see them again, but I always knew I would return here. I've been sent back to Tenebrae with a mission: to get information in order to prevent a terrible thing from happening—a catastrophe. The realms are not what you have been taught, Stella. There are places where things are done very differently from how they are done in Tenebrae.' He looked at her, his face serious. 'I told you this once a long time ago, but it is still the truth. You don't have to be a slave.'

Stella wanted to laugh but checked herself. Had Abon finally gone off the deep end? Or was this some sort of game to him? She thought she'd play along to see where he was going with this.

'So . . . are you saying that I can just decide I'm free and . . . what? Just let Nefas know?' She laughed at the thought before growing sober once more. 'And you think all the mentors have been lying to us on purpose? Hiding the secrets of the universe from us? Why would they want to do that?' She wrinkled her brow. 'It doesn't make a lot of sense, Abon. Anyway, I already know there are different people and cultures in Terra and through the chasm,' she added.

He sighed. 'I'm not talking about *in* Terra, Stella, or the chasm. And *you* know the mentors haven't told you everything. There are things they lie about, and there are things they don't know.' He studied her, gauging her response.

She had to admit he wasn't wrong about the mentors. She was suddenly starting to feel unsure and a little shaken by his words. 'What is your point?' she asked him impatiently. 'Did you really have to break into my room in the middle of the night to explain this?'

'I did,' he said firmly. 'We've run out of time. You aren't safe here anymore. You have to leave with me—tonight.'

'What?' she gasped. 'Leave tonight? Why?'

'Archer analyzed the machine readings tonight. If he hasn't figured it out yet, he will. You have to get out of here—and soon.'

'What is he going to figure out?' she asked, her stomach sinking. Abon had convinced her to lie to Archer in the first place. Did the mentors know?

A smile played on his lips. 'I don't think you realize what you did, Stella. You opened a portal from the other side *without* the Tenebrae mirror. You came back without it. I didn't even believe it at first. But it happened somehow. I would've said it's impossible. I'm still reeling from the implications. The living creatures you saw defy explanation. And then there's the key. The key was *in* the door!' he said this in the lowest voice possible, glancing about.

He looked at her. She felt lightheaded. The blood must have drained from her face because a concerned expression flashed across Abon's eyes. He pulled a blanket off her bed and wrapped it around her shoulders. Going to her cooler, he took out a bottle of boire and gave it to her, telling her to drink. She didn't argue. While she drank it, he watched her silently. He seemed to be weighing something, debating within himself.

When she finished, she suppressed the noise in her mind and forced herself to think. *Was what Abon said true?* She thought back to the lab. She remembered the machine and all the connections and wires she was wearing. And then she knew. It had pulled her in, but she somehow already knew that the mirror hadn't brought her back from the chasm. It had been something completely different that carried her, but Abon couldn't have known that.

'How can you be sure?' she asked him.

'I saw the readings.'

'You saw them?' she asked incredulously. 'How?'

The readings were the jealously guarded secret of the lead mentor and his superiors. Even the team members weren't authorized to see them.

'I have the access codes. I have help from my country, remember? Oh, and I captured Archer's fingerprint while he was distracted.' He looked amused. 'Anyway, the readings show, definitively, that you jumped back *after* the portal collapsed. It was probably close enough to be unnoticeable to the team, but Archer poured over those reports for hours tonight. He'll most likely have the tech guys run a diagnostic on the machine in the morning, but this won't stay hidden for long. We have to get you out of here.'

He glanced at her, and she was surprised to see fear in his eyes. He was afraid. And she knew why. The jumpers and contenders were treated well as long as they did what was required. They were the privileged ones, but that could change in the blink of an eye. They tried not to think about it.

So far, the scientists thought they could explain the chasm's response to her. But now, she realized, she would be an anomaly: an unexplainable mystery. And the stratas just loved to figure out a good mystery—even if it meant taking it apart, piece by piece.

She suddenly saw that Abon was right. She felt an overwhelming wave of desperation rising, but she pushed it back down. Panicking would just make everything worse.

She looked at Abon's face; it had lost that sweet boyish roundness from years ago. It had transformed into a heart-tugging manliness that she was never quite at ease with. She knew his watchful eyes and his lanky but strong build. It dawned on her that, although some of his story might be new and strange, the rest of him was still familiar and trustworthy. After all, she had known him a long time.

'What do I do?' she asked him, resolute.

His sigh of relief was palpable. 'I'll help you pack. We can only take what is necessary.'

He stealthily went through her things, choosing carefully. He dismantled her computer, removing several parts and packing them in her bag, while she changed into clothes that she could travel in.

'We need to remove your electromagnetic field. They can track you with it. Drink this.'

He poured her a small glass of a bitter, clear tonic. She drank. She watched him remove a small medical kit from his bag, open it, and begin setting things out.

'Give me your arm.'

She looked at him, surprised. He was dead serious. She took a breath and stretched her arm out to him.

'This will hurt,' he said apologetically, wiping the area with a swab and beginning to cut.

She gasped then clenched her teeth. He made an incision on her forearm, just below her crest and tier, and inserted a small device.

'This is an extractor,' he explained, not looking up as he worked.

Taking a syringe from the bag, he inserted it in the vein directly below the device. Slowly, a thick, ink-like sludge, drawn by the extractor, began to ooze into the glass vial, filtered from her blood.

Abon waited with patience until the last drops were collected, and then, carefully, he lifted it out. He removed the device and began suturing the incision up.

'There. Not bad,' he said, inspecting her arm. He looked at her. 'You okay?'

She nodded, admiring his handiwork. How had he learned to do that? What else was he hiding? His knowledge and skill both fascinated and disturbed her in turns.

He took out another device and a shipping box from his bag; he inserted the vial of black fluid into the device and switched it on.

'Now you're back online—or so they'll think,' he told her. He laid the device in the box and sealed it, placing the package in her outgoing mail shoot. The city's automated mail system would begin carrying the package to its destination without delay. 'That should keep them busy chasing their tail for a while,' he said amused.

He turned to Stella. 'We need to leave now. Are you ready?' he asked, holding out his hand.

She felt a wave of fear and swallowed hard. *I guess this is it. I'm really going to do this.*

'Ready as I'll ever be,' she answered aloud, taking his hand and trying to sound braver than she felt. She doubted that they could make it past the city walls. She just hoped that they would last the night.

* * *

The great city was still wrapped in slumber as the councilmembers assembled in their ornate chambers. No furnishing was too extravagant: no expense was too costly. The council deserved and expected the highest quality of what Terra had to offer, and their council chambers reflected that. The room's interior walls were overlayed with gold, while luxurious drapes adorned the massive windows. Beneath their feet lay an intricate, polished mosaic of extremely rare and exotic stones. Decadence and frivolity dripped from ceiling to cellar in the halls of power that overlooked the city.

The sleep-torn council took their seats as the chancellor called them hastily to order. The surprise briefing of the doctor had been news indeed. Chancellor Tallis impatiently motioned for the guards to call him in.

'Congratulations, Doctor. It seems you have not failed our trust, after all.' The chancellor spoke from the center chair as the doctor entered.

Dr. Nefas strutted across the council chambers as he approached the head of the council. He knew full well that the pinnacle of his career was being realized. He reveled in the knowledge that he was standing in the midst of the center of wealth and political influence, overlooking the most powerful city in the planet.

'Chancellor, Great Council, I apologize for the hour, but I knew that you would want to hear the news immediately. That is why I wasted no time in requesting your indulgence. Our suspicions about the girl have proven true. This clarifies everything we've grown to learn about the nature of the chasm and how it can be used to achieve the great objective.'

'Are you quite sure, Doctor?'

'Absolutely sure, Chancellor. My team analyzed the data, and full diagnostics have been run on the machine. There is no longer any doubt that we have found the one the chasm dweller spoke of. We already knew the girl was a true conductor; we just didn't understand the depth and breadth of what that would mean. It was all only theoretical until now. This changes everything in our favor.'

'Indeed, it does, Dr. Nefas,' Chancellor Tallis affirmed. 'You are to be commended. When can the girl reenter the chasm?'

'She is still very weak, but debriefing is complete. The girl isn't aware of what occurred. Communications with the chasm could theoretically be established as soon as she recovers strength.'

The councilmembers murmured with excitement and several nodded in satisfaction.

'Very well,' the head of the council responded over the growing din, 'take the Tenebrae mirror immediately, and set it up in the large ceremonial cavern on the outskirts of the city. Send men at once to collect the girl.'

77

'I beg your pardon, Chancellor, but she needs time to recover before—'

'We don't have the luxury of allowing her more rest. We are running out of time. From this moment, she must be kept under surveillance and escorted. Let no one see or talk to the girl, and send her into the chasm as soon as your team is ready. Comprenez-vous, Doctor?'

The doctor bowed patronizingly, his servile manner highlighting his mousy features. He had tried to warn the fool. If the Chancellor wanted to destroy the girl by sending her back into the chasm too soon, who was he to argue?

'Of course. You know best, Chancellor,' he said aloud, the faintest hint of smugness beginning to seep through his apparent deference.

The head of the council narrowed his eyes in annoyance. 'Oh, and Doctor,' he replied, silencing the excited murmuring of the councilmembers with his hand, 'if you fail at this, you will live to regret that you ever drew breath.'

The self-satisfied expression died on the doctor's face. He bowed again, this time in perfect Tenebrae fashion, his demeanor quickly taking on a more humble guise.

'Yes, Chancellor. I will not betray your trust.'

The head of the council waved for him to go, and the doctor backed out of the room in deference, his contrite face now pale in the dim light.

The doors closed as the councilmembers began to talk excitedly amongst themselves.

'Could it be that we are finally on the verge of a breakthrough with the outer chasm?'

'This is certainly the girl that he asked for.'

As the council conversed, their anticipation grew. In the midst of their rising satisfaction, the chamber doors were loudly thrown open, and a captain of the Tenebrae guard entered, breathless.

'What is it?' the head of the council asked, annoyed at the disruption.

'The girl, sir . . .' he said, his voice betraying his fear as he beheld the council. But gathering courage, the captain straightened his shoulders and continued, wide-eyed, 'The chasm jumper . . . Chancellor, she's gone!'

Chapter 8

The Cross-roads

Abon peered around the corner and down the dark corridor. Watching him from behind, Stella saw something in his hand. Looking closer she realized it was a handgun. How in Terra was he able to get a weapon? *No one* had weapons except the officers.

Looking back, he noticed her expression and winked at her. Then motioning to her, he disappeared into the next hall. She took a deep breath and followed him.

Tenebrae was the largest city in Terra in those days; it was made up of a series of connecting avenues and boulevards which the people used to travel in the city and the luxurious Lev train which went to all the major stops and also far away, beyond her knowledge. Abon avoided every one of these and took her instead on tracks—narrow side paths that were infrequently used, where they would be less noticed.

After a while, they came to places that she didn't recognize, and as she looked around, she felt herself begin to relax. She asked him where he was taking her.

'A place where we can get help and supplies,' he responded curtly. Abon hadn't relaxed one atom. He was scanning their surroundings continuously. The weapon was out of sight. She decided not to press him.

The track soon became wider and approached an ancient, underground lake. There were several large, opulent pleasure boats along a dock on one side.

'This is Deception Lake,' Abon told her. 'Fortified walls with guarded gates completely surround the city, except here—here, the lake is encompassed on three sides by a curtain of solid rock that extends all the way to the cavern roof. There are seldom patrols in this area because it's considered the most secure part of Tenebrae's border.'

Abon glanced around cautiously. There was no one in sight. The hour was still very early; most people were undoubtedly still in bed.

He took the track along the edge of the water, and Stella followed, admiring the lake as they went. Its mighty depth reached below the roots of Tenebrae's vast tunnel system. The beauty and extent of the lake had inspired awe and wonder, even in the days of Tenebrae's forefathers. Luminescent shades of blues and greens created the illusion of shining sapphires and emeralds submerged and swimming in the deep. It was made even more lovely by the reflection of the delicate and colorful stalagmites which cascaded high above in the wide, shimmering pool that lapped gently on the speckled-sand shore.

After a few minutes, they approached a sheer rockface that rose abruptly, soaring up vertically to the dome several hundred feet above. The track narrowed and snaked between the sheer cavern wall and the brim of the lake. Along this path Abon guided them for several hours until the boat-lined dock, the sandy shore, and even the lights of the city had all melted into the dimness far behind them.

At mid-morning, they stopped along the bank and breakfasted. 'I'm sure they've discovered that we're missing by now,' Abon told her, looking back over the water in the direction of Tenebrae. He smirked. 'Archer's going to be scratching his head wondering how we bypassed all their security measures.'

He handed Stella dried food from his pack. After examining it curiously, she took a bite. Whatever it was, it was much better than Tenebrae gruel.

Taking their canteens, Abon climbed down the short rocky bank to the water's edge. Stella sat on the edge of the track, resting.

'Even contenders need a break now and again,' she said to him. 'Aren't you tired, Abon?'

'I'm alright. You're the one who's been worked day and night,

Stella,' he said, glancing at her while he filled the containers. He looked grim. 'But you've held up better than most people would have in spite of it,' he said, passing a full canteen to her. 'I've never seen them push someone to their breaking point like they've pushed you.'

Stella said nothing and took a long draught of the cool water. *Is that what they had been trying to do? Break me?*

He returned to the water and bathed his face and neck. Stella watched him. She couldn't go any farther now without a rest, but Abon didn't seem tired at all. She wondered why. He straightened up and, coming over, took a seat next to her on the rock. They gazed out over the water together in silence, and a peace seemed to settle over them.

'Abon?' Stella asked after some time.

'Yeah, Stel?'

'What will happen if they find us?'

'Don't worry Stella. They're not going to,' he said, turning in her direction and catching her expression of fear. His countenance was reassuring and resolute. 'I won't let that happen.'

After resting awhile, they continued on, making their way along the shoreline. The track wound on and slowly narrowed by degrees, until it was a rough footpath only wide enough for one. Stella continued to follow him until, suddenly, Abon stopped. He was scanning the wall, looking for something. She looked too but couldn't see any defining features in the solid rock face.

'Yes, this is the place,' he said quietly and pulled a small device with a keypad from his bag. He entered a code into it, and a faint click was heard. In the cavern wall, a low door silently swung in, revealing a small catacomb-like passage. He motioned for her to stay, disappearing into the entrance. She glanced nervously around, but everything was still.

Several minutes elapsed before he returned, signaling for her to follow. She stepped over the rocky threshold, and Abon latched the door again behind her. He led her through a winding labyrinth of tunnels. It wasn't very long before Stella failed to keep any sense of direction and felt helplessly lost.

They turned a corner and came to a narrow stairway. They began to climb up into the darkness. After every flight of stairs, there was a landing and then another flight continuing up in the same direction. Stella's ears pressurized multiple times as they climbed. Flight after flight, landing after landing—in this way they traveled a great distance—across land and in altitude.

After they had gone several miles and Stella's legs began protesting at every rise, they reached a long landing. In front of them, along one side, was a wide metal door. Abon punched a code into the small keypad on the wall next to it, and the door immediately slid open. It was some type of cargo elevator. He motioned for Stella to get in, and with a sharp, sweeping glance behind, followed her. He entered another code on the elevator's keypad, and the doors closed, shutting them in. The elevator lurched into motion.

'You might as well get some rest; we're going to be here a while,' he told her, tossing his pack down and stretching out on the ground. 'It'll be a few hours.'

Stella nodded, relieved, and sat down, leaning comfortably against her bag. He didn't have to tell her twice. As soon as she stopped moving, she nodded off. She was deep in dreamless sleep when, before she knew it, Abon was gently shaking her awake once more.

'Stella, we're almost there,' he told her.

She opened her eyes, wondering how much time had passed. Had Abon been able to rest? As he helped her to her feet, her eyes observed his careworn features, doubting it.

The elevator was slowing and, before long, came to an abrupt, grinding halt. The metal doors creaked opened revealing a long, ascending staircase. Abon stepped out and, after a moment, motioned for Stella to follow him. Near the top of the flight of stairs, he gestured for her to wait. He continued up the rest of the flight cautiously and onto the landing above.

She peered silently over the top step. They had reached a massive cavern where many paths and stairs emptied into a great courtyard. It was clad in smooth, worked stone. It was some kind of main thoroughfare. There was a large, white stone structure in the center of the cavern, held up by intricately carved and ancient looking pillars. Stella saw that the architecture was different from anything in Tenebrae and thought it must be old, very old.

Abon was quietly moving past every entry point, pausing and listening at each one. He reached one of the far tunnels across the courtyard from Stella and disappeared from view. She didn't like losing sight of him in this place. Her heart beat loudly as she watched, waiting. After a few minutes, he reappeared and walked directly towards her.

'There are some people here who I arranged to meet,' he told her quietly. 'They will help us.'

'Who are they?' she asked nervously.

He looked at her and smiled. 'Don't worry, Stel. They're friends.'

She followed him to the tunnel and saw a man dressed in dark clothing step out of the shadows. His watchful eyes were observing her closely; there was a guarded curiosity in his glance. Abon and the stranger exchanged a few hushed words. Abon glanced back at her.

'Stella, this is Sergeant Caleb MacIntyre.'

She nodded slowly at him. She had recognized instantly that he was some kind of foreign soldier. His uniform was very different from anything she'd seen before, and his hair and beard were shaped in a strange way. The weapon he carried, strapped across his torso, was a type of gun unknown to her. And sergeant? Was that his name or his title? She had no clue. She had seen foreigners from outside of Tenebrae at times in the marketplace, but this man was altogether different.

'Hello, ma'am,' he said, speaking Exter, the language of foreigners, in a way that sounded strange to her ears. He continued, 'It's a great pleasure to meet you. Welcome to the Cross-roads.'

'May the warmth of Terra be yours,' she answered politely but haltingly in the same language.

'Thank you, ma'am,' he responded quietly and glanced at Abon. 'Please follow us now. We need to hurry.'

She nodded and silently followed Abon, wondering where they

were taking her and wishing with impatience that Abon would give her some explanation.

Ahead in the dark, Stella jumped as several soldiers, dressed in the same fashion as the first man, emerged and silently fell in around them. Abon smiled at her reassuringly. They followed the tunnel for a short time, the strangers flanking Stella with their weapons drawn. Watching their movements, she realized that they reminded her of Abon—he had moved in the same controlled, guarded manner since they left the dormitories. *These must be his people.*

They crossed a side passage, and then abruptly, the lead man held up his hand. The others stopped instantly, and Abon put his hand on her arm, signaling for her to be still. They listened. After a moment, she heard voices coming up the corridor. By the sounds of it, they were approaching fast. Hiding was impossible; the passages stretched on, flat and plumb straight in each direction without variance.

Abon led Stella away from the entrance and positioned her against a wall. 'Stay as low as you can,' he whispered in her ear, taking up a position in front of her as the others stealthily concealed themselves at the mouth of the corridor.

In a moment, she heard the approaching group begin to slow and then saw a soldier step warily into the opening with his weapon drawn. He wore the red signet of Tenebrae emblazoned on his black uniform. The others in his company followed close behind.

Seeing them made Stella's blood grow cold. She had no love for the Tenebrae soldiers. They were cruel and full of corruption, extracting bribes in exchange for protection from anyone below their rank. They served the stratas, but everyone else, including chasm jumpers, served them. They were restrained by fear of their owners and nothing else.

In an instant, the hidden men were upon the soldiers, and the sound of gunfire broke out, bouncing wildly off the corridor walls. The Tenebraeans dove to the ground, directing their assault towards Abon. A barrage of gunfire came towards them; Abon's weapon answered in rapid response. The uniform above Abon's knee was shredded open, and a dark scarlet stain appeared in the fabric spreading downward. But he continued firing without pause.

Abon and the foreigners fought with disciplined precision, and the Tenebrae men soon began to falter. The onslaught was fierce, and they had been caught off guard. Losing heart, several turned and fled as their comrades fell. Caleb sent two of his men after them with a sharp order.

At that moment, a searing pain ripped through Stella's right shoulder. She gasped as the tunnel began to spin, and she fought to stay conscious. The gunfire soon slowed and then ceased, and then Abon was once again beside her.

'Stella, you're hit!' he cried in dismay.

'So are you,' she rasped, trying to focus her blurred vision on his injured leg in worry.

'It only grazed me.' He staunched the wound at her shoulder, and another man came to help, kneeling down.

'She's losing a lot of blood,' the soldier muttered. 'Lift her up a bit, Jared.'

Abon nodded in response, lifting her carefully and turning her so the man could put pressure on both sides of her shoulder. Stella gasped in pain. Caleb came up beside them, and working together, they succeeded in slowing the bleeding.

The others soon returned from pursuing the enemy. They spoke to the sergeant in low voices. 'None escaped,' one of the men reported. 'We searched their bodies but found nothing useful.'

'Search the enemy here as well for any information we can find,' he ordered.

The men worked quickly, finding a pouch with official looking papers on one Tenebrae soldier. The sergeant scanned the documents and put them in his pack, giving the order to prepare to leave.

Turning to Abon, he said, 'I don't like the amount of blood she's lost, but we need to keep moving.'

'She won't be able to walk,' the other man commented.

'I'll carry her,' Abon told them.

The sergeant nodded. Addressing his men in a low voice, he said,

'Those soldiers were most likely searching for the girl. We have to assume they know she's missing. That means we'll need to move fast before the tunnels are cut off. Time to roll.'

'I hate to do this, but we have to keep moving,' Abon told her, lifting her carefully.

It was the one smooth, seemingly effortless motion that surprised Stella. Why hadn't she noticed before how strong he was?

He looked down at her. 'Comfy?' he asked, his eyes teasing.

'Yes,' she answered, trying to sound lighthearted, 'but I hope you know I'm not carrying you if you get shot—so don't even think about it.'

He laughed under his breath. 'Alright. Deal.'

The men set the fastest pace that they'd traveled until now. Stella could feel their tense alertness as they swiftly traveled through corridors and up endless flights of stairs—up, always up. If Abon was tired, he gave no sign.

The agony in her shoulder grew worse, and she began fighting the urge to wretch from the pain. It was mercy when the warm feeling of unconsciousness began to close around her, and she knew no more.

* * *

'. . . the defector. She's been shot. She needs a medic immediately.'

Stella became aware of the rumbling of an engine and opened her eyes. She was leaning on Abon. They were in some kind of military vehicle. He sat holding her, alert and watchful, his arm resting protectively around her injured shoulder. The sergeant was speaking to several armed guards.

A massive set of doors opened, and they drove inside a large concrete entrance facing yet another pair of reinforced doors. She glanced up at Abon, and their eyes met.

He smiled. 'Good morning, sleepyhead.'

'I used to like mornings,' she groaned.

As the second set of doors opened, she was instantly

overwhelmed by a terrible, bright light. Blinded, she shielded her eyes and cried out. Abon quickly covered her face with his arm and pulled his coat over her head.

'I'm sorry, Stella. I know it hurts; it will pass soon.'

She heard him urgently discussing something with the others and felt herself being lifted out of the vehicle and carried. She heard many urgent voices. Abon was saying something. Many people were there. Where were they? Why did her eyes feel like they were on fire?

'Abon, what's going on? How can you see?' she asked, confused.

'We are at the border of my country, Stella,' he said gently. 'We are going to the surface.'

Her head swam. The surface? What was he talking about? Didn't he know that they couldn't survive there?

'What? Are you saying . . . that you're a surface dweller?' she asked disbelievingly.

Like everyone else in Tenebrae, she had heard the tales of a primitive people who roamed above, dwelling on the surface. As the story went, they worshipped a terrible god who burned their skin and eyes with a great fiery ball that hung suspended above them. But it was just a tale for children. *Wasn't it?* She felt the panic inside begin to rise.

'Stella, please trust me. We're going to a place that's specially lit, where you'll be able to see. Here, we're almost there now—hang on.'

He carried her through a doorway, and as the doors closed, they shut out the blinding beams. She felt his arm pull away, and she carefully opened her eyes.

Abon was looking at her intently. 'Can you see?' he asked.

She nodded, slowly looking around. They were in a large medical room, next to a table. Many strangers were there.

Abon set her on the table, nodding to the two men who stood by. They spoke together in an unknown, foreign tongue as they carefully unwrapped the bandage at Stella's shoulder, investigating the damage and discussing it as they worked.

Stella turned and scowled at Abon. 'Now, will you tell me what's going on?'

Taking her hand, he said with a grin, 'I'll tell you anything you want to know, Stella.'

Chapter 9

The Western Woods

'Tell me more, Abon—sorry, I mean Ja-red. Jared? Did I say that right?' she asked, wrinkling her nose at the sound of the strange name in her ears. His real name perplexed her almost as much as the idea that Abon had been born on the outside surface of Terra. She was lying on her back, basking in the warmth of a large, wood-burning fireplace. Abon was leaning against the wall nearby, watching her.

'Yes, close enough,' he laughed. He liked hearing his name pronounced in Stella's soft accents. 'Tell you more about what?' he asked. 'You've been asking questions for a week straight. Aren't you running out of them yet?'

She had relentlessly hounded him for explanations while they were in the process of surfacing. Every few days they had been moved to a new bunker, closer to the surface, to acclimatize. Each bunker was a little more like the surface in pressure, climate, light, and temperature—among other things. They said this was necessary for people born in Terra; in the past, some had died from ascending too quickly.

When she asked him about the war he was fighting, he told her that, from the beginning, it had always been a war of ideas. The tension and corruption had mounted until, at last, the military and elected officials had fractured, each vying for control. Power structures on the surface were drastically changed. In the throes of revolution, the land had shifted into three, new, separate self-governments.

The Midland region of Arva was the largest by far, cutting a wide swath from the northern prairies to the deep south. A strategic alliance had developed between Abon's wooded homeland of Vespera in the West and the far, wind-swept Eastern Shores as a result. It wasn't enough though. Communication with the East was spotty at best, while the Midland region was undivided and had massive food capabilities and resources. They were slowly gaining in both ground and wealth. Arva was winning this war.

People were fleeing from the East and West in large numbers to the Midlands, in search of more stability and order, provisions, and, rumor had it, more freedom. Jared had lost many friends and comrades who had defected over the mountains before the last pass was blocked. The West needed a strong ally and fast.

There was a knock on the door, and Sgt. MacIntyre entered. 'Pardon the intrusion, ma'am, but there's a general come specifically to meet with you.'

He looked at her and then Abon. They exchanged a quick glance that she couldn't decipher. 'They're in the conference room,' he continued. 'I'll lead you there.'

The room was packed with military personnel. She was trying to learn the differences between the ranks and branches represented in the different bunkers from Abon, but she was beginning to feel that it was hopeless.

She was guided to a chair. She looked back. Abon wasn't there. *He must still be in the hall.* She turned around to search for him, but the door closed and was blocked by several soldiers.

She looked at them. 'Please move out of my way,' she said, perplexed. They just stared at her without responding. She could feel her stomach sink.

'We just want a few minutes of your time, Ms. Stella,' stated a deep voice behind her.

She turned around. A uniformed man, tall and broad, stood at the far end of the table. He looked to be in his late forties, or perhaps early fifties, and was decorated with many medals.

'I'm General Campbell. I have some important information I'd like to discuss with you on behalf of the Vespera government—if I may.'

'I would like Abon . . . I mean Jared . . . Jared Crux to be present before we proceed.'

'Officer Crux does not have the clearance for this briefing. He has been given another assignment below the surface. Please, miss, sit down, and I'll make this as brief as possible,' he said, gesturing to the empty chair.

'Officer Crux is still needed here. I will gladly help you in any way I can. But he has been my guide, and I honestly don't think I can manage without him.' She looked unwaveringly at the general.

He returned her gaze, measuring her. After a moment, he answered, 'It's unfortunate, but it's out of my hands now.'

'Who reassigned him?'

'I did.'

'And it's out of your hands?' she questioned.

'He asked to be reassigned as quickly as possible,' he said calmly.

She exhaled sharply. It felt like she'd just been slapped in the face.

General Campbell continued, 'He is not used to being inactive for so long, and he was growing concerned for his team under the surface. Your disappearance has put pressure on our people below. Some of them are at risk. Officer Crux wanted to descend as quickly as possible to help them.'

Well, she couldn't blame him. If she had anyone down there who she cared about, she'd be worried too. She sank slowly into the chair. She looked at the general, disheartened. 'What information do you want to discuss?'

'We were able to procure copies of the machine readings of your chasm jump. We'd like to ask you a few questions. I have some of the West's leading scientists here. You won't mind if they gather a few of your vitals, will you?'

It didn't sound like a question.

'We'd like to have you attempt the jump again. We've replicated the Tenebrae technology in our lab, and we want to see if we can have more success than they did.'

'What is your goal in all this?' she asked.

'I will be honest with you, as I hope you will be with me. I will tell you what I can. It's a simple goal. We believe the Tenebrae government is trying to create an alliance with those across the chasm. The government of Vespera would like to be included in the process so that the result will be beneficial for everyone.'

He sounded sincere. 'My jump was not ordinary,' she said, shaking her head. 'I don't know if it's repeatable.'

'There's only one way to find out, then, isn't there?' he said with the hint of a smile.

* * *

The scientists were very thorough. Stella was in the lab, on yet another stainless-steel table, having more blood drawn. She had answered their questions with caution, remembering Abon's warning in the beginning. What they never suspected, they never asked about.

They had been at this for seven days: reading vital signs, testing blood, taking machine readings, asking questions. They had tried to administer another electromagnetic field in her blood, but she had refused. She wasn't going to let them put something back in her that Abon had taken out. So, instead, they fitted her arm with a device that wirelessly connected to their machine and would guide her back. It made her think of the imported slaves in Tenebrae before they were processed. They all wore a similar-looking device.

She was tired. It was crushing that Abon never said good-bye. When the meeting with General Campbell had ended, she searched for him, but he was already gone. Even his room was empty. He must have been planning his departure for a while.

Stella glanced around the lab. The machine was massive, taking up a large portion of the room. Many computers and workstations were scattered throughout the lab. Along the far wall were a row of small containment cells. It appeared that freedom, even on the surface, could be taken away, she thought darkly.

They wanted to attempt a jump tomorrow. The scientists were all busy in their own world, consumed with various tasks. Sgt. MacIntyre was stationed inside the door, ever watchful. She knew one of his men would be stationed outside the door as well. They had guarded her continuously since the day at the Cross-roads.

The lead scientist approached. 'We are done for today. Get as much rest as possible, and we'll send for you when we're ready.' He helped her off the table and went back to his desk.

She stretched and walked slowly to the door. Sgt. MacIntyre opened it and followed her out. As they walked back to her quarters, she thought about the day they met, and she remembered Abon's warm manner toward him.

'Sgt. MacIntyre, I hope you don't mind me asking, but did you know that Abon—I mean Jared—did you know that he was leaving?'

'I don't mind at all, ma'am. I had no idea they were reassigning him. I was with him when he got the order. He was pretty shocked. They had him roll out that same hour too. I've never seen that before.'

She stopped and looked up at him. The room had been so full of people; she had assumed Sgt. MacIntyre had been among them.

'Weren't you there when General Campbell explained that he'd been reassigned? And that Jared *requested* the reassignment?'

'The brass said that, did he?' the sergeant said under his breath, stroking his beard. 'The general's men wouldn't let none of us in.'

He turned and looked at her intently. 'There's no way in Vespera that Crux wanted to leave, ma'am. I hope you know that.'

* * *

Stella was still pondering Sgt. MacIntyre's words the next morning while the team connected her to their network and monitored her vitals. It was clear to her that, regardless of whether the other surface countries could be trusted, the government of Vespera certainly could not.

After Sgt. MacIntyre's revelation, she had considered refusing to cooperate with the general, but she couldn't bring herself to do it. She knew she couldn't trust him, but her desire to enter the inner chasm was too strong. She realized that she would experience that agonizing pain again and that with every jump she was risking her life—Rafiya was never far from her thoughts—but her yearning to regain the peace she had found in the meadow eclipsed every fear.

The lead scientist approached. 'Our machine might work a little differently than what you've used in the past, but it should allow you to jump for a few seconds at least. Once you get back, we'll calibrate it and attempt a longer jump next time.'

'Just don't turn it on,' she told him.

He glanced at her in surprise and then laughed. 'It won't work without power, Stella,' he explained dismissively.

'Don't turn it on,' she repeated, the fear in her eyes giving him pause.

'Well, if you want to try it first without power, go for it,' he said indulging her. 'We'll fire it up after that. We're ready whenever you are.' He went back to review the reports that were spread around his desk.

She closed her eyes for a moment, focusing and remembering her training. She walked towards the mirror, already sensing the force from it pull at her. She slowly put her hand against the glass, feeling the familiar sensation of it yielding, softening around her hand, drawing her in. The machine immediately began humming loudly, and ink-colored mist formed in the center of the chasm stabilizer. The heads of the shocked scientists shot up, and they stared at the mirror in awe.

Stella braced herself, knowing the pain that was coming, and let it draw her into itself. All became dark as she passed through into the agony of nothingness. Once again, the suspended darkness and suffocation overwhelmed her. The complete absence of light, heat, and sound pressed on her like a great, gnawing void that she was sure would crush and consume her. At last, she dropped to her hands and knees and gasped for breath.

It was finally over; the pain of the jump slowly began to recede. She was in the meadow, and it was night. She scanned her surroundings—the sky was starless, darkened with storm clouds, and the stench of smoke filled her nostrils.

Her eyes swept down to the ground beneath her. She had fallen into something damp that she, at first, assumed was mud. On closer inspection, she scrambled to her feet, repulsed, suddenly realizing that it was blood. In horror, she looked up and saw that there was a trail of scarlet that traversed the field from the place where the girl had attacked Stella to the chasm stabilizer. It appeared as if an injured body had been dragged. She tried not to wretch as she quickly wiped her blood-streaked hands on her clothes. With trepidation, she surveilled the shadows around her, but there was no sign of the girl—or the lamb.

What had happened to the meadow? She was no longer in a peaceful field; before her lay an open space that was desolate, burned, and bare. The mighty oak that had stood proud and green was now charred—dead and stripped naked of its once majestic leaves, except for a score of shriveled and blackened husks that dangled from its lifeless limbs.

Wandering around the tree, she saw that the artesian spring, which had once bubbled out from between the tree's thick roots, was dried up—its deep streamed dusty and barren. She turned and began to walk across the wasteland towards the hill and the door set in stone. How had this place changed so much?

She climbed the now blackened foothill and looked at the door. It was barely recognizable: seared, half-hanging on its hinges, and wide open.

She stopped short in alarm. Who had opened the door? She peered through the doorway into the wide gulf, seeing only darkness. At once, she heard a voice behind her.

'Hello, Stella.'

She turned, but there was nothing there.

'I've been waiting a long time for you,' the voice continued.

'For me?' she asked. 'Who are you?'

'We are the chasm dwellers,' the voice answered.

Stella looked around but saw only the dimly lit meadow. 'How did you know I was coming?' she asked.

'I've seen your attempts and knew you would come eventually,' the voice replied.

She felt a sense of dread that she couldn't explain. This being felt powerful, very powerful. A frigid cold crept through the air and surrounded her—whether from the doorway or from the source of the voice, she couldn't tell. She began to shiver.

'How long have you been here?' she asked him.

The voice laughed, and she caught a glimpse of movement in the dark.

'A long time and a short time. Forever and not long.'

'How is that possible?'

'Stella, you know so little. Much that you think is impossible is not so. Soon I will show you just how much is within my grasp.'

She felt a chill run down her spine. Instantly, she was overcome by a strong urge to flee, but she was frozen. Her legs felt like lead anchored in place.

'What do you want?' she asked the voice warily.

'A home,' the voice responded with sadness. 'We were forced from our home long ago, by a race of brutal conquerors, and we must continually search for a new one.'

Stella felt a sudden wave of pity for the creature, despite the instinctive feeling that she shouldn't trust it. 'How many of you are there?' she asked, afraid of the answer.

The voice laughed menacingly. 'Armies and civilizations—your numbers pale in comparison.'

Something was moving closer to Stella, slowly. She saw the reflection of a viridescent light; a soft glow was beginning to radiate in the dark, revealing the shimmer of an outlined form. As the light expanded, she caught her breath. She could see him.

He was darkness and light at the same time—dreadful and very beautiful. Stella looked at him in awe. He was majestic, and a shadowy light seemed to radiate out from within him. His face was captivating to look upon; his skin glistened. His rich garments were formed of scales of verdant abalone, like the inside of a shell. He shimmered with living shade.

Hidden just beneath the surface of his great beauty, she could sense a deep well of fury within the creature's being. Stella was captivated and terrified all at once. To her dismay, the chasm dweller approached her. She backed away, frightened.

'Please don't come any closer,' she heard herself say, but her voice sounded strange and distant—a weak, quaking whimper.

Then she saw the shapes of countless beings in the darkness behind him, their bodies emitting a soft, green glow.

He laughed softly and continued towards her.

Her mind reeled. She turned quickly and fled back down the hill towards the mirror. She felt the chasm begin to shake.

'No!' the chasm dweller yelled after her.

With just a quick gesture of his hand, he pushed the Tenebrae mirror away. It slid in a fast, smooth motion, stopping to rest on the distant side of the meadow. Lifting his powerful arms, he steadied the great chasm with some unseen force. The earthquake slowly ceased.

Stella stood rooted in dread. He came and stood beside her, close enough that she felt the intense cold radiating off his body.

His cool, green eyes narrowed. 'You cannot close the chasm,' he said quietly but intensely. Turning to the door, he called, and more beings began passing through the doorway.

'Bind her,' he ordered.

The dark, glowing forms descended upon her. They would have killed her, but the chasm dweller forbade it.

'Don't harm her yet,' he commanded coldly. He signaled for more chasm dwellers to come, and they poured over the threshold.

She tried to think of something, anything to prevent or slow them, but what could she do? It was too late. The door was open. She was hopelessly and utterly powerless to stop them.

* * *

Jared heard a crisp knock on the door. 'Come in,' he said emotionlessly.

'I see you're moping about like usual.'

Jared bolted up when he heard the familiar voice. 'Caleb! What are you doing here?'

'I'm here with new orders," he announced. Jared looked like he hadn't slept in days. 'You're rolling out in the morning.'

'What? Where to?' he asked, getting to his feet.

'Back to the surface.'

Jared looked at him. 'What's going on, Caleb? Where is Stella?'

Sgt. MacIntyre studied his friend, deliberating over what to say. 'She jumped again. They attempted it way too soon. Our tech wasn't ready.' He glanced at the ceiling in frustration. 'Jared, she's still in there.'

'What do you mean?' he responded anxiously.

'She never came out of the jump. She's been in there for two days. They've tried everything to bring her out.'

'How is that possible? Nobody has the strength to keep an inner chasm open that long.'

'No one's explaining nothing. They've ordered you back to see what you know.'

Jared's jaw clenched. He should never have left—orders or not. Stella had trusted him, and he'd left her. And now she was in terrible danger. He paced the room, struggling to master the anger and frustration rising inside. He tried to think. Nothing with Stella's jumps ever happened the way they expected. Why were they so different? He had to find answers.

'We're not leaving in the morning, Caleb,' he told his friend, who had been watching him closely. 'We're leaving now.'

Chapter 10

Treaties

Stella watched the legions gathering in the inner chasm bleakly. She ached all over. She was in a living nightmare. The chasm dwellers had beat her and tormented her for hours upon hours, day upon day—except that, now, the light of day never came—it was just a succession of darkness that never seemed to end.

When they had finally tired of her, they threw her against the dead tree in the glade where she was forced to watch the chasm dwellers passing through the door. It felt like an eternity, yet they were still coming. She could see the many rows of an army assembling in the fields to her right. She watched as the units fashioned a multitude of strange and savage looking weapons, heaping them in great piles. There was no mistaking it. They were preparing for war. What purpose they had in keeping her alive, she couldn't guess. She had learned that these were cruel beings that seemed to savor her pain and fear. She tried to show as little as possible.

But her fears grew as the creature that had first spoken to her approached. 'You will be our messenger,' he told her directly. 'You will tell Tenebrae Councilman Jolon that the treaty will move forward as planned with the West and that we accept their offer of hosts from the surface. We want more than they're offering. In exchange, we will send his directions to the Westland's general who will follow their orders. Tell him that they are running out of time— our enemy will be here soon.'

'How will I tell him?' she asked blankly.

'We will send you back tethered,' he said, a smile on his lips. 'We have immense pleasure in tethering, but you might not feel the same.' His laugh shot fear to her core.

'After that, will you leave here?' she asked, stalling.

He sneered at her. 'We are never leaving here. We will always keep a battalion here from now on. And you will never be free.'

She knew he meant every word.

She felt the cold emanating from him as he moved closer. He held out his hands and began fabricating something in the air. An object began to form. A single ring appeared, hovering before him, and then another. Soon a chain began to take shape, one link at a time assembling together, suspended in the air, growing ever longer. When he was done, he smiled a slight, cruel smile at her, and the chain dropped to the ground.

He waved an arm dismissively towards Stella. Immediately, the chain seemed to come alive. Stella watched, immobile and filled with dread, as it moved in a slithering motion towards her. It reached her foot and, like a viper in a tree, coiled around her ankle and began to climb. It continued wrapping itself around her until both legs were held tightly in its constricting grasp. Then the chain stretched upward and crossed her abdomen. It slithered up slowly, encircling her body, spiraling around her diaphragm. Reaching her upper body, it paused and appeared poised to strike.

Suddenly, it sprang, piercing her skin with sharp, metal pinchers. Stella screamed in agony. It began burrowing, searching for a gap and finding one, pressing itself through her ribcage and penetrating her heart.

She clenched her teeth, feeling excruciating pain and pressure as the serpentine chain continued to dig. In disbelief, Stella watched the chain bore into her flesh, until even the end disappeared through the wound. The puncture then closed up, leaving no trace.

Then the chasm dweller lifted his hand, testing his grip. Stella gasped as she felt the chain constrict inside of her, grasping her vitals, and even her very will, with a grip of steel. She felt herself rise as he lifted her high off the ground and carried her towards the Tenebrae mirror. Without a word, he thrust her through.

Instantly Stella was plunged into the painful blackness. Suspended in the nothingness, she began to weep with anguish. She felt the flame of courage dwelling inside her begin to waver and sputter, and then it went out. No words can be found for the despair of that hour. All light was extinguished. And all was consumed by that great darkness.

Eventually the anguish of the jump began to subside, and the mist started to clear. She immediately recognized that she was in Tenebrae. Her back was held tightly against the glass, the hazy mist around her slowly dissipating.

Archer and a few others were working nearby. She heard him swear in shock, and immediately, he ran to her.

'Stella, you're alive! They told us you were dead. What is going on? How did you open the mirror?'

She tried to answer, but no words came out. Instead, she felt the firm command of the chasm dweller directing her what to say.

'Archer, get Councilman Jolon,' she gasped.

He looked at her sharply, calling one of his assistants over and ordering him to fetch the councilman without delay.

'He was just here moments ago, Stella. What is going on? The Tenebrae government is being very tight lipped.'

Again, Stella tried to answer, but it was futile. The chasm dweller held her voice in his own power.

Within moments, the middle-aged councilman appeared. He was a man lacking integrity and nerve, achieving his high position through bribes and corruption, and keeping it now through the same means.

Archer addressed him. 'Councilman, this is Stella. She was a chasm jumper here before she disappeared. We were told she was dead.'

'I know of her.' The councilman glanced at him before turning his attention on Stella. 'What do you have to say, girl?' he asked gruffly.

The chasm dweller put the words inside of her mind, and she faithfully repeated them to the councilman, 'The treaty will proceed. When you have subdued the surface, the chasm dwellers will require more hosts. The general tells us that Vespera is preparing a large offensive at the Tenebrae front two weeks from today. He awaits your orders. We must act quickly; the enemy is coming soon.'

The councilman nodded with pleasure. 'You are a great heroine to Tenebrae, girl. We will defeat our accursed enemies, after all, with your help. Tell the chasm dwellers that they will have as many hosts as they need, and tell the general to do exactly as I say.' He paused, thinking. 'Tell him to go on with the offensive as planned; we will be ready for them. When the last of Vespera's forces are broken, there will be no more resistance. Then they will gladly sign the treaty with us.'

He smiled in pleasure as he dispatched many more instructions through Stella to the chasm dweller, knowing that the girl would faithfully carry his orders to Vespera and to their covert ally, the general of the West.

* * *

Jared put his hand on the hard face of Vespera's Tenebrae mirror, watching for any sign of the dark mist swirling over its surface. Nothing was there. He then moved again across the room to the machine, saying nothing. He had arrived back at the surface lab in the Westlands to find the sensors showing that Stella was barely breathing—her vitals through the floor.

The lead scientist approached. 'We are continuing to monitor the inner chasm. It has stayed stable after a momentary fluctuation but has begun growing at an exponential rate. It can't stay stable at this growth rate for much longer. We are running out of ideas. Did she give you any clues into how this is happening?'

'No, she didn't,' he said. After a moment of thought, he shook his head, 'I don't think she understood it herself.'

Suddenly, the portal came to life, and blackness appeared on the surface of the mirror. Jared felt hope surge inside him as he saw Stella's hands emerge from the chasm. She was coming back!

Her arms and then her face became visible. But the instant his eyes fell on her pale and haunted aspect, Jared knew something was wrong. Stella's whole body passed through, but somehow, she was held tightly against the glass.

Her heart rate shot up, and she moaned. Several of the team members ran over; others stood, paralyzed in shock.

'Stella?' Jared was instantly next to her, looking at her in horror and taking in her injuries. He felt himself begin to shake with fury at the sight of her body riddled by abuse but, with an effort, calmed himself.

She focused and tried to speak.

'Stella, calm down. Don't try to talk,' a scientist told her.

She found Jared's face. The chasm dweller's power held her in an agonizing, iron grip. 'General Campbell . . . get him,' she gasped.

Jared nodded to the soldier at the door and heard him relay the message.

'What's happening, Stella? How are you being held?' he asked, urgently feeling around her limbs and torso in the mist, looking for a way to free her, frantically searching for what was keeping her fastened in the mirror. He tried pulling her towards him but stopped when her face silently contorted in pain. 'What can I do, Stella?' he asked desperately.

'Nothing,' she tried to say. Her lips moved, but no sound came out.

'I'll get you out of this,' he said intensely. 'Stay with me.'

General Campbell approached from behind Jared and stood over her. She fought the internal command wildly but was forced to train her eyes on him.

'Deal acceptable . . . need more hosts . . . will protect you . . . enemy coming.' She moaned. The pain from fighting the unseen tether was indescribable.

The general glanced nervously around and then back to her. It seemed his contact in Tenebrae had come through on his word of sending an informant after all.

'Good work, Stella,' he told her.

She nodded, but Jared, who was watching her closely, saw her eyes narrow as she glared at the general.

General Campbell cleared his throat and spoke forcefully, 'I want all personnel out. Clear the room. Now.'

As the room began to empty, Jared planted his feet. The general looked at him. 'You too, soldier. Out now.'

'I'm not leaving her.'

The general saw the determined set of his jaw and paused. 'I know you'd like to stay with your girlfriend, but what she has to tell me is classified. I'll let you right back in to visit when I'm done.'

'I'm not going anywhere,' he said with resolve.

The general looked at Stella. 'Tell him to leave until we are through—that you're okay, and he can come in after.'

Stella ground her teeth. There was no way in Terra that she would say that. But the chasm dweller's command came hard and fast. She wanted to cry out in agony but couldn't. Her mouth was determined to open, in spite of her, to order Jared away. She battled against the power of the tether, fighting to free herself from its grasp. It was all in vain. The internal chain tightened around her mercilessly, plunging her into anguish and despair. She was a slave and must obey.

She looked at him, defeated, and was forced to repeat the chasm dweller's words. 'Jared,' she whispered hoarsely, against everything within her very being, 'please leave. I am fine. We'll talk later.'

He winced, and his broad shoulders sunk. She watched him half-heartedly fight the general's men as they dragged him out.

When the room was empty, the general turned to her. 'Girl, tell them I accept. I will need the help they promised soon to defeat the players on this side. There are not enough in Vespera who want a treaty with Tenebrae, yet.'

'I have the information for you now,' Stella replied and, directed by the chasm dweller, began relating intelligence that she had gathered from the Tenebraean councilman about the upcoming battle, arms, and the number of men. Most of the information made little sense to Stella—much of it was about things that had not yet come to pass: outcomes of battles and choices that hadn't yet been made.

Stella wondered how the chasm dwellers could think they knew the future. She considered the possibility that they were all just insane. For an hour, Stella related knowledge back and forth between the two realms.

Finally, as the encounter drew to a close, the chasm dweller delivered his last orders, 'Stick to our agreement, and all will be done as discussed. And one last thing—the soldier, Jared Crux—he has become a liability. Get rid of him. Send him to the front and make sure he doesn't come back.'

Stella fought these last orders with all the ferocity that she possessed, with the whole of her passion and might, but the strength of the chasm dweller overpowered her—like surging floodwaters consume an earthen dike.

He had ground her will to dust in his merciless grip; Stella had finally been broken. She had uttered the words through clenched teeth, while her heart wept bitterly with the knowledge that she had been the vessel used to deliver Jared's death sentence.

The general nodded and retreated.

In a moment, Jared was sprinting across the lab toward her, as the science officers poured back into the room.

'Stella, I'm going to get you free. Have you got your tongue back yet?' he asked her with a grin, almost lightheartedly, while intently searching the surface of the mirror.

But she knew him better than that. She had caught the barely discernable edge to his voice underneath his practiced steadiness. He was quickly and methodically searching the chasm glass and stabilizer with his hands, looking for any variation or clue.

Stella's mind was screaming; she had to warn him. Despite the unavoidable agony, she pushed as hard as she could, once again, against the tether.

'You're in danger,' she tried to say, mouthing the words, but Jared just looked at her with questioning eyes. It was useless. Her energy was waning.

One of the scientists came up. 'Stella, how are you keeping the chasm open?' he asked in fascination.

She looked at Jared hopelessly, a tear welling up in her eye and slowly rolling down her cheek. He saw her despair. His heart wrenched.

The chasm dweller, who had been observing Jared through Stella's eyes, suddenly recoiled as he discerned a faint glow in Jared's face that he recognized as the light of Caelum. Instantly, he knew that Jared had somehow been to that realm or with those who had. He was immediately filled with loathing and blind hate, wanting nothing more than to cause him to suffer. He mercilessly tightened the tether around Stella, and she writhed painfully. He gave her back her voice, allowing her to cry out in pure and utter agony until there was no will left in her to utter a sound.

The medical assistant's voice grew urgent, 'Her vitals are getting worse . . . she's crashing.'

Jared's eyes reflected his terror; the creature drank it in, savoring it. Then he smiled cruelly and slowly began to extract her.

Her lids started to droop, and she felt herself being pulled back into the chasm.

'Stella!' Jared screamed, grabbing her arms in a vise-like grip, but it was futile. She melted back into the swirling dark. As she did, her body was stripped from his grasp, slipping through his fingers like a mist.

His hand slammed against the rigid surface of the glass in disbelief. After a stunned moment, he began punching it hard, with all his might. It was unyielding—solid and cold as stone.

He looked around him desperately, and striding to a nearby desk, overturned it; the computers smashed loudly as they dropped to the floor. He lifted the desk onto his shoulder and was about to use it to shatter the mirror when several men intervened.

'Stop! Don't break it! She can't get back without the stabilizer!' A scientist stood cowering between him and the Tenebrae mirror, his arms extended fearfully above his head. Others grabbed onto Jared, trying to hold him back.

Caleb came up beside him and, with a steady and reassuring tone, said, 'Put it down, Jared. We'll find another way to save her.'

Looking at his friend, Jared slowly lowered the desk to the ground. He glanced over to the machine monitors, trying to calm himself. He could hear the science officers still discussing her vitals. They were poor but steady. She was alive. But he had never felt so helpless in his life.

* * *

The brightly lit and well-tended street was calm and quiet, except for the soft breath of wind that unfurled a flag gracing the front porch of one of the houses. It was long after midnight in Arva. The house at the end of the lane had been dark for hours when, suddenly, a light appeared in an upper window.

The man inside had woken up in a cold sweat. Whether or not he had cried out, he couldn't say. He let his racing heart begin to calm as his eyes strayed over to his wife, stirring next to him.

'Nathan, you okay?' she asked groggily.

'Yes, Kay, don't worry. Everything's fine.'

'Okay,' she murmured, drifting back to sleep.

His eyes softened as he watched her. The young mother had spent many sleepless nights lately caring for their youngest. He wouldn't wake her now. He sat up gently.

He felt the vast weight of a great need pressing hard upon him. He knew he was being summoned. He had experienced this type of burden only a handful of times in his life, but the extensive training that he had received while serving under the high commander did not fail him. He had been taught to fight, and he knew what he had to do. Wiping the sweat from his brow and taking a deep breath, he slid off the bed to his knees and urgently began to petition the Master for help.

* * *

The dense darkness hovered over the ruin of the once peaceful meadow, the choking fumes sapping all remaining strength and life from the now consumed wasteland.

Stella woke up with a moan. She was bound securely and laying in the dirt. She tried to remember what had happened. Had she really seen Jared? What was he doing there? He must have come back. Instantly, she remembered the chasm dweller's order that she had uttered, and she fought despair.

Seized with a desire to somehow warn Jared, she was determined to find a way out of this place. She looked through the dark at the massive oak tree in the distance; though scorched and burned black, it still held its broad, spreading branches wide and uplifted in the twilight. Stella gleaned hope from that small, seeming act of resistance to the great darkness.

Suddenly, she heard a loud noise behind her. The door had slammed shut. The chasm dwellers approached to investigate. It was locked.

A commotion was heard throughout the ranks as their leader was informed and came to Stella. 'What did you do to the door?' he accused. His plan could not move forward unless the door remained open.

'Nothing,' she answered.

'Where is the key?' he demanded.

Not waiting for an answer, he raised his arm in the air toward her. Her bonds came undone, but she felt the internal chains tighten and lift her off the ground. He looked threateningly at her.

'I don't know,' she choked out in pain and fear.

He let her drop, and she was dragged toward the door by his unseen power.

'Open it!' he commanded, as he threw her roughly into it.

She stood up shakily, her newly freed limbs protesting after their long imprisonment. She tried the knob, but it didn't turn.

'I can't open it; it's locked,' she told him, her voice wavering.

His eyes considered her for a moment. 'Search her carefully,' he said to the others. 'If you can't find the key, beat her until she tells us where it is.'

'I already told you I don't know where it is,' she spat back. 'I don't have it!'

The chasm dweller turned and approached her, standing so close that she began to shiver uncontrollably. He leaned his terrifying form even closer and slowly whispered in her ear, 'I will enjoy it all the same.' He stepped back and smiled at the fear in her eyes, gaining power from it.

Then he turned and nodded to the others. With the silent command, they fell on her, searching her garments. After several minutes they became rougher, ripping her clothes in search of the key. The transmitter was torn from her arm. They were pulling and tearing at her. She bit back a cry when a chunk of her hair was wrenched from her scalp.

Don't give them the satisfaction, she thought darkly. She tried to defend herself, her arms flailing wildly, but she was struck hard from behind and fell. On her hands and knees, fighting unconsciousness, she watched a steady flow of blood drip onto her shoulders and pool in the dirt below her. *Is this how it ends? I never would've guessed this ending,* she thought to herself and almost laughed.

Then darkness overtook her.

* * *

Jared awoke with a start. He lifted his head from his folded arms. He was sitting in a chair at a desk in the lab.

The science officers were gathered around the machine, speaking in urgent tones. Shaking off sleep, he stood and rushed over to see what the commotion was about. He looked at the nearest monitor, and his blood went cold.

Chaos began to build in the lab, as the scientists, in a flurry of action, ran diagnostics, read the last printouts of Stella's vitals, and watched the mirror for signs of opening. Jared forcefully pushed his way to the front of the group standing around the machine monitors. One glance confirmed what he dreaded. There were no readings coming from Stella at all. He instantly felt numb. His worst fears were being realized before his eyes, and there was nothing he could do except watch them come to pass, defenseless.

The science officers worked tirelessly throughout the day and night to try to reestablish communications. The team of doctors endlessly discussed the situation. But they were all flying blind. It was impossible for anyone to help her return without the transmitter. Many of the experts assumed she was dead. Jared stayed close and barely slept, but even his hope was starting to wane.

After going back to his quarters at midnight on the third day, he collapsed on the bed. The scientists had exhausted every possible avenue to find Stella, but he believed in his soul that she was still alive. He had to find other help, but where? Who could help them?

Just then there was a quick tap on the door. Jared sat up as Caleb pushed the door open and walked in.

'Come on in,' Jared said, his voice dripping with sarcasm.

Caleb silently crossed the room and sat down, leaning back in the chair. He seemed oblivious.

'Couldn't sleep?' Jared asked him.

'Something like that,' he answered.

Jared nodded and said nothing. Obviously, the sergeant had something on his mind.

After a moment, Caleb sat up straight in his chair. 'We've been reassigned.'

Jared caught his breath. It felt like he'd been hit in the gut. He closed his eyes. 'When?' he asked in a hardened tone.

'Day after tomorrow,' Caleb answered.

Jared clenched his jaw. 'What's the mission?' he asked dryly.

'You already know that, after we took Stella, the Tenebraeans started picking off our guys in the lower surface-level tunnels. Well, lately, in retaliation, some of our men killed their sentries in the upper levels of Tenebrae. The West doesn't want to commit officially, of course; but unofficially, it's looking like war. We're planning an offensive op.'

After a pause, the sergeant continued, 'There's more. There's an informant leaking sensitive information to our enemies. Nobody can find him. Everything we do—our enemies seem to be expecting it. Guys are starting to say the mole is a time-traveler or a ghost.'

Jared leaned forward, thinking. He'd sworn he would never leave

Stella again. But now she was gone: a captive in a faraway place or worse—dead. No, he quickly pushed the idea from his mind. But if he stayed, would it do her any good?

It was time to do something other than wait. He was sick of waiting. He would help with the offensive. After that, he would find out what happened to Stella, even if it killed him. And tracking down the traitor seemed like the best way to find more information. Jared wondered if this 'ghost' was human enough to bleed. He'd find out.

He glanced up at his friend, resigned. 'Let's do it.'

Chapter 11

Soldiers of Caelum

The next morning dawned clear over the Western Woods. Jared watched the sunrise, drinking it in, knowing he would be going below the surface again soon. He thought of the first morning here with Stella. They had reached the surface in the evening, and she had glowed with excitement. They had talked far into the night, neither of them thinking of rest. After many hours, something caught her attention, and she had wandered over to an eastern facing window. Jared had watched her and, after a moment, came up and stood beside her.

'What is that in the distance?' she asked him, pointing to where the first traces of light were becoming visible.

'It's the sunrise, Stella,' he said gently.

Her eyes had widened in awe. As she watched the sun slowly illuminate the sky in a brilliant dawn, she had confided in him that, if there really was a sun and a surface above the earth where people lived, then the earth was a much wider mystery than she had believed, and anything else—anything she had thought to be a fable—might possibly be true. Her large, wonder-filled eyes had pierced his heart and reawakened in him the marvel of it all.

The thought of going back below now, without her, hurt; it felt like a betrayal. Jared pushed the pain and worry from his head for the thousandth time. He had tried, over and over, to drive the nagging fear for her away, but it had only grown in the back of his mind. He continued to make preparations, fervently hoping that she was safe from harm.

The night before their deployment, Jared pulled the sergeant aside, 'There's someone I have to see before we go.'

* * *

They called themselves the Way. The old house was on a dead-end street in the small town of Deluge. The moldering ruins of the faded customs buildings rose silently nearby. They were a remnant of the past importance of the parallels: the windows broken, the walls defaced by graffiti, and the crumbling remains slowly being reclaimed by nature. The unlit and tattered shreds of an ancient flag fluttered from the collapsed porch of a nearby house. Rusting and abandoned cars littered the pothole-dotted roads. Every time Jared came to the surface, it seemed worse.

He knocked on the door. The sound reverberated down the empty street. Caleb stood alert, scanning the darkness behind them.

'Who is there?' a woman's voice asked in a hushed tone.

'My name is Jared Crux. I want to speak with those of the Way.'

A deadbolt slid and the door cracked open. A woman, dressed in jeans and a white t-shirt and holding a propane lantern, appeared in the doorway. An old baseball cap crowned the auburn tresses that gently waved past her shoulders.

'Who's your friend?' her eyes held suspicion.

'Sgt. Caleb MacIntyre. He's with me,' Jared answered her tersely.

She held up the lantern and scanned each of their faces slowly, one at a time, looking at them with intelligent brown eyes.

'Wait here,' she said and closed the door.

After a few minutes, she reappeared. 'You can come in,' she said. 'Follow me.'

She led them through a hall and up a flight of narrow steps. At the top of the stairs was a door through which a gentle hum of voices could be distinguished. The men went in.

Many had come, Jared saw with relief. Although a number of faces were new to him, he was greeted by each one warmly.

Jared briefly recounted what had happened. When he finished, they all stood silently, thinking.

Finally, an old man with silver hair addressed Jared. 'This is beyond our knowledge. They are all foolish. Stella has meddled with forces that will destroy her.'

'Is she still alive then, James?' Jared asked.

After a pause, a woman came forward.

'Yes,' she said, 'she is alive. And the Master sees her plight.' She spoke with quiet authority.

James agreed.

'What is written about this?' Jared asked him.

The old man muttered to himself momentarily and then looked at Jared thoughtfully before answering. 'The Codex speaks of something similar to this.' He paused again in contemplation but didn't explain further.

James had once held the precious manuscript in his hands. He had lived long enough to remember a time when several copies of Ander's Codex had existed. But that was long ago. Now, it was said, the only copy that remained was held over the mountains, somewhere in the Midlands. It was purported that the people of the Way had hidden it there.

After a moment, James continued, 'She will be given a choice. We must hope and petition that she chooses right.'

They all murmured in agreement, but a young woman spoke up. 'She is in an unreachable place. I can't see how we can help her.'

'No one is unreachable,' the auburn-haired woman said reassuringly.

At that moment, the people exclaimed and recoiled as a light appeared in their midst—in the middle of the room. A strange man was suddenly there, his body radiating in the dimness and his face shining. He had simply appeared out of nowhere, with no warning. The light began to subside.

James had instinctively drawn back, but looking at the man's face, he drew a sharp breath and his eyes grew wide.

'Nathan!' he cried out in sudden recognition.

The strange visitor stepped forward and clasped the old man's hand. 'James, my old friend. I am glad to see you!' He smiled at James' startled expression. 'We have a lot to talk about.'

Stunned into silence, no one in the room uttered a word.

The old man had seen much in his long years of service to the

Master, but this was something altogether new. He didn't even try hiding his astonishment. 'Nathan, where have you come from? How did you get here? I thought you were in the Midlands, completely cut off from us since we lost the pass.'

The younger man laughed, his eyes merry. 'I was. Don't seem so surprised, my old friend. I remember some of your stories. Haven't you seen your own share of remarkable things? I know I have!' Nathan's eyes lit up with the thought, and his voice quickened, waxing rich with excitement, 'James, if only you could have been there when the commander fought with us last spring!'

Awe-filled wonder filtered through the room. 'What? You've seen the high commander? He fought with you?' one of the men asked in disbelief.

Nathan nodded, grinning. 'At the front we were ambushed by the Tenebraean army. I went in with the first wave of defensive troops. We were pitifully undermanned in comparison to their forces. We were quickly overwhelmed. Many gave up the cause for lost and fled. Only my men and I remained, prepared for death if that was required; we expected it would come to that.

'In our desperation, we raised a cry to Caelum that seemed to penetrate the darkness around us. We threw ourselves on the mercy of our Master, who we believed had the strength and will to help us. The Tenebraeans all but laughed at our poor defense and advanced with confidence to strike their "coup de grâce."

'In response to their advance, the high commander himself and a score of his fighters arrived through the tunnels in the heat of the onslaught and joined the battle, bringing new orders from the King. We fought shoulder to shoulder with the commander and his men, and our hope was renewed, even while the enemy's numbers still dwarfed our own.'

Nathan's eyes grew zealous. 'Prince Liam's fighters are fierce—more so than we could ever have guessed—but none of the Tenebrae men could withstand the wrath of the commander. He fights like none other I've ever seen. He's fearless and bold, and he knows warfare better than our enemies do. We followed the King's orders and defended our position until our fingers froze to our weapons. And we held. Against impossible odds, we won!'

There were exclamations and everyone was talking at once. Nathan raised his hand and laughed, recapturing their attention. 'Don't get me wrong; there is much hard work still left to do. But our King equips us.'

His bright eyes grew serious, and he lowered his voice. 'I've come from the Master's war council. The enemy is about to strike a death blow, but our King plans to counter him. We must act quickly. I have a message for someone here—a newcomer who I do not know.' His voice trailed off as he scanned the room. A low murmuring traveled through the small group.

Jared had keenly observed everything from the corner of the room. He was trying to come to grips with what he had just witnessed. What advanced tech were they using to chasm jump? There had been no visible rift or opening in the air, yet somehow, Nathan had appeared. And was James colluding with the enemy? He suddenly wished he knew these people better than he did. James was an old friend, but many of the others were unknown to him.

His eyes narrowed, looking at Nathan. Could he have just discovered their traitor? He glanced over at the sergeant leaning against the wall. He was thankful to see that he was the same old Caleb: collected and cool. Suddenly, Jared had the sense that he was being watched and darting a glance across the room, saw that Nathan was looking at him intently.

The people of the Way slowly parted as Nathan stepped towards him.

'Our King has a message for you,' he said with conviction.

Jared looked at the man in surprise. Caleb had come over and was standing at Jared's side, his hand resting on his sidearm.

After a moment's pause, Jared responded, 'Be careful, Midlander. I don't want trouble, but I am an officer of the West—even talking to you is treason.'

'That's true,' Nathan nodded, 'but I am not here to represent anyone but the King of Caelum. There is One who you owe a higher allegiance to than even the Emerald Woods of Vespera.'

Jared looked at him, startled. He spoke the truth, and Jared knew it. The men of Caelum had saved his life, years ago, and he had never repaid that debt. But how could Nathan know that?

Keeping his face unreadable, Jared asked him, 'What is the Caelum King's message?'

'Tenebrae and the chasm dwellers are forging an alliance to bring about the destruction of the whole surface of Terra and Mare. The King means to stop it. He says the time has come to renew your vow.'

* * *

The fighting in the tunnels had escalated. The Cross-roads—the main gateway between Tenebrae and the West—was impassable. It was a massive, remote cavern encircled by a vast network of intersecting catacombs, strategically situated between the two countries: the realm of Terra below and the Westlands of Vespera distantly above. Normally a busy thoroughfare of government business and state commerce during the day, now the Cross-roads was an eerily quiet, tensely guarded border flanked by soldiers and bunkers. Great, ancient pillars of limestone stood in an immense ring like menacing giants staring down upon any who approached, intricately carved by craftsmen who had been buried and forgotten for countless centuries.

Jared carefully surveyed the distant Tenebrae bunker on the other side of the cavern courtyard. An unspoken cease-fire agreement seemed to have been reached over the last twenty-four hours. Only two Tenebrae soldiers were partly visible, patrolling. All else was still.

Jared rested on his knee as he watched the patrolling soldiers move among the large bunkers. Their enemy seemed unsuspecting. Still, Jared couldn't shake the feeling that something was off. He glanced around at the large group of his fellow soldiers, hidden behind the bunker and expectantly waiting for the signal to advance. The sergeant was cleaning his fingernails with a knife. Jared smiled. Caleb never changed—always cool and calm.

Then, all at once, the command came. The West's soldiers

responded, springing into action—hurdling over the bunker and sprinting across the gateway in seconds.

Instantly, the enemy line came alive. A profusion of waiting explosives launched toward them, and the sound of gunfire from hundreds of weapons reverberated out of the bunker in unison. The onslaught was severe, and the men were mowed down around Jared as he rushed forward. He gained a few more yards and fell behind a cement barrier. The explosives began to detonate, launching bodies and debris in deafening chaos. He watched the men behind him get gunned down as they advanced over the bunker in waves. Where was Caleb? It was impossible to tell in the confusion.

Jared aimed at the Tenebrae guns and began to fire. He kept firing, taking the gunmen out one by one. His cement barrier was hit hard, ejecting powdery chunks. Jared reloaded. Their one advantage was in catching the enemy by surprise, but it was plain that the enemy had been expecting the assault. Now, Jared realized, they were being slaughtered. This was madness!

He looked around. There was hardly any cover between him and the enemy bunker. A shot tore past his ear, and he ducked his head. There was no better cover anywhere that he could reach. He took a breath and kept firing at the Tenebraeans. A barrage of gunfire focused on his barrier; a section of the concrete broke away, and Jared got as low as he could.

Another soldier made it to his position. 'Need ammo?' he asked Jared.

'Yeah, almost out.'

'Here you go, lad,' the soldier said, tossing him several clips.

'Thanks, man,' Jared replied, glancing up.

The soldier was firing quick bursts at the bunker, empty shells flying. Jared smiled grimly and joined him.

They worked for some time together, laboring to take out the Tenebrae guns. The newcomer was a first-rate shot; each round managed to find its mark. He also seemed to have an unending supply of ammunition. Jared had learned to be careful with his rounds. Vespera rationed the number of bullets given to each soldier. If they made it out of this, he would have to ask the soldier about that.

Jared realized that the waves of soldiers had stopped coming over the West's bunker. He glanced around, seeing only a small fraction of their troops that were still in the fight. The soldier next to Jared finished his clip.

As he reloaded, he asked, 'Are you ready to move? They're coming out of their bunker in a moment, and I think we got their attention.'

Jared heard a yell and saw a strong line of armored Tenebraeans leap over their bunker, charging fiercely toward their barrier.

'Time to go—follow me,' the soldier said, before springing like a hart towards a tunnel to their right.

Jared was caught off guard by the man's speed but quickly followed. They made the tunnel.

From the cover of the tunnel entrance, they continued to fire and hit enough of the enemy that the line began to waiver. A new surge of Tenebraeans came over the bunker to defend their line. Just then, Jared saw Caleb to his left, firing on the enemy from behind a pillar. His right leg was hit. He was twenty yards away, toward the enemy line. He was beginning to draw fire.

'Friend of yours?' the soldier asked, nodding towards him.

'Yeah.'

'Want to go get him?' he asked with a grin.

Jared looked at him, surprised, 'Are there slaves in Tenebrae?'

'Then follow me.' The man raised his gun and instantly darted out, running towards the Tenebraeans.

Jared ran as quickly as he could, following behind on the man's right side, firing. They made the pillar, taking shelter behind it.

Caleb looked at him in disbelief, 'Are you nuts? What are you doing?'

'Getting you out of here,' Jared said, putting him over his shoulder.

The soldier nodded once to Jared and then sprang out, firing on the line and giving the men cover.

Jared carried Caleb to the tunnel and, setting him down inside, darted back to the opening. The soldier was nowhere in sight.

'Caleb, what happened to the guy with us?' he called back.

The sergeant had started binding his wound but glanced up. 'I couldn't see. He was following us I thought.'

Jared scanned the ground they had just covered. *Where was he?*

'What uniform was he wearing?' Caleb asked. 'I didn't recognize it.'

Jared recalled it, and then it dawned on him. 'I should have known,' Jared said, shaking his head. 'He's a soldier of Caelum.'

Caleb's eyes grew wide. 'A Caelum fighter? Here?'

Jared wrenched his thoughts back to their situation and looked out onto the field of battle. This was a massacre. Their men were all but dead and scattered; the enemy line was drawing dangerously close to their location. There was no way of escape except farther into the tunnel. They would have to follow it wherever it led.

Jared returned to Caleb, hoisting him over his shoulder and plunging into a side passage. 'At least the enemy won't find us here,' Jared said to his friend.

Caleb didn't answer.

He was quieter than Jared liked. He kept talking, trying to sound upbeat, 'With supplies, you could hide in this labyrinth for weeks, easy.' Or be lost forever, he added to himself, silently. He hoped that he could keep his bearings long enough to prevent them from wandering deeper into Tenebrae territory. The tunnels here were surrounded by naturally magnetic rocks and iron that rendered his compass useless. He had a device that could help, but, to Jared's frustration, when he took it out, he saw that it had been damaged in the fight.

Shifting Caleb's weight on his shoulder, he continued to advance doggedly. Jared's thoughts returned to the battle. They had been doomed from the start; the enemy had obviously been tipped off. How many men had been lost because of it? He ground his jaw tightly. He would make sure the informant paid dearly for what he'd done.

After about an hour, there was a sharp turn in the passage. Jared stopped, setting Caleb down gently, observing him. He was very pale. Jared checked his wound. It looked ugly; the bullet had filleted through flesh and muscle, and the bone was exposed. He cleaned it the best he could and rewrapped it. Caleb grimaced deeply as he worked. He hoped that his friend could hold on until they found their way back. He took out his navigator and examined it, wondering if it could be fixed.

At that moment, they heard what sounded like light footfalls in the passage behind them. Instinctively drawing their handguns, they trained them toward the tunnel bend and waited for several moments in tense silence. Not a breath could be heard in the stillness.

The drumming of Jared's own heartbeat sounded loud in his ears. He was beginning to think they had imagined it when the faint sound began again.

Caleb glanced at him. No, they were not mistaken.

The hushed echo was now rapidly approaching. Jared took a slow steady breath and focused his aim, waiting until, at last, a man turned the corner and came into full view. It was the soldier who had helped them.

The man looked at them and grinned. 'Not the warmest welcome I've ever had . . . but then again, not the coldest one either.'

Jared let out a long breath, cracking a smile and holstering his gun. 'Welcome, friend. I'm very glad to see you again.' He extended his arm and shook hands with the newcomer.

'Same here,' Caleb said, putting away his weapon. 'Thanks for your help.'

The soldier approached him, nodded, and shook his hand.

'Where did you go?' Caleb asked him curiously.

'I thought a little enemy sabotage was in order,' the soldier said, grinning mischievously. He rested on his heels next to Caleb. 'Let's see what you've got going on here. Do you mind?' he asked cheerily, motioning to the wound.

'Be my guest,' Caleb replied.

The soldier unwrapped the binding gingerly and inspected the wound. Reaching out, he gently started removing the remaining debris and shrapnel.

Jared looked at his friend. The sergeant had turned sheet white, wincing painfully.

After a few minutes, the soldier inspected it again. 'Very good! I'm sure that's it. Now, to clean it.' He pulled a small flask out of his jacket and poured the contents over the wound. It fizzed and bubbled up.

Caleb braced himself for intense pain but then gasped in wonder, scrubbing his hands over his eyes, not believing what he saw. It seemed as if the wound was beginning to heal, slowly knitting itself together again. The clear liquid felt cool, but there was no pain at all. Caleb doubted his senses and wondered if he was perhaps delirious.

The soldier watched carefully for a minute and then began to rewrap the leg. 'Give it a day or so. It should heal well now.'

Caleb looked at him in disbelief. 'Thanks once again, friend. I'm in your debt.'

'You can call me Ian, and no worries. I give freely of what was freely given.' He straightened up, stretching, and glanced around. 'Now then, who's hungry?'

The men reclined in a relaxed circle on the ground, talking as they ate and drank and cleaned their weapons. They conversed about that day and past battles they had been through. Between stories, Ian produced a wrapped bundle in a rough-woven fabric and offered it to the men.

When Jared saw what it was, his mouth began to water. It was impossible to forget Caelum sweet bread. He took a bite, marveling that it was even better than he remembered. It held no comparison to any other bread he'd tasted in his life. Both sweet and savory, the soft, golden loaves were light and fresh, even when they were weeks old. They were sweetened with a divine, aromatic mixture of honeycomb and spices—crisp on the outside and buttery soft on the inside. They melted in their mouths. The men savored them. But the true virtue of the loaves became apparent as their weariness soon began to strip away, and, in its place, a new hope and vigor buoyed up in their hearts.

Listening to Ian's light banter and cheerful stories made the time pass quickly, awakening for Jared, old memories, long forgotten. It had been years since he had seen anyone from Caelum. Eventually, Jared asked the question on his mind. 'Ian, what made you join our fight today?'

'The King sent me, with his compliments,' Ian answered brightly.

Jared raised his eyebrows. After a moment, he responded, 'I'm greatly honored.' He considered for a minute and then asked, 'Do you know why us? Why today?'

Ian stretched out on the ground, his arms behind his head. 'The King seems to think that you may need a hand in staying alive for a bit. After today, I'm inclined to think he's right, as usual.'

They talked late into the night, and as Jared dropped off to sleep, he could hear Ian humming quietly, his pleasant voice echoing softly off the tunnel walls.

Chapter 12

~~ * ~* ~** * *** ** *~* * ~**

The High Commander

D arkness still reigned heavy in the blackened meadow of the inner chasm when Stella awoke. She groaned, racked with pain, wishing fervently that she had died in her sleep. She blinked back tears and tried to see. She was lying in the dirt, her hands tightly chained. Her back was against the door. They hadn't bothered to bind her legs. She glanced around. Two chasm dwellers were nearby, but no one else was there that she could see. She lay very still trying not to draw attention to herself.

She contemplated where Jared was and what he was doing. She wondered if he was as miserable as she was. She hoped desperately that he was alive.

She thought about the night he'd snuck into her room and pondered if she should have stayed in the dormitories that night. She could have told him then that she didn't believe his story and ordered him out of her room. She smiled slightly to herself in the dark at the thought. He wouldn't have taken no for an answer. He was too stubborn, and she gave into him too easily. He could always talk her into stupid things.

After a few minutes, the speech of the nearby guards pulled her out of her thoughts. She began to catch bits of their conversation.

'More weapons arriving tomorrow . . . almost ready for the assault.'

Great, it sounds like tomorrow will be an even bigger red-letter day than today was.

One of the guards stood up and laughed a deep and haunting laugh. She could hear him clearly now.

'Tenebrae has promised to deliver the surface to us too, and we will have all the surface dwellers we want for food and hosts.'

'No more drifting. No more endless famine!' the other laughed gleefully.

'But why stop there? Don't you see? Together, with the advancements of Terra, we will finally be strong enough to wage war against Caelum.'

Stella looked hopelessly out into the dark, their talk causing her to sink deeper into despair. But then her eye caught something in the distance. Stella saw what she thought could be a glimmer of light stretching across the horizon. Her heart still felt dead within her, but she began to think. *How long are the nights in this land?* She wondered if this was a sign that the darkness might be coming to an end.

Suddenly Stella heard a sound behind her. A knock! Something had knocked on the door. The guards stopped talking and turned around.

'What are you doing, slave?' the first one asked harshly.

'Nothing,' she answered, afraid. 'It wasn't me.'

He got up and came over, looking down at her. The other approached as well, reaching out and lifting her up by the throat. He raised his other hand as if to strike her, and she prepared herself for it, wincing.

It never came. A clear rap, rap, rap sounded on the door. He let her drop, and the guards stood dumbfounded, looking at the door suspiciously.

'I thought no one could reach the passage when the door was shut,' the first guard said, glancing at the second.

'They usually can't. The door has to be opened first. The prisoner must be doing it.'

She winced as the first guard grabbed a large handful of her hair and dragged her to her feet.

'Get up, slave. Nice try. Whatever you're doing, you're going to lose at this little game of yours.'

As she was pulled away from the door, a rap, rap, rap came again—sharp and distinct. The two guards stood frozen, their eyes fixed on the closed door.

Suddenly she heard a voice, strong and clear, call out, 'Estellah, open the door!'

Her heart leapt in her chest. *That voice!* She felt the hope, that had slowly suffocated and died in her heart, spontaneously gasp and spring to life. She didn't need to think about what to do next or debate with herself. She simply acted instinctively with everything she had left in her. She lunged for the door and, struggling with her bound hands, managed to turn the knob before the dumbfounded guards could stop her.

As the guards began to lift her with their power and pull her back, she tried to kick the door open but mostly missed, catching it only lightly with her foot.

It was enough. It slowly creaked open on its hinges.

Inside the dim doorway, the shadowy figure of a man was visible. He stood tall, clothed in military uniform. There was an insignia on his chest and helm that she didn't recognize, but Stella noticed these things only cursorily. She was, instead, rivetted to his unforgettable countenance. His face held an irresistible light that seemed to permeate the darkness around him. Stella instantly felt an unseen strength in the man, although it seemed purposely cloaked or subdued.

His sharp gaze blazed fiercely, from coal into flame, as his eyes swept over Stella and the guards who held her. He raised a long, broad, amber-toned sword; it gleamed threateningly in the shadows.

'Iudicium!' the first guard hissed and sucked in his breath, recognizing the deadly blade.

Stella watched as horror and fear spread over her captors' pale, wide-eyed faces. The guards threw her to the ground, and she heard the sharp ring of steel as they drew their own weapons.

The man came silently forward, over the threshold, into the first rays of early morning light. The guards separated, attempting to surround him as he advanced.

'What is your name?' the man asked quietly, nodding to the creature who had tormented her.

The chasm dweller licked his lips and swallowed; his eyes focused with terror on the blade that the man held.

'Ligatus,' he answered hoarsely. 'What do you want with me, Prince? Isn't it enough that you threw us from our homeland and left us as homeless beggars?'

The man's keen brown eyes focused on the chasm dweller. Stella saw that his gaze was intent, sharp, and piercing.

He answered, still quietly, but with a marked force, 'You made your choice to leave when you joined with the traitors long ago. Terra and Mare do not belong to you. They are under the protection of the King.'

The chasm dweller spat at him in response, 'I don't answer to your King!' He lunged towards the man, his sword falling with spine-chilling cunningness.

The man was ready, and with agile skill, he put his opponent's sword aside with one swift movement of his own. He struck his foe with astounding speed, running him through. As the first creature was falling, the other moved to strike the man from behind. But the man turned his blade, forcefully thrusting it back and through his enemy, almost faster than Stella's eyes could follow. The guard dropped like a stone and didn't move again.

The being called Ligatus was trying to rise, struggling with a groan. The man approached him warily. The chasm dweller saw him and cursed him with venomous hate between staggered breaths until, finally, the curses turned into a bitter laugh, 'You fool, my master has you in a corner . . . you are weak . . . exposed . . .' He gave out one more sinister and gurgled laugh and died. The green glow seeped from his body like a fog, wavered, and then went out.

Stella blinked and looked at the man. He knelt by the being, carefully examining his twisted form. He sighed grimly and then stood. Then he turned toward Stella, his eyes registering relief and care as they settled on her.

After a pause, he turned his attention to his sword; it was stained with the creature's dark blood. He carefully wiped the blade and sheathed it. While he did so, he spoke to her in a lighthearted tone.

'Do you want to stay in those chains, Stella?'

She looked down, suddenly remembering her bound wrists.

'No, sir,' she responded, the corner of her mouth edging up into a shy smile, 'they don't match my outfit.'

'Absolutely not!' he laughed merrily.

It was a joy-filled sound which created a deep happiness inside of Stella that she didn't understand.

He gently took her wrists and held them, and with a short dagger from his belt, he broke a link. The chains clattered to the ground.

'Thank you, sir,' she said, rubbing her wrists.

He nodded, observing her closely as if he saw something out of place.

Stella felt suddenly awkward and her mind raced, trying to think of something to say. Although she assumed that he must be a very important man, she mustered the courage to ask, 'Sir, who are you? And how do you know my name?'

He paused, and the smile in his eyes died slowly as he regarded her with that intense, piercing gaze. After contemplating her for a minute, he said, 'Let me ask you a question in return. Do I seem familiar to you at all?'

'Maybe—I'm not sure,' she answered, confused. She tried to sift through her punctured and frayed memory. She felt like she knew him but couldn't understand how.

He studied the ground in thought, his brow furled in contemplation. After a minute, he looked up again at Stella, and his serious eyes grew gentle. 'It's alright. You can call me Liam. Believe it or not, we knew each other once, although you seem to have forgotten.'

Stella's jaw dropped open. 'But, how? When?' she questioned.

The look on Stella's face made him laugh. 'I wish we had time for explanations now, but it will have to wait until we get to Caelum.'

'We're going to Caelum?' asked Stella excitedly. Her heart beat loud and fast at Liam's words.

'Yes, we must hurry. This is going to sound strange, but you'll have to trust me. Do you see the insignia on my tunic?' Liam asked her.

Stella looked. In the center of his tunic, skillfully embroidered in gold thread and jewels, was an emblem of a golden tree with two trunks that joined above to make an arch, bursting with leaves and fruit. Through the arched tree, depicted in sparkling gemstones, flowed a rushing river.

'Yes,' she answered.

'Touch it.'

She glanced at him with surprise.

He nodded gently.

She hesitantly reached her hand out to touch the emblem, but instead of feeling the embroidered uniform, her hand felt nothing at all. She gasped. Her hand passed through him like he was a mirage. She pulled back and looked at Liam, bewildered and suddenly afraid.

Seeing the fear in her eyes, he reached out and laid his hand reassuringly on her arm. 'Don't be afraid. It works kind of like a door. If you pass through me, you'll come to Caelum. But we must hurry,' he repeated, 'the enemy approaches.'

Shrill cries in the distance confirmed the truth of Liam's words, and Stella knew she had to act. She wrinkled her brow. It made no sense. This was all so strange—like a dream where one bizarre thing after another happens, and there is no way out except through the chaos. She looked directly into Liam's unassuming and protective eyes and decided that she believed him.

He nodded slowly once more, and without another thought, she took a deep breath and moved into him, passing through the door.

* * *

In the morning, Jared awoke, switching on his lamp in the blackness of the tunnels. Sitting up, he recalled the events of day before. He looked over at Caleb. He was still fast asleep by the tunnel wall. He turned the other way to look for Ian, but he was gone.

On the ground, in the place where Ian had been lying, was Jared's navigating device. Jared went to it and picked it up. It was in working order. He stood looking at it for a moment, a slight smile playing on his lips, and then roused the sergeant.

Caleb sat up, rubbing his face with his hands, and looked around the tunnel. 'Where'd he go?' he asked, confused.

Jared shrugged. 'That's what Caelum fighters are like. You get used to it.' He motioned to Caleb's wound. 'How's your leg?'

Caleb seemed to have forgotten it and, glancing down, quickly began unwrapping it. There was only a light scar running where the wound had been. He stood, testing it.

'You wouldn't know it looked like ground hamburger yesterday,' he said incredulously.

Jared laughed. 'Just wait,' he said, 'by tonight, you won't be able to tell it was ever there at all.'

'How do you know so much about them?' Caleb asked curiously.

Jared was rustling in his pack for breakfast rations. 'About who?'

'The Caelum people,' Caleb said the name with reverence.

After a moment, Jared paused and let out a long breath. 'It was a long time ago,' he said, reflecting. 'I was twelve. My family was traveling, and we were separated. I remember wandering alone for many hours. I was eventually found by kidnappers. They were very cruel. After abducting me, they led me far underground. They were the ones who gave me the name Abon. "Do you know what Abon means, slave?" they asked me. "It means shredded meat—and that's what you are—tasty, shredded meat," the depraved wretches told me.

'They brought me to Tenebrae, and there I was sold in the slave towers to the highest bidder. But there was a group of travelers at the towers that day. Hearing my words, they recognized my speech and guessed where I was from. They decided to act, and though the price was driven artificially high by the corruption of the slavers, the strangers, in their resolve, continued until they won the bid. Nobody there suspected that they were from Caelum.'

Jared paused, a look of gratitude swelling in his eyes. 'I suppose they bought me out of pity. They took me and cared for me, healing my wounds. I stayed with them for two and half year until they could bring me home.'

'What were the King's men doing in Tenebrae?'

'Collecting information—it was a reconnaissance mission. When their work was done, I begged them to let me stay with them, but they refused and brought me home to the surface where I was reunited with my family. I vowed to the men then that I would help them in their cause one day. When I turned sixteen, I joined the Westland military's special ops program, remembering the Caelum fighters. My first mission was to Tenebrae. That's when I was imbedded into the chasm-jumping program and you were assigned as my contact.'

Caleb nodded, remembering the first time he had met Jared—just a lanky kid with a lopsided grin. Several years of hardship, ruthless conditioning, and sorrow had all but erased that boy, leaving a shrewd, battle-hardened man with haunted eyes in his place. The sergeant had felt the injustice of sending a boy as a spy into the depths of such a corrupt and morally bankrupt place. He had exchanged some strong words with the program director, who found it fitting to discipline Caleb for his insubordination. He then offered him a transfer; Caleb had declined.

Jared and Caleb were just finishing up their breakfast when Ian came around the corner whistling a tune.

'Good morning, friends. You slept late,' he said cheerfully.

'Late nights make late mornings, for most of us anyway,' Jared said with a wry smile. 'What have you been doing this morning?'

'Intel gathering. I've been to the Cross-roads and back, looking for breadcrumbs.'

'Did you find any?'

'Enough to make the walk worthwhile.'

The men trussed their packs and debated which direction they wanted to go. Caleb wanted to go back to the surface and regroup with their fractured army. Jared wasn't so sure. As long as the informant was giving away their plans, he argued that they were fighting a lost cause. Instead, he wanted to find the spy, get any information from him that they could, and make him answer for all the misery he'd caused.

Caleb confronted him. 'Are you talking about deserting? We can't just go after this guy on some half-cocked quest for revenge. Where would we even start? We got no information to go on.'

Ian watched them debate, silently resting against the tunnel wall.

Finally, out of frustration and some curiosity, Caleb asked him, 'What do *you* think we should do, Ian?'

'If you're asking me what I would do, I think I would plug the hole in my boat before taking it out to sea,' he answered cryptically. 'But, if I wanted good information, I would go to the right source.'

'Where would you recommend we go?' Jared looked at him curiously.

'Don't you have any who serve the King in these lands?' Ian asked.

Jared paused, finding hope in Ian's words.

Caleb instantly pulled him aside and forcefully whispered, 'We serve Vespera, Jared—not Caelum. Don't get your allegiance confused. I respect their people and their King, but we got to think of our own duty.'

Jared considered Caleb's words for a moment before answering. 'It may be that the allegiance of the West and Caelum, and even the Midlands, may intersect for a time. If what Nathan said is true, then Tenebrae is about to unleash a massive attack, not only on Vespera, but over the whole surface. But you're right; we've got to consider our duty.' He paused in anxious thought.

Finally, Jared decided. 'Our path leads past the Way. We'll ask them for information. Then we'll regroup with our men.'

Chapter 13

~ ~~~ *** * * ~ **** * ~ **** ** ~* ~~* ***

House of Death

When the men surfaced in Deluge, it was dark. The small town felt even more abandoned—if that was possible. They weaved their way through the car-strewn and trash-lined streets towards James' old farmhouse.

Knocking, Jared glanced at his friends. Caleb faced the street behind them, as before, alert and watching, his fingers playing lightly on the rifle strapped at his side. Ian was looking out at the neighborhood with a quiet sadness. It was eerily quiet.

They heard a man's voice from behind the door, 'Who's there?'

'Jared Crux and two friends.' A bolt scraped, and the door cracked open.

'What do you want?' he asked in a gruff, low voice.

Jared didn't recognize him. 'I need to speak with James. I have questions for the Way,' Jared replied softly.

The man eyed them suspiciously and told them to wait, closing and rebolting the door.

'Their hospitality could use some improvement,' Jared said under his breath.

They waited for many minutes. Jared was at the point of knocking again when he heard the bolt sliding once more. The door opened, and the man stepped aside.

'James is in the room straight ahead,' he told them. The man was clearly on edge, Jared noted to himself.

James met them as they entered the room.

'Jared, my boy! We asked the Master, but it seemed impossible that help could reach us so soon.' He took Jared in a hearty embrace and then glanced hesitatingly at the soldiers who stood behind him.

Jared gestured to his friends. 'James, you remember Caleb—he was with me before. And this is Ian. Both are friends of the Way.'

'You're both very welcome here,' James nodded.

Jared detected a tense note in his voice that he'd never heard before. 'What kind of help have you been asking for, James?' Jared inquired, searching.

The old man sighed and offered them seats. 'After your last visit, we had other visitors—from the government of Vespera. It seems they don't like . . . how did they put it . . . unauthorized chasm jumps. I'd never heard of a chasm jump until they came tearing in here, accusing us of all sorts of crimes with strange names. They searched the house, leaving it ransacked. They took several of us in and questioned us at length about Nathan's whereabouts. They think we're harboring him. They've been watching our movements ever since.'

Jared raised an eyebrow. 'Are you harboring him?'

'If you mean is he staying here? The answer is no,' James replied honestly. 'He left shortly after you did that night. He never said where he was going. I think he must have realized there would be trouble and was trying to protect us.'

'If the Western government finds him, you know what will happen to him, don't you?' Jared asked, alarmed.

'Yes, I know. I told him to be careful.' He shook his head and then chuckled. 'I'm gratified by your concern. Ethan here thinks we can't trust you—that maybe you were the one who reported a chasm hop.'

A faint smile appeared on Jared's face. 'It's called a chasm jump.'

'Hop, skip, jump—can't keep it straight,' James laughed. He gestured toward the man who had answered the door. 'I told Ethan that I trusted you like my own son.'

'I'm glad some of your people are showing caution,' Jared smirked. 'You, on the other hand, can be reckless.'

'My Master has never steered me wrong. I'm not about to stop trusting him now, in my ripe, old age,' he said with a wink. 'Now, I was told you have questions. What can I do for you?' he asked.

Jared dove right in. 'There is an informant divulging our every move to the enemy. Our offensive op was going to be a swift victory. It turned out to be a bloodbath; we were decimated. It's clear they had plenty of advance warning.'

He leaned forward and looked imploringly at James. 'I need your help to petition Caelum's King. He has the power and resources to help me uncover and eliminate the traitor.'

James leaned back in his chair, contemplating all that Jared had told him.

Just then, Ian, who had been peering out at the street through a drawn curtain, spoke, 'I don't like to interrupt, gentlemen, but someone is planning to join our little party. They already have the house surrounded. There are at least fifteen—well-armed. How many are in the house?' He drew out his gun and chambered a round as he spoke.

The men jumped up and moved to the windows.

James answered Ian, 'There are two other men here, besides me, with their wives and children—and you three.'

Sgt. MacIntyre began barking out commands to the men in rapid succession. 'Get the women and children into the basement! Keep them away from any windows! Barricade the exterior doors. Find anything in the house that can be used as a weapon.'

They moved quickly and were still barricading the front door, when a loud, crushing weight slammed against it. The door buckled and groaned but held.

Jared swore under his breath. Whoever they were, they weren't messing around. The sound of loud, shattering glass pierced the air, and he saw a smoke grenade bounce across the floor. Ian caught it and lobbed it back out the window in one smooth motion.

Caleb's voice thundered, 'Cease your attack or we will open fire!'

The ramming paused, and Caleb could see the attackers hesitate. After a moment, he watched them retreat behind a vehicle.

'They're going around back!' Ethan yelled, looking out a side window.

They quickly took up new positions.

'Trespassers,' Jared hollered out at them through a broken pane, 'identify yourselves!'

A shot rang out in response and embedded in the wall behind him. The men all dove low and opened fire. They exchanged gunfire for several minutes; then they suddenly heard the loud, battering sound resume at the front door.

Jared crawled across the house to the front window and opened fire on the attackers by the door. Several fell, and the rest fired back as they retreated. It was evident that they had expected the house to be poorly defended. They quickly fled to waiting vehicles and began speeding away.

Ian leapt through the broken casement onto the ground and gave chase, firing after them. He struck the tire of the last car, and it lost control, veering into an abandoned truck. The men jumped out and fled on foot. Ian lunged and caught one man's ankle, bringing him down hard.

By the time Jared and Caleb caught up to them, Ian had secured the man's weapons and was tying his hands tightly behind his back.

'Nice catch, Ian,' Caleb said, impressed.

'Yes, the bird's been caught; now let's bring him home and see if he can sing,' Ian replied, hauling him to his feet.

The men returned to the house with the prisoner, pushed him into a chair, and fastened him to it.

Jared looked at the man. He couldn't have been much older than eighteen but had been well-equipped with Kevlar and weapons. He had a smaller build with dark, cropped hair, chiseled features, and black eyes. There was a fresh, bleeding scrape running from the bridge of his nose to the far side of his chin. There was also a symbol tattooed on his right forearm that Jared noticed with surprise. Tattoos on anyone under the age of fifty were extremely rare on the surface; Jared had never seen one outside of Tenebrae. After the revolution had begun, the art had slowly died out since no one could afford the luxury.

'Who are you?' Jared asked the man.

He looked at Jared with hard eyes and said nothing.

'Why did you attack us?' he asked.

The man didn't respond.

Caleb sauntered over to him with a grin. 'I would love nothing more than to take the fingers off this trash, one by one, until we get the information we want—or until he can't hold a spoon.'

A faint flash of fear appeared behind the man's eyes.

Ian tore a strip of fabric from a kitchen towel and wetted it. He walked over to the man and dabbed his bleeding mouth.

'No one is going to take off your fingers, lad,' Ian said gently. 'Fear may be a powerful tool in our enemy's hands, but there are stronger tools.'

He turned to Jared and James. 'They will be back within a day or two with a much stronger force. They didn't expect a fight. They will next time.'

'How do you know, Ian?' Caleb asked him.

'Do you see the brand on his arm?' Ian asked, gesturing to the prisoner. 'I've seen it before. It reads Siwang Zhi Jia: house of death.'

'House of death?' Caleb repeated and glanced at Jared.

Jared nodded, a knowing look in his eyes. 'It's not the first time I've seen the symbol either. I've had dealings with them in Tenebrae. They're called Maison de la Mort there. Those with connections hire them for certain jobs, like the attack tonight, but I've never seen this symbol on the surface.'

He paused, contemplating. 'Whoever sent them has a lot of power and money and wants the threat in this house eliminated quickly. They're afraid of something.'

James and Ethan looked at each other. 'Afraid of us?' James said with a laugh and, after a moment, turned to Jared. 'We are nothing but a group of outcasts in our own dwindling town. And, if you and your men hadn't come tonight, our lives would have been a finished chapter. We are grateful beyond words,' he said with emotion and then nodded to Ian. 'If what you say is true, and I don't doubt you, we have no choice but to leave. But where will we go?'

Ian said nothing but sent James a penetrating glance.

The other people in the house had gathered around, listening while the men talked. Now James stood silent, in thought. Slowly, his face began to dawn with understanding. He finally spoke.

'I think the Master has been preparing me for this for some time.' He seemed to have resolved something in his mind as he gazed at the men and women of the Way. 'Prepare yourselves to approach the Master. We're going to consult him.'

They murmured in anticipation.

Jared felt a thrill course through him. It had been rumored for many years that there was a line of direct contact between the two realms. Whispers spoke of a powerful nobleman in Caelum who had forged lines of communication between the King and these unlikely ones: the people of the Way.

The method made little sense to Jared, and frequently he was left confused by the King's responses; but after witnessing their strange communication with Caelum as often as he had, Jared couldn't deny its authenticity. It was uncanny how the people of the Way received information that they could not have known otherwise and garnered help that went laughably beyond coincidence. He was struck with wonder every time he experienced them receiving a message from the King.

They petitioned him now. Jared watched with fascination as they spoke with confident faith in a mysterious communication. He felt the air stir around him, and the hair on his arms stood on end. The atmosphere began to grow electric as a strange intensity penetrated the room.

He glanced at Caleb. He was hanging back, silently watching the group with curiosity, his hat in his hands.

Jared's eyes traveled to Ian and fixed on him, marveling. Ian's upturned face was filled with an expression of pure and utter joy. It seemed to Jared that there was a brightness coming from within him; like a luminescence radiating from behind a thin layer of gauze, it lit up Ian's already engaging features, rendering them brilliant to look upon.

The people of the Way were petitioning their Master with sincerity and great reverence. After the last was done speaking, they stood in silence. No one moved or made a sound. All was still. The clock in the hall chimed the quarter hour, yet they stood unmoving, waiting.

Then, abruptly, a man broke the silence, 'The Master says that, if any of us remain, the attackers will return and kill all in the house.'

The people gasped in dismay.

He paused and then continued, 'He says we need not be afraid. He has heard us and calls us his people. He has not forgotten us. He says we must leave the place we know, but he will not leave us on our own. We must turn our eyes to the mountains.'

They looked around at each other, the ramifications of what they heard sinking in. They were filled with sudden urgency but, at the same time, a deep sense of well-being. In unity, they prepared to go. They packed only essentials, keeping their bags as light as possible, since they would be walking far; they all understood now, as with one mind, that they needed to take the long journey to the Midlands.

While the people prepared, Jared and Caleb stood aside and discussed this new development in hushed tones. They both agreed that regrouping with their men would have to wait; these people needed their help. It seemed that the Way was being targeted by someone in power. The soldiers recognized that the group's best chance laid in slipping away, out of their attackers' grasp. The King's advice was sound. However, it was a risky and treacherous journey, and they were a group of families with young children.

James joined them, and the three men briefly deliberated about which route the group should take, debating whether they should go through the east-running tunnels that delved under the mountain ranges or travel on the more exposed, rough, and broken trails that snaked through the wilderness. Both routes had many known and unknown hazards. They eventually agreed that the tunnels held greater risk and, if they were discovered, offered little chance of escape. In addition, they reasoned that resources would also be harder to come by below the surface. Despite the elevated risk of being tracked, the men determined that the group should stay above ground unless it became absolutely necessary to go below.

As the people filed out of the farmhouse, the old man paused and looked slowly and sentimentally around his home. The house had been passed down from his father and built by his grandfather before him. It was where he had brought his bride home on their wedding day, and his children had all been born within these walls. Each one of his family members had been taken away, one by one, save himself.

He surveyed the simple, old place slowly, one last time, committing it to memory. He pushed down the stinging drops that unexpectedly threatened to rise to his eyes. Then he walked quietly out of his home and, for the last time, shut the door behind him.

* * *

Stella blinked her eyes. The pain and darkness she had grown to expect from chasm jumping were completely absent. Instead, she had traveled through Liam's door in light and without pain, instantaneously.

Everything came sharply into focus, and it made her catch her breath. Looking around, she was awestruck by the bright, vibrant surroundings—renewed like the shades of nature after a spring rain. All was saturated in light and color.

She was standing in the midst of a resplendent, massive stone and timber-frame building, which seemed to extend on indefinitely, with thick, richly carved pillars that rose from the floor to the ceiling that soared high overhead. It was refined yet filled also with beautiful, heart-rending tones and textures of natural wood and stone. The palace was rich in splendor and unlike anything she had ever seen or heard of.

She was on a balcony of the second level. A giant fireplace burned cheerfully behind her; its large stone chimney rose to the lofty ceiling. In front of her, a broad, polished-stone staircase descended to an expansive court below. The ancient luxury and magnificence of the place was overwhelming and bespoke the wealth and power of the kingdom.

Hearing footsteps, she turned and saw a man approaching her, followed closely by two livery-clad guards. Dressed in comfortable, unadorned, flowing clothes, the young lord was fair to look upon, with carelessly waving dark hair that fell to his jaw and remarkable eyes that were dark and strikingly intelligent. Stella discerned an unmistakable resemblance to the commander, in both his face and manner, and guessed that they were closely related.

'Welcome to Caelum, Estellah of Tenebrae,' said the man in a warm, pleasing tone.

As he introduced himself, Stella heard what sounded like the hint of an accent.

'I am the Duke of Esen—but, please, call me Jonas. The King and, indeed, all of Caelum are thrilled that you're here.'

Stella curtseyed low to her knee in Tenebraean fashion but did not know what to say. She couldn't understand what she had done to receive such a welcome.

She suddenly felt very out of place in her dirty and torn clothes. She glanced down at the muddy rags that she wore; they seemed even more degrading in these opulent surroundings, under the watchful eyes of the high nobleman. She thanked him with what grace she could muster. Her discomfort and her rags either went unnoticed by him or he had the grace to overlook them.

'If you'll follow me, my lady,' he said gently, 'I will show you to your quarters.'

She thanked him again and let him guide her down the long corridor.

The soldiers stood guard at intervals, each raising a salute, in honor, as the duke passed. Stella breathlessly admired the house of the King as they traversed its many halls. The grandest houses in Tenebrae were cardboard dwellings in comparison.

Stella saw several groups of people elegantly arrayed throughout the palace. All paused their conversations with curious glances but bowed deeply as they passed, murmuring the name 'Lord Jonas' with reverence. It was evident the people of Caelum held the Duke of Esen in high honor.

He was attentive and very kind to her, asking her questions and telling her stories of Caelum and the palace as they walked. He possessed a razor-sharp wit, and it was apparent that he liked to laugh.

For Stella, he was not as easy to read as Liam. He seemed to use his eyes more to search her thoughts than to reveal his own. Stella also perceived an unsafe, edgy quality to the duke. She had a vague sense that he probably liked to rock the boat now and again. As they spoke, the conviction grew in her that he would be a most powerful friend, but to cross the Duke of Esen would be to court disaster and death.

He led her down a hall lined with windows, displaying a spectacular view of the grounds. They stopped in front of an oversized, intricately carved pair of solid walnut doors.

'This is your apartment, Estellah,' he said, as the guards opened the giant doors in unison.

Stella caught her breath. Inside was a large, beautiful room where several elegant ladies seemed to be awaiting her arrival.

'The King has announced that a banquet is to be held in your honor tonight,' the duke informed her. 'These attendants will see to your wounds,' he continued, nodding to the ladies, 'and help you prepare.'

Stella glanced down at her torn and mired clothes.

The duke caught her pained expression and reassured her. 'The high commander has provided fitting apparel for you to wear. Is there anything else I can do for you before I go?'

Stella shook her head, speechless and still stunned at his news.

He gave her an encouraging smile. Bidding her good day, he left the room, closing the doors behind him.

'Welcome to Caelum, my lady,' one of the ladies said sweetly as she came forward. 'May we help you bathe and heal your hurts?'

Stella nodded dumbly and let them lead her to the steaming bath that was already prepared. As she sunk into the bubble-filled tub, she sighed deeply. It felt so good; she didn't think she would ever want to get out. One attendant washed her hair, and another gently scrubbed her filthy arms and legs. After a while, the water began to cool, and Stella felt cleaner than she had ever been. They helped her out and into a soft-lined bathrobe.

Stella gasped, looking down at her skin. Her many wounds were beginning to heal. Before her stunned eyes, the sores were closing

143

up and her bruises were beginning to fade.

'How is this possible?' she asked, stunned.

'The waters of Caelum heal all kinds of injury, my lady,' an attendant explained.

As she stood struck with wonder, the ladies gently guided her to a chair. An attendant dried her hair and then began to dress it, cleverly weaving fine strands of pearls and diamonds into the smoothed and curled tresses.

'Are you excited about tonight, my lady?' one attendant asked as she opened the tall wardrobe, taking out a long, extraordinarily graceful dress and laying it on the bed.

Stella's eyes stung with fresh tears as she beheld it. It was the finest thing she had ever seen, much less worn. She remembered that it was Liam who had provided it for her. She blinked, the reality of it suddenly coming home to her.

'Yes, I'm excited,' Stella answered timidly, 'but I'm afraid, too. What is the King like?'

'All who see the King revere him,' said a second attendant, 'but you need never be afraid of him when you come as a guest of the high commander. The King honors all his son's friends.'

Stella nodded thoughtfully, digesting what the ladies told her, and then paused. 'Are there others who should be afraid?' she asked hesitantly.

'Of course, my lady,' the first attendant answered. 'The enemies of the King are given no quarter. They should be greatly afraid.'

Her hair was finished, and the attendants helped Stella into the rich layers of cloth. They were light-filled, flowing robes of soft, silk charmeuse and satin. She ran her fingers gently along the garment's finely embroidered border. It was decorated with intertwined irises and gladiolus, and precious stones of many shapes were cleverly sewn into the design, portraying sparkling, multi-shaded leaves and petals in bloom. One of the attendants presented her with an accompanying pair of embroidered silk slippers; stooping down, she placed them onto Stella's feet.

Several ladies entered the room, clearly excited, holding two velvet boxes. 'The King sends these for you to wear to the banquet, my lady,' one of them told her animatedly.

Stella hesitated and then opened the smaller box. The ladies squealed in delight. A necklace of many majestic, deep blue sapphires set in silver laid glittering next to a matching set of fine, shimmering sapphire earrings.

'These are from the royal vault, my lady,' one of the attendants said breathlessly.

When she opened the large box, Stella's eyes grew wide. There, on a plush velvet cushion, laid a delicate, intricately woven crown of fine silver. Large, sparkling sapphires adorned its design.

The ladies buzzed excitedly as they dressed Stella in the stunning jewels and grew quiet when the tiara was placed on her head. They stood admiring her for a long moment and then carefully tidied the room and gathered Stella's old things.

'The King will send one of his servants to fetch you when it's time to go down,' said the first attendant. 'Is there anything else we can do for you, my lady, before we take our leave?'

'No, thank you. I have all I could possibly desire,' she answered.

As they left, closing the doors behind them, Stella exhaled slowly. What was going on? There certainly must have been some kind of mix-up. Didn't they know who she was? The thought of being discovered as an imposter suddenly gripped Stella, and the feeling of peaceful bliss was replaced by a dread that weighed on her heart like iron.

She turned to face the gilded mirror and saw the reflection looking back at her. She barely recognized herself. The girl staring back at her was all grace and elegance. She looked like a noble lady, sparkling with the light of a thousand gemstones, and her eyes shone out of the mirror with life and zeal. Stella felt strange as she gazed at the unfamiliar girl, wondering when she would wake—for the thought kept crossing her mind that this was all just a lovely, vivid dream that must, as all dreams do, eventually come to an end.

Chapter 14

The King's Banquet

S tella walked slowly through the suite of rooms, exploring her apartment. It was large and luxurious and gorgeously furnished. To the left of the fine entry with high ceilings and the spacious sitting room, Stella soon discovered a paneled study, lined with a plethora of leather-bound books. She wandered through and admired the many volumes. Pieces of exquisite art were interspersed between the bookcases, and the room was adorned with an ancient-looking stone fireplace, in front of which rested a tufted fender seat and a comfortable pair of overstuffed, high-back chairs. Another door off the main area led to a large, comfortable bedroom which contained another, smaller sitting room.

Wandering back to the main area, Stella saw doors of paned glass that opened to a large balcony overlooking the landscaped grounds. As she opened them and stepped out, she saw a fireplace and sunken pool on one side of the balcony. On the other, there was a table for al fresco dining and an outdoor lounge area. Climbing plants and cheerful flowers filled the space with even more beauty.

All these things were soon forgotten. Her attention was, instead, wholly arrested by what lay beyond. From the balustrade, she breathlessly surveyed the land before her. The King's house sat atop a lofty mountain range, at the very pinnacle, and was surrounded by lower, cascading peaks that fell away abruptly, giving way to pleasant, green hills and fertile valleys that rolled gently into the far distance where another mountain range stretched across the horizon on the very edge of sight. A fine glacier spring, whose source was found in the rocky heights, swelled as it passed over the mountain, becoming a mighty river and waterfall as it flowed from the King's house and provided water to the fertile fields beyond. The land of Caelum stretched out proudly before her, the breathtaking views continuing in every direction.

After admiring the King's vast lands for many minutes, she finally turned back to her apartment. Moments later, Stella heard a knock. She went to the door and, opening it, saw the commander. He had changed from his uniform into rich, flowing garments, befitting a prince of Caelum. His helm had been replaced with a jewel-set crown.

'High Commander,' she said, surprised, as she curtsied.

'You look lovely, Stella,' he said with pride. 'Please, call me Liam. I've come to bring you to the King. Are you ready?'

'Yes, my lord, Liam. I didn't expect you to take the trouble of coming to get me,' Stella said, training her eyes down.

'I wanted to, Estellah,' he told her. He reached out and lifted her chin. 'I don't remember you being at all shy. You can hold your head high in this place or any other, for that matter.'

Stella wondered how that could possibly be but was afraid to contradict or question him. After an internal struggle and knowing that she might not get another chance, she worked up the courage and forced herself to speak.

'Why is that, my lord? I don't know how I could deserve anything in this majestic place. Will you tell me how you can possibly know me, and what I have to do with this realm?' She paused but then added, 'And why do you call me Estellah?'

'Because that is your name,' he said calmly.

After a moment, he sighed. 'Walk with me,' he said, offering her his arm, 'and we can talk.'

Stella took it and let herself be guided by him through the many halls. As they walked, he seemed to be debating within himself.

After a few minutes, he spoke. 'There is much we need to discuss; I wish I could answer your questions fully. But the King must be the one to decide how best to . . . reacquaint you with your past. I believe he would want to be careful until you have regained some of your memory and until we can gauge what influence the enemy has had over you. Do you have any idea what has caused you to forget?'

'I don't know for sure, my lord. I really have no recollection of anything before my early teen years. In Tenebrae, they have a technology that makes you forget your past. I was told many years ago that it was used on me.'

His posture grew tense. She glanced up at him, startled, wondering what she had said wrong. His jaw was tight, and a black look had darkened his eye.

After a moment, he responded quietly, 'I'm aware of this technology. It's a form of mind manipulation. This is how the enemy has been able to keep you in bondage for so many years.' He shook his head. 'When you forgot who you truly were, you forgot how to find freedom too.' He contemplated for a moment. 'I'm able to explain a part of your history to you, but only what I am certain the King would wish you to know.'

He stopped, turning to look at her. 'You are not originally from Tenebrae, Estellah. You were born here—born and raised in the realm of Caelum until the day of your thirteenth birthday. That day, everything changed.' His eyes held the pain of some distant memory.

'Suffice to say, Stella, I searched for you long, fearing that you'd fallen into the enemy's grasp. But I was comforted because I knew you could return to us if you chose to—never suspecting that you had lost the memory of who you are. Years passed until, finally, my scouts began to hear rumors of your whereabouts. I set out immediately, and as soon as I found you, I acted. And, thankfully, you opened the door. Therefore, my question for you is this: what made you listen if you didn't know me?'

Stella thought about the moment she heard his voice and tried to explain. 'Something . . . a thought or a voice . . . I'm not certain which . . . but it drew me and reassured me that I knew you. Even though I didn't remember you . . . I felt like I knew you somehow. It made no sense to me, but your voice was as familiar to me as my own. And I knew in my heart that you were good and safe, like . . .' Stella sought for, but couldn't find, the words to explain. The idea of home only reminded her of cruelty and her own inadequacy, and other words that she might have used held no meaning for her in the life she had known.

'Like a friend?' he asked.

Stella thought of Jared: the only real friend that she had ever known. Picturing him brought a smile to her face.

'Yes—that's it—like a true friend.'

She paused, seeing her opportunity, and grasped at it. 'Speaking of friends, my lord, I . . . I had a friend in Tenebrae. I think he may be in danger. Could we possibly . . .?'

Liam raised an eyebrow, amused at her partially formed question. After a long pause, he answered her, 'Perhaps you would like to ask the King about your friend?'

Stella sighed and nodded, 'Yes, my lord.'

'What is your friend's name?'

'Jared Crux, my lord.'

Watching her closely, he asked, 'Is he dear to you?'

Stella hesitated, not knowing what she should say. Jared's life was of more value to Stella than her own, and she would do anything to save him if she could. It felt like it had always been that way and always would be.

'Yes, he's very dear to me, my lord,' she told him simply.

'If that is the case, I will ask the King about him myself,' he reassured her.

As they approached the banquet hall, the guards were waiting, and, bowing low before the commander, they opened the great doors.

The resounding voice of the herald announced, 'His Royal Highness, Liam, by the grace of the King; the High Commander of Caelum; Prince of the Realm; Duke of Lux; Marquess of Lexis; High Knight of Astra Septem; Protector of the Crown—with his honored guest, Lady Estellah of the realm of Caelum.'

They swept into the banquet hall, and all the guests in that great room—the mighty nobles and the high people of Caelum—in a wave of motion, rose to their feet. Stella felt confused, elated, and unworthy all at once, as Liam led her through the elegant sea of people to the head of the room.

The banquet hall was wide and stretched out before her. It was filled with long tables at which the great multitude of guests stood. The commander escorted her to the seat of honor, in front of the King's raised table, and took his place beside her. Everyone remained standing. Looking around, Stella felt humbled and shy; she was surrounded by beauty and stunning brightness, and the glittering people of Caelum dazzled her.

A hush soon fell over the room, and the deep voice of the herald began, 'His Grace of the Great Realm and Hosts of Caelum; Emperor of Vita Arbor; Governor of Potentia; Lord of Via Lactea; Ruler of Sapientia; Defender of the Realm of Terra and Mare; Wielder of Iudicium, the blade forged from the plates of Aereus; the Ancient One; His Great Majesty . . . *The King!*'

A reverent murmur rose over the banquet hall. Stella caught her breath as the King entered in great glory and splendor and proceeded through their ranks. He was clothed in long, flowing robes, and illumination seemed to emanate from him as he walked. His countenance and his beauty struck her with such force that the impression would never fade from Stella's mind, even for the remainder of her life.

She guessed his age, at first glance, to be at the peak of a man's strength, but as he approached, she saw that, below the majestic jewel-set diadem of gold, his hair was a glimmering silver-white. As she beheld him, she began to suspect that he must be much, much older. To Stella it seemed that his face and bodily strength were untouched by time, yet his glance seemed brimming with age and hidden knowledge. *He is old and young all at once!* she thought to herself.

He exuded the same power that she had sensed from the commander—intense, fierce, and potent. With the King, however, it was not restrained or hidden. Instead, it was richly and bountifully displayed, bursting out of his being—vigorous and strong. The whole room perceived it and stood trembling in awe.

He moved up the aisle to where Stella and the commander stood, stopping in front of them. The commander bowed low. Stella curtsied, shaking; she was unable to lift her eyes to the King.

Then the unthinkable happened. It made Stella's heart leap. It caused her mind to race and falter. She suddenly felt herself embraced in the strong arms of the King. He lifted her off the floor and spun her around in the air with a joyous laugh before placing her down again. She swayed on her feet, but he held her securely within his strong arms, steadying her.

'Welcome home, my dear Estellah! Let me look at you.' He held her out for a moment by her hands and smiled. 'You are beautiful,' he declared, pronouncing the words with pride. 'All these long years of separation, and now, finally, you are here. It's enough for me to weep and laugh all at once.' The King's eyes shone.

Immediately, he saw her confusion and glanced at the commander; his mirth sobered at the grim expression on his son's face. They surveyed one another, their bright eyes intent, searching each other's thoughts. To Stella it seemed as if they exchanged a store of information in the silence.

Finally, the King spoke. 'We will speak more of this in the council tomorrow. Tonight,' he said, turning to Stella and taking her hands softly, 'we joyfully celebrate your long-awaited return.'

The commander bowed again. Stella followed suit, curtsying low and forgetting to breathe, as the King continued up the steps, taking his place at the raised banquet table in front of them. Lifting his arms, he gave his blessing, and then the guests were seated. The attendants began to serve.

Stella tried to calm her nerves, her mind racing. Why had the King done that? How could he possibly know that she even existed? And why should he care at all?

Musicians began to play sweet, enchanting sounds on beautifully carved stringed instruments. All the while, singers' harmonies blended with the strings in a foreign tongue.

Stella, finding no sufficient answers to her many internal questions, finally pushed her bewilderment away for a time and, instead, listened to the song in growing wonder. The words floated masterfully on the soft sounds, and as Stella listened, after a time, their veiled meaning slowly formed strange pictures in her mind.

She saw a fire—red and intense—burning at the hands of a smithy who was working in the billowing heat. It was clear that he was a master at his craft. Stella could see the detailed, metal shape of some dreadful, fiery creature emerging from the center of the light and heat. It was a heinous, writhing sea serpent flawlessly depicted in the dancing flames. The grotesque reptile was in its last throws: impaled and dying upon a long, deadly spike. The master smith continued crafting the image with great strength and care. Long she watched the riveting vision, mystified, until at last, it faded as a dream upon waking, and Stella came to herself once more.

She looked around her. The commander was in deep conversation with a man seated across the table. Perhaps in his early to mid-twenties, he had bright eyes and a pleasing countenance. The commander, observing Stella, politely curtailed his speech.

'We will go over it tomorrow in the council,' he said to the man. 'The King wants you there to discuss it.'

'Yes, my lord, High Commander,' the man answered, 'I would be honored to be there.'

'Good,' he replied, pleased. 'But now, no more talk of business. Lady Estellah,' he said turning to her, 'I would like you to meet Sir Nathan Connelly. He has served me faithfully for many years. We have been through many tight spots together.'

Stella smiled and held out her hand to him. 'I'm afraid I don't know the proper forms of greeting in Caelum, but I am happy to meet you, Sir Nathan.'

The commander smiled. 'That works perfectly, Stella.'

'It's a pleasure to meet you as well, my lady,' Nathan answered, taking her hand. 'Have you only recently arrived in Caelum, then?'

'Yes, just today,' she answered him.

'Ah, I'd say that's recent. Where did you come from before that?'

'From Vespera. But I actually lived in Terra, in the city of Tenebrae. How about you?'

'I have lived my whole life in the big sky country of Arva, ma'am. And no place makes me happier than the Midlands, except Caelum, of course. I hope everything here is to your satisfaction.'

'Oh, yes, Sir Connelly. How could it not be? I still feel as though

I'm dreaming,' she said with shyness.

He nodded knowingly. 'It takes a while to adjust. I think I pinched myself a dozen times on my first visit. Were you enjoying the music just now?'

'Yes, it is so . . . beautiful,' she answered, though the word fell short of what she was trying to say. 'I . . . I saw pictures in my mind, yet I don't know what they mean or what they're singing.'

'The music here often has that effect on people. They are singing in the ancient language of Caelum. It is the lay of Aereus; the tale tells of the forging of the bronze sword long ago. The meaning can't really be expressed fully in any other tongue. Such as it is, I can translate if you'd like.'

'Really?' Stella asked, surprised. But she added quickly, 'Please, if it's not too much trouble.'

'It's no trouble, but it isn't a perfect rendering, by any means,' Nathan answered. 'Roughly speaking, it runs something like this:

'Our mighty King took up Aereus,
Whose ancient script our law displayed
The plates of Bronze harmonious
Betwixt the hammer and Anvil laid

Within the fires, a brand was wrought
Upon the Blade, the law for man
To quell his foe, the tool he sought
No mind could fathom the good King's plan.'

He paused. 'That's about as far as I can go. There are more verses, but they become even harder to put into common words.'

'Do you know what it means?' Stella asked him.

He gave her a thoughtful glance. 'Not entirely. No doubt the King will reveal the true meaning in time.'

The banquet continued for several hours, and Stella, as she began to eat, became cognizant that she was hungry—as hungry as she had ever felt in her life. As the food was served, she was hit with the realization that the most sumptuous food and drink in Tenebrae had been but a poor imitation—tasteless, colorless, and unappetizing in comparison to what was before her now. The table of the King was vibrant, aromatic, flavorful, and bursting with variety. The rich, savory food was ambrosia. Delicate glasses were kept filled with jewel-toned, piquant nectar that satisfied even the deepest thirst. Stella ate and drank until she had her fill.

Finally, when all the guests had eaten and were satisfied, the King stood, signifying the end of the meal. He left his table, passing through the hall, pausing to speak with a subject, here and there, as he traversed the room. The commander turned to Stella, offering her his arm, and they followed the King. They passed through a wide arch to an adjoining, brilliantly lit ballroom. It held a raised dais at one end where the King took his seat, motioning for Liam and Stella to be seated nearby.

As the guests were streaming into the room, the King turned to the commander. 'You have done well, Liam,' he said, putting his hand proudly on his son's shoulder.

Then he turned and regarded Stella again, his eyes gentle. 'The enemy held you long in his grasp. You may not have known it, but your very life hung in the balance until you opened the door for the commander. Fortunately, you acted quickly, and Liam was able to rescue you. But there is much to set right; Odhrán has used you to accomplish considerable evil that has set off an avalanche of consequences.'

The King surveyed the commander. 'There is much to set right,' he said again quietly, with intensity.

Stella thought she detected pain behind his eyes. She remembered the chasm dweller and his cruelty, and she felt shame thinking that she may have unwittingly played a part in harming the King or his people.

After a moment the King shook his head, dispelling his air of melancholy. 'But enough of that. Tonight, we are celebrating happier times to come, and our guests crave music and dance. They shall not be denied.'

He motioned to the conductor, and the musicians began to play—this time a quick-paced, lively reel. There was a flurry of excitement as the guests formed into lines and began the dance.

The commander turned to Stella with a smile, 'Do you want to try it?'

'Oh! No, thank you, my lord. I don't know how, and I feel very tired all of a sudden.'

The King shot her a surprised glance.

'Yes, it can be an adjustment when you first come here,' the commander said with a nod. 'You will grow stronger over time. Would you like to retire for the night?'

'I think so,' she confessed, adding hastily, 'if, my lord, the King will not be displeased.'

The King rose. 'Of course not, my dear. Take all the rest you need. You have freedom here. I welcome you again as my honored guest, Estellah. I want you to feel at home. I am very, very pleased you have come.'

He beckoned, and an attendant approached with a bow. 'Please show Lady Estellah to her apartments.'

Stella curtsied low before the King and the commander. For a moment, she was speechless from the King's words of great kindness. Finally, finding her voice, she replied, 'Thank you, Your Majesty.' She paused, and before turning to follow the servant away, she added sorrowfully, her voice wavering, 'I . . . I am sorry for any pain and trouble I have caused, Sire.'

'The King regarded her for a moment and answered kindly, 'I know.'

Stella curtsied again and, hanging her head, followed the servant out.

The King watched her go and then turned to the high commander. 'Does she retain nothing of the past?'

'She's forgotten everything, as far as I can tell.'

'Then she won't understand the ramifications of all that has been set in motion.'

'Odhrán's men tortured her for days before I found her,' said the commander, his eyes hot as embers. 'Odhrán could have relayed the information in other ways, without Stella.'

'He used her deliberately,' the King said darkly.

The high commander nodded. 'He chose her and waited until the timing was in his favor. He wanted her to be the one to betray the surface.'

The King frowned. 'Odhrán knows our laws well. He knows we will have to try her for treason under Caelum's laws.'

'He'll be counting on it.'

'Liam,' the King took the commander's arm, 'if she is tried, she *will* be found guilty,' he said with gravity.

The commander looked at the King with solicitude.

The King continued, 'And she will be executed for treason.'

'There must be another way,' the prince said in protest.

He surveyed his son. At length, he spoke, 'There is one other way, but you know this is just the beginning. You've seen what Estellah is going to do.' The King said gently, studying him.

'Yes, I know.'

Grief flashed across the commander's countenance. He paused, stung by the King's reminder. He let the emotion pass and continued in a determined voice, 'I've also seen her remorse and your love for her, Father. And I have seen her doom. I'd like to spare her from it if I can.'

The King sighed but did not protest. 'Then it is up to you, my son. You understand where this will lead us.'

'I do,' Liam said, determination hardening his jaw. 'Above all, I trust you, Father.'

'So be it,' the King said with sober finality.

Chapter 15

~ ~ ~** *** *~ *~~

The House under the Trees

Ian stood observing the distant, serene, grey hills through the dim forest trees, his mind slipping between thought and memory. He watched the waxing moon slowly rise in her celestial path as the night deepened and drew on. The generations had passed since Caelum's civil war, and the great war continued now beyond Caelum; hope and despair had woven a complex tapestry together throughout the ages of men. Throughout it all— betrayals, deep misery, and many defeats—the King had held fast to his former promise to the realm of Terra and Mare; it was under his wing, and he fought for its people, even when they seemed only to cause him grief.

The Caelum fighter looked through the tree-filtered moonlight towards the small, ragged group of Westerners sleeping on the forest floor. He contemplated, again, the deep mystery of the King's great love for this unassuming people and the marvel of how he had promised to adopt them into the peoples of Caelum— granting, to those who chose to accept, the full rights of citizenship.

Ian had seen much suffering caused by the hand of men, but this group had slowly stirred his admiration. They were weak and vulnerable, lacking much knowledge, and very young: babies in comparison to Ian's long years. But their unwavering trust and faith in the King was irresistible, and that had won Ian's respect.

He knew why the King had chosen to make them his own. It wasn't for their own deeds or abilities. He certainly didn't need them. But he loved them. Ian's eyes smiled softly on them as he continued his silent vigil, guarding their peaceful, slumbering frames throughout the long watches of the night.

* * *

The day dawned cool, shrouded in mist, with moisture-filled clouds laying low over the mountains; a heavy fog was settling in the lowlands. Jared awoke and watched as the sun fought to break out from behind the threatening veil of grey which was growing ever thicker over the jagged and lofty range to the east. They would be wet before the day was old.

Turning, Jared glanced at the group—sprawled out, encircling a smoldering campfire, still wrapped in sleep. They had waded through a sea of sword fern, moss, and wild huckleberry under the towering, evergreen giants of the vast, costal forest. All the while, the great shadow of the mighty snow-capped sentinel, Kulshan, loomed overhead. Jared was eager to gain as much distance as possible before their flight was discovered by any pursuers who might attempt to track them. He had relentlessly urged the travelers forward, in consequence, far into the night.

They were an oddly mismatched collection of old and young, mother and guide, soldier and captive. Ian had insisted on bringing the prisoner and allowed him to walk next to him unbound. The young man seemed to take to Ian almost immediately. Although he said little, he was still with them the next morning, Jared noted, surprised and amused. He had suspected the boy would disappear in the night. However, there he was, sleeping against the rough bark of a fallen cedar, and instead, it was Ian who had slipped away sometime before dawn.

Jared rekindled the fire, setting the lion's tooth coffee on the grate, and surveyed the rest of the group. Besides himself and Caleb, there was: James, snoring lightly on the outskirts of their camp; Ethan and his wife, Sophia; their teenage daughter, Zoe, and ten-year-old son, Zack; and the young, newly married Kenny and Faith were asleep side-by-side, closest to the fire.

Jared's eye rested for a moment on Faith. She was in a deep slumber, her hand resting gently on her heavily pregnant middle. He wondered, with disquiet, how much time they would have before the child came. It couldn't be long.

After a few minutes, Caleb stirred and sat up, scanning the camp; his eyes landed on the place where Ian had kept watch. 'Gone again?'

'Yep.'

'Hmph,' Caleb grunted, rolling up his blanket and getting to his feet.

'Coffee?' Jared asked, handing him a steaming cup. He took it greedily. Jared smirked, taking a swallow of his own.

They discussed their route for that day, consulting their worn and outdated maps and considering how they would get over the multitude of rivers that intersected their path. Neither man had been this way in several years, although they remembered much from past travels. They knew for certain that the prominent bridges had been gone for some time. The rest was a wild guess as to what infrastructure still remained.

The prisoner stirred and woke. He glanced around and slowly stood, hesitating before walking over to the two men.

'Where's Ian?' he demanded, his dark eyes haughty and accusing.

Caleb spit. 'Boy, you've got to learn to drop that chip on your shoulder.'

Jared chuckled and walked to the fire, refilling his mug.

The young man stood silent for a moment, weighing how to respond. After a brief pause, he asked in a more disarming tone, 'Do you know where he went?'

Caleb looked at him carelessly. 'Nope.'

The boy's eyes narrowed.

Caleb leisurely walked to where Jared knelt stirring the fire and, taking a mug, poured a new cup of coffee. He walked back to the young man.

'What's your name boy?' he asked.

The prisoner looked at him steadily and, after a tense moment, answered, 'Alex.'

'Well, Alex,' he said, handing him the mug, 'Caelum fighters are like that. You get used to it.'

Alex looked at Caleb in disgust. 'Are you for real? You really think

I'd buy that Ian's a Caelum man?' he scoffed.

Caleb shook his head. 'Not trying to sell you anything. You can believe what you want,' he told him with a shrug.

Alex was incredulous. 'Did he leave to hang out with his buddy Skookum and ride re'ems?' he mocked, still refusing to be taken in.

Jared and Caleb looked at each other and chuckled; the kid was funny.

'Like I said,' Caleb continued, 'believe whatever you want.'

He turned back to Jared, and they continued discussing how they might cross the swift river that they were approaching.

As they talked, Alex stood reasoning while he absently drank from his mug, and as he did, his features progressed in stages from doubtful mistrust to uncertainty. Finally, the uncertainty in his eyes slowly dissipated and, in its place, astonished wonder began to spread over his countenance.

Meanwhile, it was becoming painfully clear to both Jared and Caleb that neither was satisfied with their options. Finding a way to get the group over the river was proving to be a bigger challenge than either of the men wanted to admit. After many minutes of their discussion bearing no fruit, a voice behind them interjected, 'We could make a bridge.' The men turned and saw that it was ten-year-old Zack.

His mother, Sophie, had risen and was busying herself with breakfast. The smell of fried potatoes began to permeate the air.

'Yes, I suppose we could,' Caleb allowed slowly, keeping his expression serious, 'but bridge making is hard and long work. It is a wide river, and we need speed and secrecy.'

'Well,' the boy said after a moment of thought, 'then we could swim across. My dad says I'm a strong swimmer,' he added proudly.

Caleb nodded slowly, rubbing his chin. 'Yes, swimming would do the trick, but what about the ones who can't swim?' he said, motioning to the group.

Zack puzzled his mind for an answer. 'I guess I could carry them on my back,' he announced finally.

'You are very brave,' answered Alex, joining the conversation unexpectedly. 'That might work in the summertime, but the water is very swift now, in flood season. The strongest man might be dragged under by the current in that river.' He approached Zack and, kneeling to his level, spoke in a surprisingly gentle tone, 'You wouldn't want to drown yourself and whoever you carried.'

The boy shook his head, wide-eyed. Caleb was about to ask Alex if he had any better ideas when they heard a noise approaching their clearing. They all froze, listening. A whirring sound was coming on fast.

'*Drone!*' Jared yelled.

The travelers, responding with frantic haste, grabbed their possessions and scattered to the trees. Jared quickly broke down the fire and doused the flames before scrambling into the nearby underbrush. He looked up through the branches. An armed drone was hovering above the clearing and slowly circling as it descended. It approached the campfire, gathering data. Jared held his breath as he watched it study the coals and the tell-tale signs of their hastily abandoned camp.

His eye caught movement across the clearing, and he tensed. He could see Zack hiding in the branches, watching the drone in awe. His older sister, Zoe, was trying to pull him into the denser branches, but he shrugged her off. The drone became aware of them.

Turning to their location, it advanced. Jared heard a shrill whistle from the nearby trees. *Was the sound a signal of some sort?* He was almost certain of it. The drone stopped in the clearing next to where the young people were hidden, and, without warning, it opened fire on them. Jared had his weapon in hand instantly, but before he could fire a shot, at that very moment, a large hawk swept down from somewhere above and attacked the drone, clawing and gripping it in its deadly talons. Ripping and biting, the bird wrenched off the shield on the drone's underside and, violently gutting it of its wires, downed the machine. It all happened in a matter of mere seconds.

Jared quickly crawled out from under the branches, urgently rising to aid the boy and his sister. Just as he regained his feet, someone pushed him hard onto the ground. He looked up.

Before him was a stranger, streaked with dark green paint across his face and torso—a pair of shorts his only attire. He was holding a long rifle pointed at Jared's face. A dozen others, dressed in the same style, were bringing the rest of the group into the clearing. They pushed them together roughly and then to the ground at gunpoint.

In the distance, Jared could see some of the strangers standing over Zack with their weapons, discussing something. He was lying prostrate at the edge of the clearing. He had been hit. Jared couldn't tell how bad it was, but his sister, Zoe, was weeping. The strangers pulled the teenage girl to her feet and spoke in their own language while examining her.

Zoe's father was, at the same time, being led into the clearing, and, although he had never been a violent man, when his eyes beheld the plight of his children, he was overcome with rage. He threw off the man holding him with sudden strength and charged the others. Seizing one, he grappled with him, until another man came behind and struck Ethan hard on the back of the head with the butt of his gun. He crumpled to the ground. Sophie and Zoe began screaming.

Jared, taking advantage of the confusion, sprang up suddenly, bowling over his captor and knocking the rifle from his hands. The armed men raised their weapons with the intent to fire, but at that very moment, Alex ran from the woods, with arms upstretched, and leapt between them. He shouted at the men in a strange tongue, and they immediately lowered their guns, responding tersely in the same dialect.

'Drop your weapon,' he shouted over his shoulder to Jared.

Jared and Caleb exchanged an uneasy glance, and Jared slowly tossed his gun to the ground.

Alex continued to converse with the men and approached the boy, Zack, observing his wounds. He seemed to be directing the men. Two of them stooped and lifted the boy. They began carrying him into the woods.

'Where are they taking him?' Jared demanded.

'To get help,' Alex responded, turning to him. 'We need to follow them; it's not far.' He gestured to the armed men who were also lifting Ethan up onto his feet; he was conscious but unsteady. 'They're going to help us.'

The captors melted silently into the woods with Zack and Ethan while Jared retrieved his side arm and went to the others. They were shaken and pale but unharmed, thanks to Alex's intervention.

The day had progressed but remained dark, buried behind a wall of dense cloud. They left the clearing just as the grey mist was turning to a steady rain, keeping up with Alex's quick pace as best as they could. The strange men moved through the trees as silently as cats. They were soon out of sight, but Alex hung back just enough that the group might follow.

For many minutes, they heard the growing sound of rushing waters. Emerging from the trees, they saw a mighty flowing river coursing across their path. In the fog on the gravel bank, rested three dugout canoes. There was no sign of Zack or Ethan.

Two of the strange men were waiting for them, and as they approached, the men quickly dragged the canoes to the water's edge and got in, leaving one canoe empty. Alex, without pause, took this last canoe and pulled it into the shallows, directing them to get in. They divided their number between the three boats: Caleb and James in the first; the young couple, Faith and Kenny, in the second; and Sophie, Zoe, and Jared in the third.

They pushed off into the churning river, the men turning immediately downstream and guiding the boats in single file. Debris and logs protruded haphazardly out of the rushing water, but the men smoothly navigated around the obstacles, steering the vessels confidently with their wooden oars from the rear of each canoe. The shoreline blurred past as the floodwaters carried them, their small crafts slicing through the turbulent swells.

Sophie and Zoe were consumed with worry. Jared tried his best to comfort them. He watched Alex out of the corner of his eye, maneuvering his craft as deftly as the strangers.

After a time, the men wordlessly changed course and crossed the river, steering into the shallows of the opposite bank and, springing out, pulled the canoes with strength up onto the rocky bank. They helped their passengers out and then pulled the boats under the trees, covering them with a layer of freshly cut Douglas-fir and cedar boughs to shed the rain or perhaps hide them from view.

The men disappeared into the trees once more, and now the people of the Way found it difficult to follow even Alex, who was fading more and more into the forest. They hurried through the trees, glimpses of him becoming less frequent in the mist ahead of them, until they stopped seeing him at all.

They continued forward, however, until the undergrowth of the forest grew denser. The group slowed and came to a halt, though no one had spoken. Jared glanced around. There was no other way that he could see for them to go. He signaled for Caleb to continue pressing through the undergrowth, while James and the rest of their companions followed close behind.

Coming out of the other side of the dense hedge of brush, Jared stopped and looked ahead in wonder. Before him stood a large house, but there was no clearing; the forest grew up against the edges of its lofty log walls, and several mighty trunks towered out of the very roof of the structure, spreading their evergreen canopies wide over the dwelling, shielding it from view above and on every side. The door of the house opened, and one of the strange men appeared, beckoning to them.

Entering through the narrow door, they saw that the house was longer than it had appeared, stretching far out ahead of them. Large fires were lit in the center of the house between the mighty trunks, which rose like pillars, traversing its length and great height. Large and colorful woven tapestries adorned the long walls. It was clear that many families dwelt within. The man led them through the length of the structure to the largest fire in the heart of the house. A large crowd was seated there, relaxing on many tiered benches encircling the round, main hearth. He gestured for them to wait. A few of the folk glanced at the newcomers, but none spoke to them.

After a considerable time, Jared finally saw a group coming towards them from the far side of the long house. The people grew quiet as they approached. Jared observed that Alex was there, speaking deferentially to a woman who was encircled by counselors.

She had a proud bearing, exuding a regal presence that was hard to define. The woman had passed maidenhood but possessed a face still round and fresh, giving her an air of extended youthfulness. She wore an earth-toned woven garment girded with a thin belt of hide. A worked-leather bag hung low on her hip, and on her other side, was a long knife. Her flowing, dark hair was adorned with the feathers of eagles. Her countenance held wisdom and her voice was rich and pleasant.

Jared and his companions heard her speak with delight, though they could not understand the meaning of her words which were spoken in the language of her ancient people. The ministers surrounding her and those who sat on the terraced benches regarded her with respect. For before them stood Lannai: the pride of her people, daughter of an unbroken line of chiefs who had served their nation since before the dark years.

Since the death of her father, she had guided her nation, the people of the mountain. Now, as they listened to her, the people's faces reflected a general feeling of celebration and lightness. The woman ceased speaking, and Alex responded to her in the same language, saying each of the Way's names, one after another, introducing them to her.

He turned to Jared and addressed him in their common tongue, 'I would like you to meet our . . .' Alex paused, thinking for a moment. 'Though it doesn't convey the whole meaning, I believe the closest title for her in your language would be princess,' he said.

And then he continued, 'This is Lannai. She's my mother.'

Chapter 16

The People of the Mountain

J ared nodded his head in respect, and Lannai turned her gaze upon them. 'It is not our custom to welcome strangers or bring them into our midst, revealing to them our hidden paths. But, today, you are honored guests of Tan Lálam,' she said, extending her arm in a welcoming gesture. She spoke without hesitation and with the accented speech of their region. 'You have brought my son back to me; for that, I am beholden to you and grateful beyond words. Your injured friends are being cared for. Perhaps you would like to see them? A great feast is being prepared—for all my people rejoice with me that my son has returned.'

Jared nodded. 'Thank you, my lady, for such a welcome. You are right to assume that we're worried about our friends. I'd like to see them as soon as possible.'

'Of course. I will take you to them now.'

She turned without ceremony and led them down the hall to one of the many woven tapestries that hung along the length of the main house. She looped it up onto a hook, exposing a doorway. They could see now that the long, woven blankets concealed rows of rooms extending along the length of the house on either side, the coverings lending a form of separation to each family that lived there.

'These rooms are for your people to use as long as you have need of them. Please rest awhile until all is prepared.'

They thanked her and passed through the opening. Jared glanced around as he entered. It was a comfortable room; the wide log walls were hung with decorative woven blankets, and it was warmed by large cast iron plates, at either end of the room, that had been heated in the main fires. The floor was strewn with lush firs. To the left, shelves and hooks hung along the wall where many items were stored in orderly fashion, and a ladder led to a loft above.

To Jared's right was a doorway through which he could see several more interconnecting rooms. Zack was lying on a fur-covered cot in the adjacent room's center, and Ethan, with bandaged head, sat on a low stool next to him. He rose as they stepped inside.

'How is he?' Jared asked the boy's father.

'He's still sedated. They removed two bullets, but his wounds were not life-threatening. No organs were damaged, thank the Master,' he said in a relieved tone. 'Their medical people know what they're doing—that's for sure.' Respect was in his eyes. 'They told me they've seen wounds like this many times before,' he continued. 'They have been dealing with armed drones for years it seems. They said my son should be able to make a full recovery within a few weeks.'

'That's great news, Ethan,' Jared responded. 'How's the head?' he asked, gesturing to the bandage.

'I'll be fine,' he told him. 'It could easily have gone another way, you know, Jared,' he said, shaking his head. 'We could all be dead, but the Master had other plans. For some reason, every last one of us was spared.'

Jared looked at Ethan and raised an eyebrow. 'Your son was attacked by a drone. You got hit hard enough to give you a headache into next week. And you're saying the Master planned this?' He shook his head. 'Don't get me wrong, Ethan, I trust him. I know the King is very powerful and has many servants throughout the realms. And it's clear he wants to help us, but Caelum is far away. There must be limits to what even he can do for us here.'

Ethan cocked his head, looked thoughtfully at Jared, and smiled slightly. 'The people of the Way believe that the Kingdom of Caelum resides here,' he said, tapping lightly on his breast, 'in the hearts of each of the Master's servants—no matter where they are. And that being so, there is no limit to what he can do for us. The

167

ancient accounts speak of a time long ago when the Master's servants, living out this principle, performed unexplainable acts of power.'

'You believe the legends, then?' Jared said, surprised.

Ethan looked at Jared, and there was an intensity kindling in his eyes. 'Every word.'

They had all feasted, seated around fuel-heaped blazes, while elders stood and recounted stories of their people: some brimming with humor, others holding pain and loss, but all with lessons hard won, passed down in the fire glow to each succeeding generation.

After the elders had spoken, Lannai rose. 'An account of my son, Alexander, must now be given. Over two years ago, my sons left to do the work of our people and never returned. Only Snake's Terror, my younger son's ever-faithful hawk, returned injured and grasping, in his sharp and bloodied talons, my son's leather pouch. When we searched for them, we found that the fields they had been sent to tend had been utterly destroyed. And though the loss of our winter store was a disastrous blow and impossible to mend, it was much harder for our people to accept the disappearance of the two eldest grandsons of Chief Hotsim.

'Our people searched long, but nothing more was ever found of them. Emissaries were sent to our cousin tribes, but none had any new knowledge concerning them; though separately, they each sent back reports of their own significant troubles. Now that he has returned, my son will tell us his tale and uncover the mystery of that dark day for us all.'

She nodded to him, and Alex slowly stood, taking his place next to the flames. His skin glowed red and his eyes seemed like black coals as he recounted the memory of his ordeal.

'That hot summer morning, I had set out early from Tan Lálam with my brother, Javier, to do as we were bid by the elders—to check the far grain fields, the wheat and the barley, and also the corn in the next valley and to water them, if necessary. Our hawks, Snake's Terror and Black Talon, circled high in the overcast skies while we walked along the eastern ridge. There, Javier and I distinguished the scent of smoke, and we briefly sought its source, for fire is ever our enemy in the late summer months. But before we could learn its origin, the wind shifted, driving the scent away. The air became sweet once more, and we were forced to give up our search.

'The sun was high when we finally approached the valley of wheat. I observed with satisfaction the well-growing, blonde stocks waving and glistening in the heat of the day. Before resting, my brother and I climbed the foothills and broke the dam of the high pool, for the grain wanted water. We rested then in the cool shade, watching the water flow down the canal and slowly fill the trenches that we had dug with our people throughout the planted rows the previous spring. We allowed the water to fill the trenches and spill into the barley ditches that laid beyond them. When the ground had finally received its fill and standing water remained in all the trenches, we remade the dam, blocking up the pond once more.

'My brother and I then continued beyond the valley of wheat, making our way to the next valley where the ears of corn would be ripening on their stocks in great number. As we crested the foothill, the valley of corn laid before us. Fully expecting a tall sea of green stalks and their long, golden tassels swaying in the breeze below me, I cried out and froze in alarm at what my eyes beheld instead. The valley was a charred and smoking ruin, black and burned. We hurried down the slope and wandered speechless through the blackened and smoldering stocks where I perceived the ripe ears had not been harvested but had also been scorched, still bound in their husks. Studying the field and the ruin closer, it became clear to us that the blaze was fresh and had not been a natural occurrence. The destruction had been done by human hands or, at least, by human will.

'Javier and I were discussing these revelations when Snake's Terror, who had until this point sat soberly on a branch above us, suddenly uttered a shattering cry and mounted up to wing. He dove hard and extended his claws to strike. I turned to find his target. Men were there. Snake's Terror was on the closest man in an instant, gouging at his face and eyes. Black Talon dove close behind.

We joined their attack—I drawing my knife and my brother swiftly nocking an arrow. But before I could reach the hawks, another man raised a weapon and struck the faithful bird hard across his side, knocking him from the man's face to the ground. He was lifeless and unmoving. Black Talon shrieked and bore down on them fiercely. I cried out and charged the men while Javier's bow sang; at least a dozen lay at our feet before many minutes passed.

'We were overpowered, however, by their sheer numbers, for they were many. Black Talon was shot out of the air and fell. I was thrust to the ground with a bullet in the side and then disarmed and restrained. Javier was also injured and captured. One of the men—the one who had been attacked by Snake's Terror—approached. He was bleeding profusely from his nose and lip but still had the gall to kick Snake's Terror where he lay in the dirt. I spat on the man for he had no honor.

'They struck me and then carried me back the way I had come, over the foothills, towards the wheat and barley fields. The men pointed and motioned for me to look out over the valley. I turned my eyes to the place, and to my horror, I saw men and their machines dousing the freshly watered fields with fuel. The men laughed cruelly at me as they carried me to a vehicle, locking me in the back of it. Javier was already inside; he was badly injured but bore it patiently. As the vehicle pulled away, I saw a faint glow over the hill, and as I watched, smoke and flame began to rise from the valley. I lost all hope then for the provision of my people. Nothing would be left by evening.

'The men took us to a government facility where there were many containment cells. There we were separated, and it was the last time I saw my brother. I beheld in that place the strength and size of our enemy. They have numbers and weapons that make us appear as little children armed with sticks and pebbles. I saw that we could not win against such force.

'There, they meant to break me—and, indeed, I was much broken. Fine-tuned methods of deprivation and torture were their tools, and after many days, I was but a shadow, no longer son of Lannai nor grandson of the great Hotsim, forgetting all that I had once been.

'I became a servant of darkness: tracking those they sent me to track, killing those they sent me to kill, knowing only the fear of my captors mingled with much hate. It was in this state that the people of the Way found me. I was sent by my captors with a group of men to kill them all—every last man, woman, and child. But they didn't fear us. The other captives and I had never met such determined resistance. They held their ground and fought with much valor and skill.

'Overwhelmed, we fled. But I was caught by one of them. My comrades observed my capture and yet abandoned me to them. I believed that I would be tortured once again, and I readied myself. But, instead, they showed me only kindness.

'As I observed them, I felt the chains on my mind slowly begin to loosen. And I began to remember many things that I had forgotten as I traveled with the people of the Way. I spoke little but listened closely to all that was said. I heard them speak of a great mission of their King. The one who had caught me, Ian, spoke to me of many things. He told me that they were returning me to my people. When I awoke one morning, he was gone; he had left in the night. Only then was it revealed by the others that Ian had come from the country of Caelum.'

Gasps and exclamations followed this declaration. A fevered excitement spread over the house as Alex continued, 'Our people have heard of the fame of Caelum's King and his distant kingdom before now and have often wondered if the reports carried to our people from far off held any truth; but we have been unable to search it out. Now I am convinced that the reports we have heard are trustworthy. I have seen that he acts as a good king. He provided soldiers to protect his servants when I and other men had been sent to destroy them. And I saw with my own eyes how their King guided them with messages when they asked for his help.

'My people, the stories of our ancestors are true. They passed their knowledge to us of the days of Yochanan, the sojourner, who bore the message of the great King of Caelum. How did we forget it? They knew then of his greatness and fame. They learned his name. Emissaries were sent to Caelum and treaties were there signed. They returned with tales of the vast kingdom and a blessing from the King for our people.

'Life and light sprung up then in the hearts of our nation, and an age dawned over them like none that had ever been seen before. But the King's enemies among our people soon multiplied fear and caused many to doubt him, spreading a covering of lies that the people harkened to. The dark years followed; the sun dimmed and the crops withered as we turned our hearts away, forgetting the great King and his blessing.

'Regret and sorrow have bitten at the heels of our people since those days, and no new choice has been presented to us—until now. My people, I propose that we seize this chance and turn once again to the King of Caelum. He is a good ruler, and he is powerful. Let us send a new delegation with these—his servants—the people of the Way and learn if he might forgive our past bond-breaking and renew the ties between our peoples; for only he can protect us from the deadly weapons of our enemies.'

There was a burst of excitement and much talk, as the people debated over Alex's words. Many spoke afterwards—some vehemently rejecting Alex's plea but numerous others agreeing with Alex and his plans.

Lannai watched them debate from the shadows, her wise face and sharp eyes keen in the firelight, yet she did not speak. Her son had spoken well, swelling her heart with pride, but she understood her people. They would require time, and she would allow every last voice of her nation to be heard, before calling for the votes of the elders to be cast.

Far into the night, after most had sought their beds and the main fires burned low, Jared lay awake on his cot, listening as the sound of movement and voices gradually settled into a hushed stillness. The turn of events made him smile and shake his head in wonder. With interest, he had watched the people debate heatedly over Alex's words. Most of the people seemed to want another treaty with the King if they could secure one.

Jared wondered what the King's response to an emissary would be. Would he speak with them? He wondered how many more people would be placed under his protection if an envoy was sent with them. If this was the King's doing, then he certainly had a strange sense of humor.

He chaffed at how long it might take before they could continue their journey. *A few weeks.* Jared frowned. The boy needed a few weeks. He was relieved that the boy would recover, but the delay frustrated him. A few weeks for the informant's trail to disappear. A few more weeks before Jared could regroup with his men. A few more weeks before he could pursue any trace of Stella. But what else could be done? The boy had to be given time to recover before they could go on.

It seemed that all of Jared's plans, one by one, had been derailed or gone sideways. From the beginning, he had sought out the Way only for Stella's sake. Then, when that seemed too much to ask, he had settled on asking for help to find the traitor so that he could extract information from him about Stella. But even though he had asked James repeatedly, there had, as yet, been no word of response to his requests from the King.

He thought about Ethan's words concerning Caelum and the old accounts. Some of the ancient stories were pretty wild. Jared believed some of the tales, but what of the ones that defied all nature and reason? He pondered for several minutes. Anything was possible, he decided with a shrug. What was harder for Jared to understand was his own situation. If the King truly had the power to help him, why didn't he? Why was he not even responding to Jared's requests? Jared wondered vaguely if he had done something to earn the King's displeasure.

There must be something more at play, if what Ethan believed was true. An all-powerful king, if he was good, would not sit idly by while his enemies caused destruction across his lands. The King would have a strategic plan.

Jared paused in thought. Maybe that was what Ethan had been trying to explain to him—the King's plan. Jared suspected there was more to Stella's situation than he could understand. Perhaps the King wasn't idle. In all fairness, maybe there was just a bigger plan than Jared could see. Ethan had alluded to a great power made available to them by the King—one that laid at their very fingertips.

Well, it was sorely needed. He hoped, for all their sakes, that Ethan was right.

A fair morning followed. Jared left his bed, being careful not to wake the others. Slipping out through the tapestry-drawn doorway, Jared glanced up and down the wide hall of the large house. All was still.

He made his way to the front of the house and, quietly opening the door, crossed over the threshold. Nothing could be seen in the denseness of the underbrush, except a series of worn footpaths that led from the doorway, disappearing in different directions under the forest eaves.

Jared chose a wide-worn path leading around the side of the house and through the trees towards the north. It wound for some time, through the living pillars of Douglas-fir and hemlock, eventually opening on the edge of a ridge which overlooked a steep, east-facing valley that stooped low and then rose again in the distance.

Here he lingered, and breathing in deeply the sweet, new scent of the morning, he surveyed the wide sky before him. The clouds had broken in the night, uncovering a freshly washed canopy of clear blue in the dawn's pale rays. The melodies of many birds rose with the sun's spreading flames on the eastern horizon, bathing the world in light and song. It promised to be a warm day.

Jared heard a dog barking and some commotion in the trees farther along the path. He left the ridge, following the sound curiously. The noise grew. Turning a corner, the trees fell away to reveal a wide clearing in the woods. Many of the tribe were there. The children were playing with a number of dogs.

Beyond the boisterous group stood a large, rough structure where Jared saw several men were gathered. He crossed the field towards them. As he drew closer, he could see that the structure was surrounded by netting and housed many hawks. Several birds were loose, and the men were using a series of calls and whistles, drilling the birds through maneuvers. Jared watched in fascination as the birds soared high above and then dove with staggering speed, following the commands and finally coming to rest on the men's outstretched arms.

Alex was there working with them. He turned and saw Jared. 'Good morning!' he called. 'We've been running the hawks through their exercises.'

He approached holding one of the great birds. 'Truth be told, I need the practice far more than they,' he admitted, smiling. 'But it's a comfort to know that, even after all this time, they haven't forgotten me.'

'They're certainly magnificent creatures,' Jared said, admiring the hawk on Alex's arm.

'They are a proud and faithful race,' Alex replied in agreement. 'My people did not keep them in the days of old but respected their majesty even then, and they worked together at times for a common goal. Now, we live in friendship and unity with the hawks. They are our eyes and ears to the outside world, and we offer them food and protection.

'This is Snake's Terror,' he said, holding the great bird aloft, 'my old hunting companion and friend from my youth. Throughout all my misery in the last few years, I never thought that he still lived.' He stroked the bird's head fondly as the creature nuzzled his fingers with returned affection. Alex's voice was thick as he continued, 'To hold him once more is a gift unseen but greatly cherished nonetheless.'

When the men had finished running the birds through their maneuvers, they renewed the feed and fresh water while the hawks played, racing each other and the hounds across the length of the field and back. Jared watched them with heightening regard. The people of the mountain were a stern and free people. Their ancestors had taught that, for years beyond count, they had been subjugated and systematically weakened. Indeed, the story of the slow defeat of their people was well-known; they were but a shade and a memory of what had once been, long ago.

The Westland's government knew that they would lose control, if rejected as the people's benefactor, so they began a systematic destruction of their livelihoods. No one took responsibility for the attacks: the destroyed crops and homes, the poisoning of their water supplies, the strange diseases that suddenly ravaged the wild goat populations. No one bothered to ask who was responsible. The people didn't have to. They already knew. But they refused to be dispirited. They dug new wells. They planted more crops in remote areas away from their village. And they built new houses, keeping them well hidden.

Amid this battle, Lannai stood like a stalwart lighthouse against the onslaught of a raging sea. When her sons had disappeared and their tribe's food stores had been decimated, Lannai had not submitted to the terms of help that the West had tried to force upon them. Instead, she had given all that she had and fought to find a way for her people to survive and maintain their freedom. And, against all odds, free they had remained.

Now her son had returned, revealing to her the extent of their enemy's strength. It was almost enough to make her finally lose heart. It was folly to think they could withstand such might. After his revelations, Lannai had seen the wisdom in her son's solution; sending an envoy to Caelum was their only hope of not falling under the control of their great oppressor. The elders had cast their votes, and their opinions had coincided with Alex.

It was decided. An emissary requesting an alliance with the King would be sent over the mountains with the people of the Way.

It was night. All had been still for hours while Jared lay awake in thought. The boy, Zack, was recovering more quickly than expected, and preparations had already begun for their departure. Jared was calculating the days of supplies that they would need to make it to the Midlands.

Suddenly, Jared sat bolt upright on his bed and listened. The unmistakable sound of distant gunfire was reverberating deep in the woods. He rose and began to hurriedly dress, and as he did, the sound of many drones was heard passing over the house, high overhead, heading southward. He sprang out through the tapestry covering and saw men darting out of the main door.

Jared followed wordlessly, sprinting down the wide path behind them. Dawn was still hours away, and the night was overcast and dark. As he approached the large field where the birds were kept, Jared saw a reddened glow. *What have they done?*

There was great tumult. The hawk enclosure was on fire, the flames darting, furious and high, into the night. In the dancing light, Jared could see that the hutch was riddled with bullet holes and the netting was slashed and shredded. Many men were already there, rushing from the nearby well and dousing the enclosure with water. Jared joined them. After laboring together for some time, they were able at last to extinguish the flames, plunging the field once more into darkness.

The men groped in the shadows of the now hissing and dripping enclosure, making their way towards the hutch. Jared held his breath, fearing what they would find. Not a sound could be heard issuing from the enclosure. The birds were utterly silent. They opened it and continued to search. Where were they? The waning moon broke through her thick shroud of vapor and shone upon them in the clearing. The men could see well enough now but to no avail. There were no hawks for them to find inside—great or small, living or dead. The hutch was empty.

Stricken and dumbfounded, the men stood in the steaming remains of the structure, trying to understand the riddle. They didn't have to wonder long. A shrill call echoed in the night sky over the trees, and Alex gave a shout. A great hawk descended from the mist and alighted onto his shoulder. It was Snake's Terror. He gave a piercing cry and was answered by the call of many birds.

The men turned towards the welcome sound and saw them descending before the eastern ridge, in great numbers, with the moon in their wake. The hawks were diving and circling above a lone man who was walking towards them; his bright eyes shone between the rays of moonlight and shadow.

The newcomer, being forewarned, had reached the birds in time, stealthily setting them to flight before the enemy's guns had drawn nigh. He came now, bearing their young in his arms. He advanced, and, when Jared saw the man's face, he grinned.

Ian had returned.

Chapter 17

Mountain paths

T he arrival of Ian created quite a stir. Everyone in the tribe wanted to touch him and ask him questions about his home. But Ian had lost none of his good humor. He was very patient with them, lightheartedly answering their questions and helping them in their work.

Jared noted that Alex was a permanent fixture by Ian's side. When the elders named Alex as their choice for the delegation, Jared breathed easier. It would have been hard to separate them. Anyway, he had grown to like the kid.

The date of their departure was set. The evening before they were to leave, a great feast was held by Lannai and the elders to honor them. At her bidding, Lannai's ministers brought forth many gifts that had been specially prepared for them. They were equipped with food and supplies: dried berries, nuts, jerky and smoked fish, a compass, flint, blankets, and many weapons.

A set of fur-lined and leather clothes was provided to each in their party. They were well made, well fitting, and warm; for by Lannai's order they had been fashioned, and she had overseen their making with added care.

'These garments are the winter garb of our people,' an elder explained with solemn pride, 'and carry with them the blessings of our nation. None other wear them. Our friends and brothers, our cousin and sister tribes, they will all honor you and leave you in peace, letting you pass unhindered with these, our tokens. And they will assist you if they find you in need.'

At dawn, Alex's people rose to see them off, and after all things were ordered and made ready, Lannai spoke to them for the last time. 'May you find favor with the King,' she said, 'and may the blessing of the people of the mountain go with you.'

Turning to Alex, her eyes glistened, but her voice held strong and proud, 'Guide these, your companions, faithfully through the mountain passes of our people. Stray not off their paths in the darkness. Fear not the wind nor the floods, but walk in the courage of your fathers and the heritage of your ancestors.'

They held each other in a long embrace, but finally they withdrew.

Alex turned, his face set in stern resolution. Nodding to Jared, he silently started on the eastern path, guiding the travelers from his village towards the towering white-capped crags that rose menacingly on the horizon.

For many days, they moved under the soaring canopy of ancient trees without trouble or hinderance. The eastern peaks remained aloft, only growing larger and more foreboding at intervals. Lannai's son guided them with confidence; he had traveled these mountain paths countless times.

Birds chirped and cawed, calling to each other cheerfully, as the group made their way under the solemn watch of the giant boughs. Next to their path, a rapid, bubbling stream flowed pleasantly over moss-covered stones for many miles. The weather was fine at first and held as they traveled through the sheltered, bright, neon green of the fern-adorned valleys. But, by the fourth day, the landscape and climate had changed; the sky became overcast, and the temperature dropped notably. Their progress slowed as their path grew rough and began to abruptly climb. Then the thinning trees opened to pine-adorned, panoramic lookouts, where they caught glimpses through the mist of the rugged, snow-capped heights that lay beyond.

Crouching low one morning, several weeks into their journey, Jared peered down the tree-lined banks of a steep, rocky gorge, weighing their options. The path that Alex wanted to follow gave Jared serious misgivings. But the risk of discovery was high if they tried turning back now; they had barely made it through the pass undetected, and he doubted that their luck would hold if they attempted it again.

The dawn had broken, clear and brisk, with thin wisps of cloud hovering over the mountains. Searching tendrils of cold mountain air found their way down from the heights and caused the people of the Way to shiver and button their coats, making them thankful, once again, for the thick, well-made garments of the people of the mountain. Everything was quiet and still.

Jared looked at Alex once more and, noting the confident look in the younger man's eyes, relented. Glancing behind, he nodded to Caleb, who silently motioned for the group huddled behind him to follow.

They came up slowly, in a line, anxiety revealed plainly on each face. Ian brought up the rear, his usual cheerfulness checked by his silent, sober assessment of the path before them. This was the most dangerous part of the crossing. Trees kept the path mostly concealed, but the gorge was treacherous. If one of them lost their footing, sending a shower of rock and gravel down the steep bank, it would be equivalent to shooting off a flare for the soldiers below to see.

Vespera's and then Arva's forts along the border had been circumvented without incident. Moving past one lone Midland patrol in the gorge was all that remained. Alex was leading them on an unmapped trail. His people had discovered this hidden crossing by accident some years ago, and it had been chosen now for its secrecy.

As they advanced, James asked the Master fervently under his breath that they pass undetected. The group picked their way carefully over the rugged course, working across the uneven, narrow shelf that jutted out from the rock face. Peering over the edge, Faith nervously noted how the narrow, rocky track fell away abruptly to the distant gorge floor below.

When they had almost all passed the most precarious stretch, Jared looked back and felt himself begin to relax as each person cleared the rocky outcropping and moved, one by one, over to the wider, more stable trail. Kenny and Faith were nearly finished crossing the narrow portion, with Alex and Ian close behind.

Then, without warning, the footing below Faith and Alex collapsed. Ian instinctively grabbed Alex and was pulled down with him. As they were skidding down the steep embankment, Ian managed to shove Alex toward a small ledge several feet below them and to their left. Alex landed hard on the outcropping.

At the same time, Faith was sliding down in a cloud of rock and dust. Ian lunged after her, catching her arm, but there was nothing solid for him to grasp to break their fall. As the group watched helplessly, the two slid swiftly down the embankment and fell over the edge.

Caleb was the first to act. 'Move!' he shouted to the group, shoving them forward roughly. He reached out and pulled Kenny, paralyzed with horror, onto the wider path.

'Hold on!' Jared called down to Alex, who lay unmoving on the ledge below them. 'We're coming to get you.' He threw down his pack, taking out a harness and rope.

'Give the harness to me, Jared,' said Caleb. 'I can get Alex. We're better off splitting up if you think you can track the others.'

Jared looked at Caleb and nodded. He knew they didn't have a lot of time. Dividing the rescue attempts was their best option.

'Alright. I'll go after Faith and Ian. You get Alex and then get these people out of here,' Jared said, handing Caleb the equipment.

'I'm going with you!' Kenny said from behind them.

Jared and Caleb turned, observing him closely. His face was as white as a sheet.

'No, you're not,' Caleb told him, shaking his head. 'Jared will go. He's used to this terrain, and two will only draw more attention.' There was understanding in his eyes as he laid a hand on the young husband's shoulder. 'He *will* find her. Trust me. But we can't help her from an Arvan jail cell. I need your help to get Alex and get the rest of these people away from here. We need to move—fast.'

A commotion in the camp below warned them that the alarm had been raised. Kenny looked distraught, but he nodded.

Caleb gave Jared a grim look. 'Don't get caught.'

'I won't,' he replied, chambering a round.

Without another word, Jared leaned over the ledge, spotting a way down on the boulders some distance to the left of Alex. He crossed back over the partially collapsed ledge and stepped carefully over the side, picking his footing with caution.

Caleb put on the harness and secured the line to a nearby tree. Lowering himself swiftly, he came to the ledge where Alex was sprawled. With relief, he could now see that Alex was unconscious but breathing. Kneeling by him, Caleb shook him gently. He immediately came to and began to sit up.

'Whoa! Slowly, Alex!' Caleb said, supporting him. 'It looks like you hit your head pretty hard when you landed.'

'Yeah, I can feel it. How long was I out?' Alex asked, trying to get his bearings.

'Not long,' Caleb told him.

'You're joking, right? It's at least an hour after sunset,' he said.

Caleb's face shot up and fixed on Alex's eyes; he was staring into the distance. 'How much can you see, Alex?' he asked him gravely.

'Not much. Shadows. Just dark shadows,' he responded.

Caleb whistled low. 'It's not yet noon, Alex,' he said in a low voice.

Alex tightened his jaw and said nothing but nodded slowly in understanding. Caleb examined his injury and bandaged Alex's blood-stained head.

'Here's the harness. Let's get you up, and then we'll worry about the rest.'

Caleb strapped Alex in, and, together, Ethan and Kenny lifted him safely to the main path again. Then they lowered the harness for Caleb. As soon as they hauled him up to the ledge and he set foot on the trail, Caleb wasted no time. He began giving orders as he unharnessed himself.

'Ethan, Alex is injured and can't see well. You'll need to stay with him. Take his right arm over your shoulder like this,' he said, demonstrating with Ethan's arm. 'The rest of you stay close behind them. Kenny, you're gonna bring up the tail.'

Caleb took the lead, starting down the path at a brisk pace. The group followed. A silent and desperate plea to the Master was on their lips as they descended the mountain trail and headed into the wilderness. Caleb guided them off the path as soon as the terrain began to level out. He guessed they had only minutes to be clear of the track and out of earshot if they wanted to have any chance of escape. He earnestly hoped that the Midlanders didn't have dogs.

Plunging directly into the thick forest undergrowth, he led them on a straight trajectory, away from where he guessed the patrols would be searching. The tense minutes were some of the longest in their lives, but their pleas to the Master were not wasted. They continued in the same direction for several hours without incident.

Finally, footsore and spent, Caleb called a halt in a low, sheltered gully. The group dropped their packs and collapsed on a mossy bed of grass and clover that sprawled out around a trickling glacier brook. Patches of snow were scattered throughout the high altitude, but the sun had advanced high in the day, burning off the cloud cover of the morning and making the day pleasantly warm.

Despite their fear and grief, the group's exhaustion overtook them almost immediately, and they began to doze. Caleb felt his eyes grow heavy as well; he stood, shaking off his weariness. He had to stay alert. He walked to the stream and bathed his face and neck with the icy water. He refilled his water bottle.

Choosing a spot where he was partially screened but could still command a wide view of the surrounding areas, he took out his old map and settled down against a tree. He studied the map. It was the best one he could find in the West and had cost him much effort and a small fortune to acquire. In reality, however, it was heavily marked and incomplete, with frustratingly less detail of the mountain regions than Caleb needed. They had narrowly escaped their enemies, but he knew it would all be futile if he now got them hopelessly lost in the vast mountain wilderness.

Caleb spat. He hated the Midlanders. He understood war was war, but they had killed too many of his friends on the battlefield. If they hurt Jared, Ian, or young Faith, they would live to regret it. He vowed silently that he would track every last man down and make sure of it. He marveled that Jared had convinced him to go to the Midlands at all. The West might not be perfect, but, in

Caleb's mind, Arva was the home of the ultimate corruption. Everyone knew they were crooked. The evening news was always reliably full of stories of the failures of Arva's leaders. Jared would figure that out one day.

He wondered how Jared was faring and if Ian and Faith had somehow, against all odds, survived the fall. He desperately hoped so. But, replaying the scene again in his mind, he seriously doubted it. The drop had just been too far. If either of them was alive, they would have extensive injuries, and Jared would have trouble moving them to safety without being seen.

It was much more plausible that Jared had discovered they were already dead and was, even now, tracking their group in order to rejoin them. He wouldn't have too much trouble finding them. He knew the younger man's skill, and Jared had known where they were headed, Caleb reminded himself. Though he felt heavy from the likely loss of Ian and Faith, he let out a slow breath. Jared would join them before long.

When the group had rested an hour, Caleb roused them. 'We need to keep moving until nightfall,' he told them. 'We'll head towards the river and follow it at a distance.' He figured that was the safest course to keep them from losing their way. Caleb watched with respect as the people of the Way, though still weary, got back on their sluggish feet doggedly and continued on.

The light-filtered woods soon opened to a rocky plateau looking east, and they stopped for a moment, admiring. The view was magnificent. They could see that the craggy mountain range, marching from the north and bending away to the southeast, was nearing its borders. After a series of rolling foothills beyond, the landscape fell away to a rich, fertile plain as far as the eye could see. Big Sky Country—they were almost there.

As the group gathered new hope and courage, their cares suddenly felt less burdensome. It wouldn't be long until they reached the freedom and safety that had beckoned to them from afar, guiding them into a new land beyond the West.

* * *

The scouts had returned in the dead of night, unlooked for and bearing grim tidings. Before dawn had broken, the King was in his council chambers, deep in deliberations. It had been confirmed that the enemy was planning a large-scale rebellion on Terra and Mare.

The Duke of Esen spoke. 'If you want to save her, and also all the citizens of Terra and Mare, it is the only viable option,' he said with conviction. His clear mind had already played out every possible outcome. 'There is no other way.'

The duke's words hung heavily over the King's council chambers. Although the King had commanded that every other alternative be sought out and explored, he knew the law of his country. Jonas was right.

'It is as we thought, Father,' Liam said, after a time. 'If there is another way, I know it will be found.' He looked at the King. 'In the meantime, Jonas has uncovered a course that might prevail against the enemy and prevent the destruction of Terra and Mare. I say, we take it, if a less costly way cannot be found.'

The King considered his son's words and then looked at the duke. 'You are certain that the realm will rebel?'

Jonas' eyes met the King's. 'I have seen it.'

The King nodded. 'It must be decided then.' He sat observing his son and his councilor for a few long moments and then continued, resigned. 'Let us proceed. We will follow your plan, Esen.'

The duke addressed the commander. 'Your troops will have to be trained to obey even the finest fibers of your orders, Liam. One misstep could be catastrophic. It will be hard for them, and they won't understand. They cannot be told the whole plan, or the enemy may suspect what we are about to do.'

The commander returned his glance with determination. 'They will be ready, Jonas.'

The duke saw the expression in Liam's eyes and nodded in satisfaction; the same resolve was reflected in his own. The prince would prevail—he must—the future of their kingdom hung in the balance, and the survival of their people depended on it.

* * *

Jared watched silently as the patrol passed by on the road. He waited and then moved on, keeping well hidden and quiet in the brush. He had been searching for hours, yet there was still no sign of Ian and Faith. The patrols were apparently still searching for them as well. They were on high alert.

He reproached himself again for his poor judgment in allowing Alex to take them over the mountain gorge. The people of the Way weren't wilderness savvy or trained soldiers. Now the young expectant mother and Ian were both probably dead because of his foolish choice.

He heard voices and paused. More troops seemed to have been called in, and Jared was getting nervous. Suddenly, he heard the click of a round being chambered behind him; his heart sank as he froze.

'Turn around real slow,' a man's voice ordered.

He lifted his hands slowly, palms out, and turned.

Two men in military gear stood with their sights trained on him. 'Don't move,' the first man commanded, keeping his aim on Jared as the other soldier approached and disarmed him. He pushed him to the ground roughly and restrained him. Jared offered no resistance.

Once they had pulled him back onto his feet, they plied him with questions. 'Who are you?' the other soldier asked. 'And what are you doing here?'

Jared realized that the truth would probably be the swiftest way to help Ian and Faith so he answered the Midlanders with studied calm.

'My name's Jared Crux. I'm looking for some friends of mine who need help. They fell from the gorge earlier,' he turned and nodded to the spot where Faith and Ian had gone over, 'and must be badly hurt.'

The men exchanged glances. 'We've been looking for them for three hours. We saw them fall, but they are nowhere in the gorge,' the first man told him. 'We searched the few outcroppings that they could have struck, but there was no sign of them.'

'It's like they fell and vanished into thin air,' the second man added. He looked hard at Jared. 'What were you and your friends doing here?'

'Fleeing Vespera,' Jared said simply.

The men weighed his words. It wouldn't be the first time people risked life and limb to get out of the West.

'Then where are your friends now?' the first man asked suspiciously.

'I don't know,' Jared answered truthfully. 'I hope they're still alive and it's not too late to help them.'

The men nodded and stopped questioning him. 'We have to take you in,' the first man said in a more sympathetic tone, 'but others are still searching for your friends.'

'I appreciate that,' Jared responded.

They took him down the trail to an awaiting, open-air jeep and hoisted him in, cuffing his hands to the roll bar.

'It's a half-hour drive over some bumpy terrain,' the first man warned as they climbed into the front seats and started the engine.

They rolled into motion. Without the use of his arms, it was an immediate struggle for Jared to remain upright. This was going to be a long drive.

The men chatted back and forth with each other as Jared's mind worked feverishly to figure out a way of escape. Precious time was being wasted; he needed to find Faith and Ian.

Without warning, the vehicle suddenly lost power and died, coasting to a stop. The driver tried the engine. It cranked but wouldn't turn over. The man swore and popped the hood. As both soldiers got out and stood in front of the engine, troubleshooting the problem, Jared suddenly noticed movement in the trees to his right. Someone was moving in a concealed, stealthy manner towards the road. He watched intently for a moment. The figure drew closer, briefly passing a thin spot in the bushes. He couldn't believe his eyes—it was Ian. Jared stifled his urge to call out.

Ian motioned for quiet and approached noiselessly. He reached over the side of the vehicle to Jared's handcuffs. As he touched them, they opened wide with a click and fell off. Jared grinned and shook his head in silent wonder. He stood up and looked around cautiously. The guards were still busy on the other side of the hood.

Jared stepped gently out of the back and followed the Caelum fighter into the undergrowth. Ian led him soundlessly away from the patrols a safe distance before either man spoke.

Finally, Jared asked in a low voice, 'Where's Faith? Is she hurt?'

Ian glanced at him with his bright eyes. 'She's right as rain. A friend of mine is taking care of her.'

Jared breathed his thanks. 'How did you do it, Ian? How did you survive that drop?'

Ian looked at Jared with surprise. 'With all you have seen, do you not yet understand the power of Caelum?'

Jared furled his brow, wondering what Ian meant. 'Are you saying Caelum has power over the gravity on Terra and Mare?' he asked.

Ian chuckled, shaking his head. 'You have much to learn even about your own realm.'

The sound of voices on a road somewhere close at hand warned them to curtail their speech. Staying low, they edged away from the sounds and towards the dark, towering woods beyond.

* * *

Stella giggled so hard she almost spilled her tea. The laughter of the ladies was infectious. Her days in Caelum had been the sweetest of her life—filled with beauty, love, and more happiness than Stella imagined possible. She knew she never wanted to leave this place.

A knock on Stella's door caught the attention of the group, and an attendant announced the visitor, 'Cebrail, High Knight of Caelum, Honored by the King, and Defender of the Crown.'

'Welcome, honored Sir Cebrail,' Stella said, rising to her feet as he entered. She recognized him as one of Liam's guards, although she had never spoken to him. Broad and athletic, with dark hair and a swarthy complexion, it was evident that he was expertly trained and battle hardened—a fearsome foe for any who would oppose him.

When she first came to Caelum, Sir Nathan had explained to her the difference in rank between the knights and high knights. 'The high knights earned that title long ago,' he said, 'during the Great Rebellion, the civil war of Caelum. They are the ones who fought with distinction during the great battle and were made high knights in consequence. None have received the honor since. Many of the Duke of Esen's men were made guardians of the realm for their valor, and some of the high knights also received the honor of defender of the crown that day and became the commander's elite force—his personal guard.'

Stella recognized that Sir Cebrail must be one of those elite few. The ladies quickly rose to pay him honor as well.

'Hello, Lady Estellah,' he said to her. 'The King has asked me to fetch you to his council chambers.'

Stella tried not to act surprised or concerned, but it had been several weeks since she had been summoned before the King. She felt a sense of foreboding. What could the King want with her? Had she done something wrong?

Despite her hesitation, she answered the high knight with courtesy. 'I am honored, Sir Cebrail. I will come immediately.'

Regardless of her fears, making the King wait was the last thing she wanted to do. Bidding farewell to her ladies, she took the arm that he offered her and headed in the direction of the King's council room.

'Do you know why the King wants to see me?' she asked him.

'No, my lady. He asks to see us both, but I don't know why,' he answered.

Stella nodded and said, 'Many are talking of war, Sir Cebrail. Do you know if it's really as imminent as they are saying?'

'I believe so, my lady. Men have been sent to summon the reserves. It won't be long now.'

They chatted as they made their way through the palace halls to the large council room doors. Two guards opened the doors for them, and they entered.

The King stood before a table with his back to them. He was leaning over it, studying something. As Stella approached, she saw that it was a detailed map traced with many strokes and markings.

The King glanced up at them. 'Lady Estellah, Sir Cebrail, please come in.'

They bowed low before him. Stella had forgotten how overwhelming it was to be in the King's presence. His unbridled power and energy were enthralling and terribly frightening all at once.

Turning to her, he took her hands in his own. 'It has been a great pleasure having you in my house once again, Stella. This season of rest has come to an end, however. It is time for you to accomplish those things which have been ordained for you. I am sending you to the surface of Terra, where the Way will teach you many things you have still to learn.' There was unfathomable love in his eyes.

After a moment, he turned to the high knight. 'Cebrail, I am charging you with Estellah's protection. Bring her to the Way.'

The King paused and chuckled, 'Ian could use your help as well. They're keeping him on his toes. More instructions will follow shortly.'

'Your Majesty,' Stella said, taking a breath, 'the commander said he would speak with you about a friend I have in the Westlands.' She said the words quickly, in a breathless voice. Her heart pounded in her ears when she spoke in his presence.

The King regarded her for a moment, with gentle eyes, and then answered calmly. 'The commander has spoken to me of your friend. What can be done has already been done. Do not fear for him. I am watching over him and will continue to do so.'

'Thank you, Your Majesty.' Stella let out a long breath, relief washing over her features. She curtsied deeply and continued in a choked voice, 'I've been so afraid for him.'

'Give no rein to fear, Stella. You were made to be fearless.'

His eyes brimmed with compassion and wisdom as he regarded her. 'The opposite of fear, Estellah, is love, and it will always win out and lend courage for the tasks ahead. Now, we must say goodbye for a little while. In all that happens, please remember my love for you. It will never waver.'

He reached out and pulled her to himself, enveloping her with his massive, protective arms.

She grasped him back. A wave of love and a feeling of safety swept over her and almost overwhelmed her.

After a moment, he let her go, and turning to Cebrail, he said, 'Go now, Sir Cebrail, with my blessing.'

'Must we really leave now, Your Majesty?' Stella asked him.

'You must,' the King told her gently.

Stella blinked. The saturated color and brightness of Caelum was gone, making everything appear even more grey and dismal than normal. She glanced down at herself. Her beautiful, flowing robes had transformed. Instead, she wore plain, unassuming clothes in the style of the surface of Terra and Mare.

Cebrail stood beside her, dressed in the same common fashion. She barely recognized him. Gone was the heavily decorated uniform of the illustrious High Knight of Caelum. Nothing gave away his rank or nationality now, except perhaps his stunningly vibrant and penetrating eyes, not uncommon for the men of Caelum, and a faint illumination about his face.

'Your face is glowing, Sir Cebrail,' she told him in surprise.

'Yes, that's understandable after where we've been. Yours is as well. It will fade as time goes on—now that we are away from Caelum and the King.'

The thought seemed to weigh on him as he scanned their surroundings.

'Do you know where we are, Sir Cebrail?' Stella asked him. She could see that they were in the parking lot of a small-town grocery store. It seemed well cared for. Colorful hanging baskets adorned the front of the store and large flags hung from its posts. Though it was small, it seemed to be thriving. A steady stream of customers was coming and going through the front doors. She could hear people calling friendly greetings on their way in and out. Several cheerful groups stood chatting here and there around the entrance. Stella had never seen a place on the surface like it. It seemed . . . happy.

Cebrail nodded. 'Yes, I know this place. We're near the border of the prairie lands,' he told her.

'The prairie lands? Is that in the West?' Stella asked him.

'No, this isn't Vespera, Lady Estellah,' Cebrail said with a smile. 'We're in the Midlands now.'

He glanced over to the vehicle next to them. It was an old, dirt-covered, extended-cab truck with a for sale sign on the dash. The owner had just exited the store and walked up to his truck.

'Hey man, how much for your rig?' Cebrail asked him.

The man looked up, clearly impressed by the size of the Caelum fighter, and answered with a measure of respect. 'Five hundred. Gold-backed Midland only though. I never take East or West pesos.'

Cebrail nodded and, reaching into his pocket, produced a wallet. The exact amount that the man had specified was inside.

'Can I buy it now?' he asked, holding out the cash.

The man paused for a moment, adjusting his grocery sack. Then, taking the cash, he grinned.

'Sure, if you'll give me a lift home.'

Chapter 18

The Oath of Caelum

S tella wondered where Cebrail had learned to drive as she watched him expertly shift gears, guiding them through the hairpin switchbacks of the winding foothill pass. The area was remote, and as they turned off the paved road onto gravel, it became even more so.

'Where are we going?' Stella asked.

'To the border—to meet up with a friend,' he responded.

They traveled the dusty track for an hour, until they reached an opening in the pines. A lake, nestled in the shelter of the foothills, spread out before them. There were no other vehicles or people in sight.

Cebrail pulled over and got out of the truck. Stella followed his lead. She climbed out, stretched briefly, and then walked over to the lake's edge. A group of ducks floated placidly by as she drank in the beauty of the quiet setting.

Cebrail stood nearby, waiting. He was scanning the edge of the trees, looking for something or someone.

A crow uttered a shrill caw overhead, shattering the stillness. The ducks took to flight, calling loudly and spreading wide, rippled wakes across the calm surface of the water.

Stella heard a sound and, turning away from the lake, observed a man emerging from the woods. He walked directly to them.

Cebrail immediately approached the man, and stretching out his hand, they grasped forearms, greeting in the way of the men of Caelum. They conversed for some time in their own tongue, the newcomer speaking with Cebrail in urgent, hushed tones for several minutes.

Stella observed that he had the same bright eyes and unusually pleasing countenance as Cebrail, leaving no doubt that the stranger was one of his countrymen. Their conversation seemed to resolve as they turned and walked towards her.

'Lady Estellah, may I present Sir Ian,' Cebrail said to her.

'It's an honor to meet you, Sir Ian,' she responded politely.

'It was a blessing to be in Caelum when you returned home, my lady! Your long-awaited return caused such a celebration that it echoed across the realms,' Ian said in his pleasing tone. 'I saw you there with the King and high commander shortly before being deployed. It is a great honor to meet you, Lady Estellah.'

'Ian guards the King's servants,' Cebrail told her. 'There is a young woman with child who he asks us to bring to safety; he cannot abandon his post.'

'Of course, I would be glad to help her. Where is she now?' Stella asked.

Ian turned to the trees. A very pregnant young woman stepped out hesitantly towards them.

'Faith, this is Estellah and Cebrail. They will take you to the others,' Ian said encouragingly. She was visibly relieved.

Ian said something more to Cebrail in the Caelum tongue and, bidding them farewell, turned and disappeared under the shadow of the trees.

Faith addressed them, 'Thank you so much for your help. How did you know we'd be here?'

'The King sent us,' Cebrail answered.

Faith's eyes grew wide, and she slowly smiled. 'The Master has never failed me,' she said with gratitude, her eyes shining.

'Nor will he ever,' Cebrail answered assuredly. 'You can be certain of that.'

Faith took the bench seat in the back of the pickup and was soon asleep, sprawled comfortably across the padded vinyl. Cebrail told Stella he was driving them back in the direction of the nearest town.

'We'll get food for you both and find her friends there, my lady,' he explained.

'Thanks, Cebrail. That sounds great,' Stella said, feeling suddenly hungry, though she knew that nothing would compare to the bounty that she had grown accustomed to in Caelum. Thinking of Caelum made her feel even more hungry. 'I'm going to miss the great feasts and banquets of the kingdom,' she sighed with melancholy. She already longed to go back.

The knight's eyes glanced at her knowingly.

'Sir Cebrail, can you tell me the history of Caelum?' she asked. 'I know so little about your country.'

'It is a long history, my lady—so much so that the volumes would fill all of Terra and Mare and still would only just scratch the surface.' He smiled. 'But I can tell you a few stories of our kingdom, though there is much grief and sadness in many of our tales. What would you like to know?' he asked her.

She thought for a moment. 'Will you tell me about the people of the Way? How are they connected to your kingdom?' she asked.

He glanced over brightly and nodded. 'For many long years, there was very little communication between Caelum and Terra,' he told her. 'The breach had started not long after the people had been made stewards of the realm. Alas, how quickly they forgot who gave them their autonomy! The King is a patient and kind ruler, though fierce in battle, and he did not want to use force against them if it could be helped. However, darkness was being nurtured and bred in the realm, and the King was grieved at the state of things. So, as a token of goodwill and peace, he sent a messenger to Terra to deliver a dire warning.

'He was called Yochanan. He went far abroad reminding the people that the Kingdom of Caelum held jurisdiction thereof. He spread the news that the King who had appointed them to care for the realm would be returning. He warned them that they should put away their insubordination before it was too late, otherwise the King would consume them with his great wrath. Many laughed at Yochanan and paid him little heed, for he was a man of the wilderness, wearing rough clothes and living in the forest among the beasts, gleaning his food there as he moved from town to town. They called his words uncouth, being accustomed, instead, to those words that tickled the ears and stroked vanity. The leaders of the people threw him from their palaces and banished him from their villages.

'But others were cut to the heart by his words and heeded the message of Yochanan, asking him what they must do. He advised them, "Each of your families must send emissaries to Caelum as soon as possible, renewing your oaths to the King and asking for his pardon, for he is a forgiving ruler. Then he may relent of the judgment that is coming upon your people." His counsel seemed good in their eyes, and they did all that he suggested.

'The King responded to the envoys with great kindness and renewed his contract of peace with all who requested it. The leaders of the people saw this, however, and were eaten up with jealous rage, for they saw the hearts of the people were with the King and the numbers following Yochanan were increasing daily. So, they seized Yochanan and confined him to a cell, hoping that his people would disband. But they did not. Instead, they multiplied.

'Driven at last by their great fear of the King and hatred of his followers, they took hold of Yochanan and dragged him into a great public square. There, they executed him for treason. "Terra and Mare belong to us," they told the people that day. "Anyone who speaks the name of the Caelum King or Yochanan will be treated likewise." Great oppression followed, and many objectors were executed in like fashion; the rest were treated harshly and scattered. But, through it all, they remained faithful to Caelum. The Way continues to this day with the help of the Duke of Esen, even though in many places they must now meet quietly and keep their movements secret.'

Cebrail fell silent.

'Will you tell me more about the Duke of Esen?' Stella asked when Cebrail had finished. 'Who is he? I mean, what is his position in Caelum? The people of your country seem to revere him.'

He smiled. 'Now you are asking much. Who is Lord Jonas, Duke of Esen?' He paused for a long moment, reflecting, before going on. 'Lord Jonas is very old, although you probably wouldn't guess it. Many of our advancements are due to him. He has traveled far abroad and has a vast well of knowledge—so much so that some consider him a seer. He is the King's counselor and confidant.'

Stella nodded in silent thought and was still pondering Cebrail's words as they pulled up to the small-town diner. Stella roused Faith gently, and they went in. It was a classic hometown gathering place with wobbling tables, warm service, and a sprawling menu. They ordered, and as the waitress brought out their meals, a large party came in.

Stella looked up, observing their weather-beaten appearance and their leather and fur apparel. They were of the same style that Faith wore. As her eyes fell on the leader of the group, Stella jumped out of her seat and cried out, 'Sgt. MacIntyre!?!'

'Faith!' Kenny exclaimed at the same time. He ran to her and pulled her into his arms eagerly. She began to cry.

The tumultuous confusion in the little restaurant lasted for some time but eventually settled and gave way to many questions. Tables were pushed together, and they all settled in, ordering hot food and drinks, preparing to be amazed at the explanations each group had for the other.

Caleb couldn't wait any longer. He got Faith's attention and asked, 'Where is Ian?'

'He went back for Jared,' she explained reassuringly.

'Wait! What? Jared?!?' Stella asked. Her eyes snapped to Caleb. 'Where is he?'

'How do you know Jared?' Faith turned and asked her, confused.

People started talking all at once. Caleb held up his hand, trying to restore some order. 'Whoa, slow down. Don't everyone talk at the same time. If y'all would hush, I'll explain.'

He took a slow, deep breath as they quieted and then began. 'I think I'd better back up to the beginning. Jared and I met Stella when on assignment . . . in a distant country. We brought her to the West, but she was abducted,' he explained.

He glanced at her grimly, wondering how she had been able to escape. He briefly related all that had happened to Jared and him after Stella had disappeared in the chasm. Their reassignment, the battle, meeting Ian, the attack on the Way, and their journey through the mountains all followed in due course.

When he explained how Nathan had appeared with a message for Jared, Stella gasped, 'I met Nathan in Caelum! I think I overheard the commander talking to him about going, although I didn't realize it at the time.'

James smiled, nodding. 'Nathan has been close to the high commander for many years, although he is still young. It doesn't really surprise me that the commander confides in him.' He looked proud of his young friend.

Caleb nodded. 'You may not be surprised by any of this, James, but, I'll admit, I am.'

He looked with astonishment at Faith. 'I'd like to know how you and Ian survived that fall. You should be dead, and you don't have a scratch on you. How'd you manage that?'

A smile played on Faith's lips. After a moment of reflection, she answered, 'When the path gave way, I fell so fast. There was nothing to grab on to. I thought for sure it was all over. I knew the cliff was just too high for anyone to live through a fall like that. I didn't mourn so much for myself as I did for our child.' She laid a protective hand on her stomach.

Kenny leaned over and put an arm around her, pulling her close. Faith smiled at him and continued, 'Ian suddenly grabbed me, and then we were both falling. We fell for what seemed like long, extended minutes; but somehow—I can't explain it—I wasn't afraid. A peace filled me. As we fell, I saw the rocky outcropping where you were all standing disappear into the distance as the broad sky circled above. I watched as the tops of the trees below became clearer and clearer and began approaching at a nauseating speed.

'Then, at the last moment, Ian spun us around somehow and pulled himself under me. He yelled at me through the roaring blast of the wind, *"Hang on, lass!"* And as I did, I closed my eyes tightly and begged for the Master to help us.'

She paused and looked at them. 'And then everything just . . . stopped. I felt like I was floating, drifting—I don't know for how long.' Even now, there was wonder in her eyes. 'When I finally woke, I was still filled with a sense of peace and comfort. I was lying on the forest floor under a thicket of trees; it was like I had dreamed the whole thing.

'Ian was standing nearby. He was unharmed, so was I, and so was my child.' Her eyes fell to her protruding waist. A tear of gratitude welled up in her eye and overflowed, slipping down her cheek. 'Ian led me a long way through the woods to a lake, where he had somehow arranged for Stella and Cebrail to meet us so they could bring me back to you. Ian told me then that he was going back to find Jared.'

The group sat silent, pondering her words. After a few moments, Caleb raised an eyebrow. 'Who is Cebrail?' he asked.

Stella looked around her, suddenly realizing that Cebrail was nowhere in sight.

'He was the man with us when you got here,' Faith explained, glancing around the diner for any sign of him.

'There was no man with you, Faith,' the sergeant said. 'You two were alone.'

Faith's mouth dropped open.

'Wait!' James interjected. 'Do you mean *the* Cebrail? The knight from Caelum who has performed countless feats in the ancient legends?' His eyes grew wide.

'Technically,' Stella corrected teasingly, 'he's a high knight.'

James looked starstruck.

Caleb crossed his arms and leaned back in thought as the others continued the lively discussion. There had been no man with Stella and Faith when he entered the diner. He was sure of it. Had the women imagined him? He thought of Ian and the uncanny way he had come and gone as he pleased. Caleb had lived his whole forty-some years without seeing anyone from Caelum, and now, apparently, two of the King's men had suddenly and separately sprung into his vicinity within weeks. *What are the chances of that?*

It was an old legend that Caelum fighters showed up more often when there was action at hand. He had always discounted the talk as idle tales, but now Caleb wondered if there might be a sliver of truth in the rumors. Or perhaps this group of the Way were just slowly losing their grip on reality. That was a definite possibility.

Regardless, things were certainly heating up. He felt it. If he didn't know any better, he'd think large-scale war was on the horizon. Caleb glanced at Stella; she was talking and laughing with the others. She had been in the center of classified communications with Vespera's general. Caleb knew she must know a great deal, and yet she hadn't said anything about it.

He wondered again how she had been able to escape and end up here, of all places. The chasm dweller's hold on her had seemed unbreakable. It dawned on him that she would be the perfect asset for the enemy to use to gather intelligence. He suddenly doubted her for the first time. Jared trusted her completely and would do anything to protect her. But Caleb wondered, *Where did Stella's loyalty lie?*

He signaled for the bill. The waitress approached, smiling. 'It's been taken care of,' she told him, refilling his coffee.

'Who covered it, ma'am?' he asked her, glancing around the diner.

'The tall man that came in with these ladies,' she said, gesturing to Stella and Faith. 'The one with the nice eyes—he paid,' she explained cheerfully and, clearing the table, carried the dishes away.

* * *

Jared stooped, taking a drink, and splashed his face in the frigid glacier spring as the sun sank low on the jagged, western peaks in an array of fiery crimson and majestic purples. The day had been spent avoiding the roads and skirting patrols in wide berths. The intersecting valleys had filled with patrolling teams of men, and, more than once, Ian had silently warned Jared of a nearby soldier he hadn't noticed.

They had been forced to move painfully slow, but as the day advanced, the patrols had become fewer, until many hours passed without them seeing or hearing any sign of them. Trusting that they had gone beyond the search's perimeter, they made camp in a low, sheltered spot. Ian, finding an abundance of dry wood, had set a small fire. He was now fanning the dry kindling into flame.

The air was rapidly cooling with the coming dusk. Jared filled a small pot from his pack in the stream and carried it to the fire. Ian produced a woven pouch and emptied its dried contents into the water, setting it in the flames. As the broth warmed, he threw in an assortment of fresh herbs that he had gathered. Before long, a rich, pleasant aroma began to rise from the pot, wafting out on the night air.

'What are you making, Ian?' Jared asked, curious. They hadn't stopped to eat since before Faith and Ian had fallen from the gorge, and Jared's appetite was awake and keen.

'I do not know what it would be called in your tongue,' Ian said thoughtfully. 'But in Caelum we call this medela. It has been eaten there for many years.'

As it simmered, Ian kept Jared entertained with various histories and legends of his homeland. When it was ready, Ian passed him a steaming bowlful. Tasting it, Jared found that it was a hearty, deliciously seasoned stew, with broth and spices that both warmed and comforted.

'I'd love to see your country one day, Ian,' Jared told him.

Ian's eyes brightened as he spoke. 'There is truly no place like it,' he told him, 'and no words outside of the Caelum tongue can do it justice.'

'Do you miss it?'

'Yes,' he said, 'but, more than the kingdom, I miss the King. He fills all those privileged enough to stand in his presence with life and purpose.'

Jared nodded. He recognized the deep love for his King that Ian shared with his countrymen. It made Jared's own desire to see the King sharpen inside of him. The men were silent for a few moments in thought.

Ian glanced up and froze, his eyes fixed intently on something beyond the firelight.

Jared followed his gaze and then started; there was a man standing nearby, leisurely watching them on the shadowy edge of the trees. Jared caught a glimpse of a long sword at the man's side, gleaming in the shadows. He sprang to his feet and instantly drew his sidearm, fixing it on the stranger. No one moved.

After a moment, the man gently raised a hand in a disarming manner and spoke just one word. 'Jared.' His voice was calm, and he spoke with quiet authority.

Jared hesitated. He was conscious of a sense of great power in the stranger. At the same time, however, he was alive to a coexisting compassion in him. Suddenly flooded with peace as he beheld the man, Jared somehow knew that he was in the presence of an ally. He slowly lowered his weapon.

'If you're a friend, come and warm yourself by the fire and have a bite to eat,' Jared said to the man guardedly.

Ian had remained motionless and silent, but his bright eyes were glowing, and he never took his gaze from the man.

'Thank you,' the man said, moving into the firelight, 'it's good to finally get a chance to meet you.' He approached and offered his hand to Jared. 'You can call me Liam.'

Jared took his hand with caution.

'I've heard much about you from a friend,' Liam continued, and then glancing down at the fire with interest, he turned to Ian. 'Is that medela I smell?'

Ian rose to his feet and grinned, stealing a glance at Jared. 'Yes, my lord. Help yourself.'

Liam extended his hand to the Caelum fighter, and they grasped forearms warmly in Caelum fashion. 'It's good to see you, Ian and to hear you speak so of the King.'

Ian bowed low. 'It's a great pleasure to see you as well, my lord, High Commander,' he said with a beaming countenance. 'Even more so because it is unexpected.'

Liam grinned. 'It would be a shame to be too predictable.'

The commander sat down by the fire as he ate, and Ian and Jared settled in comfortably around him with second helpings. The night was clear, and the stars were crisp and bright. The thin, crescent moon had risen in her orbit.

Jared studied the commander as he ate. He had heard many legends and countless tales of Caelum's high commander throughout his life, but Jared had never imagined that he'd have the opportunity to meet him. He had the bearing of a nobleman and carried himself like one who had received extensive military training. Jared noted, however, that there was also an unassuming, casual quality to the young-looking prince. He was struck by the commander's keenly intelligent glance that seemed to miss nothing. He wore the striking blue uniform of Caelum, decorated with many honors. The crest emblazoned on his tunic was the symbol of Caelum: a river flowing between two trunks of a flourishing tree that joined together at the top to form a living arch.

Jared's eyes traveled to the sword strapped at Liam's side. It was a large broadsword, fashioned with masterful skill, beyond any handiwork that Jared had ever seen. *Iudicium.* The famous blade was well known in lore throughout Terra and Mare. Its amber scabbard glimmered in the firelight and seemed to throw back and multiply the light that glinted off its faceted surface. It was engraved with spellbinding, strange symbols amidst the flowing Caelum script.

Sitting there in the dancing light, to Jared, the commander looked as though he embodied the formidable cunning of a modern-day general, combined with the fierceness of an ancient warrior of legend. *If this is the kingdom's crown prince, then Caelum is indeed secure. The most glowing reports of him haven't come near the truth!* Jared marveled at the sight of him.

The commander had finished his meal and turned to look at Jared with piercing eyes. 'You have risked your life to help bring my people to safety,' he said, his eyes searching. 'Why?'

Jared looked at him, caught off guard, but after a pause, he answered, 'I had to do it. They were under attack, and I knew they couldn't make it on their own.'

The prince glanced at him. 'What about your oath to the West?' he asked.

Jared hesitated for a moment before continuing. 'It was an unusual situation. I'll just have to explain everything to my superiors when I report to them.'

The commander nodded silently in thought. After a long moment, he spoke again. 'And what of the oath you swore to Caelum's King?' he asked.

Jared's mouth went dry. The oath he had sworn with his whole heart as a boy still tugged at his conscience even now. For years, he had longed to serve Caelum but had no clue how to follow through on that promise in a tangible way. The country was a far-removed, distant realm.

'What about it?' Jared asked.

The commander held him in his piercing, intent gaze. 'Will you abandon your first allegiance and reject Caelum's summons now, when the battle is nigh?' he asked.

Jared swallowed. The commander pulled no punches. He could deceive himself no longer; Nathan had been right. The summons had finally come. He had been longing for it and dreading it at the same time.

'I cannot fulfill both oaths,' he told the commander, almost apologetically.

'No, you cannot,' Liam said simply, an intensity in his eyes.

Then Jared finally understood what the commander was asking of him. His heart was divided. He knew that he must choose once and for all where his allegiance lay. He felt a knot in the pit of his stomach.

He thought of the West's Emerald Woods and of his men. He thought of Caleb; they had been through much together. Then he thought of Stella. The West's government was directly responsible for the danger Stella was in. Jared was dedicated to Vespera, but as time went on, it seemed more like he was fighting for a tainted image rather than his beloved home. He thought of the times he'd watched his own government hurt the West's citizens in a thirst for wealth and control. The leaders were, even now, squeezing the lifeblood out of their own people to remain in power. He loved his people and wanted to protect them, but Jared knew Vespera was rotting from its head. It was impossible to protect his people from their own leaders.

His thoughts turned to Caelum's King. He was known for his integrity and his peace-loving heart, but he had no pity on those who betrayed him. Loyalty was Caelum's highest law, and rebellion was punishable by banishment and death.

Whatever choice Jared made, he knew there would be no going

back. It would be all or nothing. But, if he had the courage, fighting for Caelum would be the adventure of a lifetime. At that thought, his heart raced, and he felt a thrill shoot to his very core.

But would the King even want to accept him when he had already sworn fealty to another nation? The question caused Jared to suddenly understand himself, and for the first time, he realized just how deeply he longed to join with the forces of the kingdom. He believed the King of Caelum was worthy of his allegiance. For all Jared knew, this might be his only chance, and he didn't want to lose it. If he blew it, he knew he would regret it for the rest of his life. He made up his mind.

Looking boldly at Liam, he said, 'If the King will have me, I will honor my pledge to him, Commander.'

The prince nodded approvingly and stood. 'Then kneel, Jared Crux, and renew your oath.'

Drawing Iudicium from its scabbard, the commander took the blade and, turning it, set it tip-down before Jared. Then the starlit firmament above and the Caelum fighter standing watch nearby bore witness as Jared knelt before Caelum's high commander and repeated the words he had said so long ago as a boy—words he had never forgotten:

'I, Jared Crux, do pledge myself

and swear that I will be faithful

and bear true allegiance

to His Majesty, the King of Caelum,

my Liege Lord and Master

and to his heir, according to law,

defending them in service, obedience,

and true faith,

from this day forward

until my death.'

'So be it,' the commander affirmed as he sheathed the amber-toned blade. 'Rise now to mighty deeds, soldier of Caelum.'

As Jared stood, Ian approached and clasped his shoulder. 'Welcome to the fight, lad,' he said, a spark in his eyes.

Jared smirked. 'What have we been doing until now?'

'Oh, that was just a bit of inclement weather,' Ian told him, grinning. 'Welcome to the storm.'

Chapter 19

Preparing for Battle

S weet was the comradery of that evening. Jared observed in awe-filled delight how much Ian came to life with an unrestrained zeal in the presence of Caelum's prince. He hadn't yet recognized it, but the commander's subtle but unrelenting influence was already beginning to change him as well.

As the night deepened, Jared began to feel as though Liam was relating to him not as a commander with his subordinate but as a man with his close, trusted friend. He answered Jared's many questions with patience and opened up honestly to him about the next steps in the offensive. Liam gave Jared information that none but those with the highest security clearance would typically have access to.

'The enemy is in the midst of mobilizing their forces,' Liam told him. 'They are preparing for an assault on the surface—the likes of which has never been seen before.' His expression grew dark as he explained. 'Their plan involves gathering enough leaders of the surface to betray their own nations. In exchange, they've promised wealth and quarter for the traitors and their families. They are very close to achieving their objective. Now is the time for us to act,' the commander said with gravity. 'While the enemy is distracted, we will attack them in their own territory with speed and precision.'

Jared knit his brow at the thought. There was a time when an attack on Tenebrae would require a hundred thousand troops if there was to be any hope of success. But the commander was right. Their borders had become gradually less defended and laxly guarded as their leaders became sure, and even arrogant, in their impending victory. Jared considered the commander's plan. It could actually work. It might be possible to slip in undetected with a modest force if they were careful.

'What will we do in Tenebrae, my lord?' Jared asked, a feeling of excitement rising in his chest.

'We will cause the enemy to hemorrhage beyond repair,' the commander replied. 'The King has seen the great suffering of the souls in Tenebrae. He has commanded me to carry a message of hope to them, to bring to them the healing waters of Caelum, and to lay liberty before their feet.'

There was a gleam in the prince's bright eyes. 'The time has finally come to rescue the captives of Tenebrae.'

* * *

Early the next morning, they were joined by the commander's elite guard and preparations for the assault began to take shape. The following days were full of intense training and much labor for Jared. Liam's men were trained to a staggering level of skill and perfect obedience to his orders. With a sharp word, hand signal, or even a look, they discerned his directions and instantly responded to their leader each time without fail, as only the knights of Caelum could. Jared worked hard to learn and become familiar with the many signals the prince used to make his orders known.

They broke camp almost every morning and followed the commander wherever he led them. Most days they traveled a great distance, over the rocky terrain, before stopping to make camp once more. At night, the prince and his men conducted raids against the outlying enemy strongholds. Jared was tasked to guard the camp and supplies but would listen with great relish the next day while Ian recounted to him lively stories of their exploits.

One day during training, after many weeks had passed, Jared sparred with several other Caelum fighters as Liam watched. Afterward, he called Jared to himself and asked, 'How would you like to come with us tonight?'

Jared grinned. 'I thought you would never ask.'

'You'll need this then,' the commander told him, holding before him a sheathed sword. Jared, with admiration, took the burnished weapon in his hands and slowly drew it from the mouth of its scabbard. Unlike Iudicium, this blade was not bronze but, instead, a lustrous, silver-toned steel. The grip was remarkably well formed and sat comfortably in Jared's palm.

The prince nodded in approval. 'Now your training begins in earnest.'

From that evening forward, Jared joined them on the raids with Ian at his side. He learned much about surprise tactics and guerrilla warfare from watching and fighting alongside the commander. Jared's mind still reeled at the implications of what they were going to attempt. The commander and his men had been smuggling slaves out of Tenebrae for years, but this was something entirely different. They were going to attempt to free the entire population of slaves in the dark city. The sheer scale of it made his head spin.

It had been many days since Jared had begun to think of Liam as more than his commander; he had become his closest friend. His admiration for him and his men had grown as they worked and fought together side by side, and Jared had whole-heartedly thrown himself into learning any skills the commander or his men would teach him.

His mind remained anxious, however. Finally, finding an opportunity one night while they were sitting by the fire, Jared asked the commander the question that had laid heavily on him for weeks. 'My lord, do you know anything about the girl who was trapped in the chasm?'

'You're thinking of Stella of Tenebrae.'

'Yes, my lord,' Jared responded, his mind racing. *So, the commander knew about Stella.* He asked his next question hesitantly, fearing the answer. 'Is she still alive?'

'She is,' Liam replied.

Jared let out his breath, a tide of relief washing over him.

How many spies did the King have to gather such news across the realms? An uneasiness slowly rose inside of him as he wondered what the commander thought about Stella's involvement with the chasm.

The chasm dwellers were the sworn enemies of Caelum and had been for centuries. Stella's actions, even if coerced, might still be seen by Caelum's crown prince as traitorous.

'Is there anything we can do to help her?' Jared asked him carefully.

The commander glanced up at Jared with a knowing expression, as though reading a portion of his thoughts. 'You can stop worrying,' he reassured him. 'The King sent me to rescue her from the chasm dwellers several weeks ago. I took her to Caelum. She is greatly loved there. The entire Kingdom of Caelum rejoiced when I found Stella and brought her home.'

Jared breathed deeply once more, letting the news sink in. *Leave it to Stella to win the hearts of a kingdom*, he thought to himself and smiled fondly, shaking his head at the news. 'She's alright then,' he said aloud.

'Yes,' the commander nodded with a smile.

'I'm grateful to you,' Jared told him, leaning back, relief clearly written on his face.

The commander eyed him thoughtfully. After a moment, he gently spoke his name. 'Jared?'

'Yes, my lord?'

'How fully do you trust me?'

Jared looked at him. 'I trust you completely, with all I have, my lord. I meant it when I pledged my loyalty to you, and I won't fail you in that,' he assured him.

Liam nodded. 'And how much are you prepared to give up for Caelum?'

Jared paused, wondering at the commander's question, thinking his words through carefully before he spoke them. 'I have found meaning and purpose, beyond myself, fighting with you, Commander. I've given myself for this cause. There is nothing that I will withhold from you if you ask, my lord.'

The commander let Jared's words hang in the air for a moment before he responded. 'Even Stella of Tenebrae?'

Stella. Jared looked hard at the commander but said nothing. He was speechless. He had the strange sensation of fading out of a pleasant dream into a waking nightmare.

The commander was silent, watching the flames for a while in thought. Then, leaning forward on his arms, he held Jared in his serious, steadfast gaze. 'How much do you care for Stella?' the commander asked Jared with sudden earnestness.

'Very much, my lord,' he answered firmly. 'I would die for her.'

The commander nodded, understanding. 'So would I.'

Jared flinched and felt his throat tighten. So, this is what it came down to. Jared was ready to lay down his life for Stella if necessary, but this was something else. If he was hearing right, he was being asked to prove his loyalty by letting her go. How could he possibly do that? Jared thought about what the commander had just told him. The prince had rescued her. He had been able to find and protect Stella when Jared had been helpless to save her.

Jared could see enough to begrudgingly admit that the commander cared for her. He wondered how Stella felt about him. After a moment, however, he stopped and shook his head in shame. How could she say no to an offer from the Crown Prince of Caelum? Why would she? Jared could never compete with the life that Stella could have with the commander. Stella, no doubt, knew that the commander would be able to care for her and protect her much better than Jared, try as he might, ever could.

'Are you asking me to give her up?' Jared questioned, his voice edging on resentment.

'I'm asking you to entrust her to me,' Liam answered with gentleness.

'You ask more from me, Commander, than I know how to bear,' he said, broken.

Prince Liam looked at Jared with compassion. 'I understand that I'm asking you to let go of what you hold most dear for Caelum. Only one question remains: do you trust me, Jared Crux?' the commander asked once again, his eyes piercing Jared's heart.

Jared bowed his head. He had believed—he still believed that the prince was worthy of his trust. Liam's words reverberated in his thoughts. *She is greatly loved there. The entire Kingdom of Caelum rejoiced when I found Stella and brought her home.* Jared had pledged himself to serve Caelum; he must abide by the consequences.

He gradually felt his resolve harden. *So be it*, he decided grimly. If this is what the commander and Stella wanted, he wouldn't argue. He would entrust her to the Prince of Caelum—for Stella's sake and for the good of the Kingdom—even if he had to rip out his own heart to do it.

* * *

Pull over. Nathan blinked his eyes as the command pierced through his thoughts. He signaled immediately in response and pulled off the road into the parking lot along the old highway. His other errands would have to wait. He instantly recognized the voice and knew enough not to argue or delay. He pulled the passenger van he was driving into a nearby parking spot and waited. Several minutes went by but nothing happened.

Glancing left and right, he closely observed the few stores and restaurants around him but noticed nothing out of the ordinary. There was no one nearby. *Well, now what?* He began to question if he had heard the Duke of Esen correctly. He had been so sure.

After sitting for some time, he thought he would stretch his legs. As he got out, the door of the old diner in front of him swung opened. James walked out. Nathan started with surprise, but James just smiled and walked over.

'Well met, Nathan!' he said, shaking his hand warmly. 'I was just hearing how you have been busy in the service of the King.'

'James, my friend,' Nathan responded with a bewildered smile, 'in the Midlands, while I live and breathe. How . . .?'

James' only response to Nathan's surprised expression was to throw back his grey head and let out a big, booming laugh of pure joy.

The others, hearing the commotion, came out of the diner. When Stella saw Nathan, she laughed too. 'Couldn't miss out on the fun, I see,' she teased.

Nathan smiled and approached her. 'Lady Estellah! You're here too! This is quite the surprise. I didn't know that you knew James and the Way.'

'I didn't until today; it's actually quite a long story.'

'Unless you've got other plans, why don't you all come back to my place and tell me all about it?' Nathan offered.

Caleb narrowed his eyes as he stood at Stella's side. He didn't trust this Midlander. He seemed to have quite the knack of showing up unannounced at strange times, and Caleb didn't believe in coincidences. They did need help for Alex though, and at the moment, they didn't have a lot of options. They were now fugitives caught between countries in conflict. In this position, Caleb was wise enough to not spurn anyone who was offering them a hand.

'We appreciate the invitation, but what we could really use is a doctor,' Caleb told Nathan plainly with his usual pragmatism. 'Our friend was injured, and he's lost his sight.'

'I didn't realize the urgency,' Nathan said in surprise. He pondered for a moment before speaking. 'I think I know someone who can help. He's a friend of mine. I'll take you home and then fetch him to take a look at your friend—if you'd like.'

'We'll take any help you can give us,' Caleb told him. 'Thanks.'

'I was on my way to return this van before I was . . . stopped,' Nathan told them as he unlocked the doors to the twelve-seater. 'But I can do that later. I normally drive a small car, but my cousin asked to use it for a couple of days—so we switched.' He laughed. 'It's like the Master knows what we need even before we do.'

Chapter 20

The Slaves of Darkness

J ared watched silently for the high commander's signal. As he waited, he observed the dark slave towers jutting dramatically into the Tenebrae skyline, remembering his despair the first time he beheld them as a boy. The angular, ebony structures had held terror for him then. His eyes narrowed, thinking of the many lives that had been extinguished in those hideous, forsaken spires.

It was time to bring them down-—every last inch of the whole, accursed system. He gripped his weapon in anticipation. He was going to enjoy this. Suddenly, a beacon kindled in the guardroom of the edifice.

The signal!

The commander's unit had succeeded in infiltrating the first tower. Instantly, the awaiting men surged into action, sweeping towards the opening. The iron gates swung wide on their hinges as the men stealthily poured into the very heart of the enemy's vast domain.

The Tenebrae soldiers, caught by surprise, leapt up in confusion as the King's men rushed upon them in the vestibule. Jared charged, hurling himself at the nearest guard, silencing him quickly before he had time to raise the alarm.

Ian, seeing Jared in the crosshairs of another Tenebraean, plunged towards the man and cut him down before he could fire. Within minutes, the other Caelum fighters had subdued the rest of the guard, and silence fell thick in the antechamber. Regrouping, the King's men continued along the corridor, heading towards the detention wing. All was quiet. The fray had been short, and Jared had hope that they had avoided alerting the enemy to their presence.

The commander's team had neutralized and secured the prison quarter and were throwing the doors of the detention cells open by the time Jared and his men reached them. They worked together swiftly, sweeping floor by floor, freeing all the captives they could find in the deep recesses of that dark place. The slaves emerged from their prisons, gaunt and hollow-eyed, afraid to hope that freedom was in their grasp.

As they saw the prince, however, Jared could see a change come over them, and the realization of what was happening spread over their features with rapid force. 'Oan . . . Oan has come,' they whispered to each other, using the name of the freedom-bringer in the lore of Tenebrae.

Another floor was cleared, and the commander sent Jared's company ahead to the level below. They quickly obeyed. Jared was busy opening cells on the lower level when Ian put his hand on his shoulder, signaling for silence. Jared froze and glanced at him questioningly.

Suddenly he felt the hair on the back of his neck rise. *What was it?* He broke out in a sweat as fear took hold of him. He saw nothing in the light, but he felt the presence of something deeply menacing in the shadows beyond. Something was coming.

Ian silently holstered his guns and drew his sword, holding himself in a ready stance, facing the darkness. Out of the corner of his eye, Jared saw the other Caelum fighters do the same. Then, around the bend ahead of them, Jared saw a soft, green glow in the darkness.

Its intensity slowly grew, and then Jared heard it—a sinister echo of deep, gurgling laughter. The enemy was laughing at them, mocking them. Their dark, threatening voices filled his mind. Then he saw them. Twisted shapes of glowing shadows drew near and filled the corridor. There were many. *What were they?* Then Jared remembered Rafiya's labored words about grotesque creatures as she lay dying next to the Tenebrae mirror; he had no doubt that the same creatures now approached.

The freed slaves around him collapsed to the floor, stopping their ears and whimpering in tormented fear. Those still in their cells cowered in terror. The enemy had come.

Jared stood rooted, paralyzed with dread, but Ian and the fighters advanced, bright swords in hand, seemingly untouched by the foul voices of the enemy.

At their approach, the shadowy figures laughed at them, spewing curses and drawing forth their own gruesome weapons.

'Flee now, accursed servants of Odhrán,' warned Ian sternly, 'or the abyss awaits you.'

His warning was met with harsh laughter. 'Perhaps it is you, Ian, and your pathetic troop that should flee before you are destroyed,' a dark shape retorted. 'You are out of your depth, Caelum Knight.'

He spat as he said the words, and the dark shape's menacing tone then changed to taunting. 'Or perhaps we will be merciful and take you captive. Under the master's hand, all are shaped into his powerful, new creations. None can resist him.' The creature laughed. 'You would be re-made into our image, old friend.'

Ian looked full on the creature and was undaunted. 'Save your breath, Scelus,' he told him. 'I do not fear you nor your devices. You know that you have only a short time before the King destroys you all.'

'Then I won't waste time or breath on fools,' Scelus snapped but then paused. After a moment, he continued in a more subdued tone, lacing his words with sudden benevolence, 'Though I would have *you* join with me, Ian. You are outnumbered, and I have not forgotten our kinship of old. Scarce did I think that I would remember our bond while you cast it aside. But so it is. Will you suffer to be proven so utterly faithless?'

Jared glanced nervously between Ian and the chasm dweller. There was apparently a history here that he knew nothing about, and he grew suddenly fearful that the offer from the dreadful creature might prove a temptation to the Caelum fighter.

Ian observed the shadowy form warily and stood valiant and unflinching. 'You have no resemblance to the ally I once knew, Scelus. Your words are devoid of truth and betray your self-deception,' Ian returned, shaking his head. 'You were once great, serving proudly before our King in his glory.' His voice hardened as he continued. 'Your accusations are more fit to be turned on your own head, chasm dweller—on your traitorous head and on the false-hearted hoard behind you for your treason to Caelum!'

At his words, the chasm dweller gnashed his teeth and lunged at Ian with the fierceness of a striking viper. The beings behind Scelus, salivating with eagerness to inflict pain on their enemies, leapt forward towards the King's men and engaged them in battle.

Jared looked back at the slaves who lay on the ground helpless before the enemy, senseless in their terror. He cried aloud to the Master for help and, wiping the sweat from his eyes, looked forward, towards the warring soldiers. Seeing his comrades fight, he swallowed hard and forced his fear down with an inner hand of iron. He drew out his gun and aimed at the nearest attacker. His hand shook as he pressed the trigger. His aim was good, but the bullet traveled through the chasm dweller's form as through wind and shadow.

Jared clenched his jaw. *Of course.* He had forgotten how useless his old weapons were against the true enemy.

Although the creature was untouched, Jared had succeeded in catching his attention. The chasm dweller's green eyes bent in his direction, and, filled with loathing, the shadowy being leapt towards him.

He dropped his firearm and drew forth the sword that the high commander had given him. *Move!* he commanded his wooden limbs and advanced. With each step, he felt less afraid, and when his blade met the scimitar of the twisted, shadowy form that came at him, Jared forgot his fear in his determination to hold back the enemy.

Across the passage, Ian had sprung back just in time, the curved sword of his attacker slicing the tunic of the Caelum knight. He responded with a sharp thrust of his blade, but the chasm dweller parried it, knocking it from his hands. Weaponless, Ian was nearly pierced by his adversary's next swing, but, twisting away, he dove to the side and rolled, reclaiming the blade where it laid some feet away. The creature lurched toward him. From the ground, Ian countered, striking up at the chasm dweller, slicing deeply across his right forearm.

The creature bellowed and recoiled, cursing with furious hate, and then he bore down hard and fast over the Caelum knight, slashing fiercely with the wickedly formed steel. It glanced off Ian's blade, forced wide. Ian's surging counterstroke came up with power, impaling the chasm dweller through his core. The maimed creature shrieked as he turned away and fled.

At the same time, Jared remained locked in fierce battle with his opponent—struck at again and again by the chasm dweller—but his training had not been wasted. He blocked the series of blows, deflecting the enemy each time, but the being was staggeringly strong and didn't seem to tire.

The chasm dweller thrust forward, knocking Jared back. As he stumbled, the creature rose above him threateningly, and their blades met with a high-pitched clash. Jared's sword was forced down hard toward his own head. He struggled with all his might to keep the blade aloft. The press of the chasm dweller increased, and Jared let out a labored groan as he strained against the force, his mind racing as he tried to remember the commander's training.

Ian turned and, seeing Jared's plight, abandoned the pursuit of his fleeing foe. He instinctively rushed towards him, but as he came, two mighty chasm dwellers blocked his path.

Jared ground his teeth and pushed against his assailant with newfound vigor, and though, for a moment, it seemed as if the chasm dweller might waver, the enemy doubled down. Jared, in dismay, felt the creature's immense power increase once more, and his arms began to give way. His own double-edged blade pushed towards him and came to rest against his face menacingly, piercing his skin in a thin line.

At that moment, the shrill ring of unsheathing bronze brought the chasm dweller's gaze up from Jared, and a look of pure terror registered in the enemy's serpentine eyes. There was a flash like branched lightening as Iudicium flamed brightly across Jared's vision. The chasm dweller's head was swept away from him in one smooth motion. The greenish glow of the creature's twisted body faded and went dark as it slumped to the corridor's floor.

Jared looked up. The commander stood above him, his eyes ablaze with hot fury, wielding the forged bronze as a flaming brand before his scattering foes.

Confronted with the unbridled wrath of the high commander, a howl of terror arose from among the ranks of the chasm dwellers— none could contend against him. Abandoning their assault, they turned and scattered like vermin into the darkness, away from their enemies.

The battle was now decided. By the time the council was roused to the threat within the city walls, the commander had a firm grasp of control on both towers, and the opposing troops had fallen into chaos. The Tenebraean defense that assembled was quickly dispatched by the commander's men, and the rest were helpless and overwhelmed by the sheer number of the escaped slaves. Those who remained in the streets, trying to restore obedience by force, were targeted by the now massive crowd or trampled. Most accepted defeat and silently slunk away.

'Burn them down,' Liam ordered his men, nodding to the now emptied slave towers jutting high into the blackness. He shouted another command to the rest of the force, and they sped across the city towards the university.

The troops found the gates abandoned. The Tenebrae guards had fled at the rumor of the coming of Oan. Forcing the doors wide, they steered towards the science wing and plunged into the depths of the building.

Jared soon recognized the curving halls before him. He had been here before; it was the place where he had rescued Stella. With urgency, Jared went to work, joining the other soldiers in breaking open the cells. He hastily threw open each door, one at a time.

As he breached the locks, the Caelum fighters poured past him into each cell. They emerged with many bound slaves and quickly began removing their chains. Two of the newly freed girls, recognizing each other, ran and clung to one another with tears. After several minutes, while Jared continued in his labor, he saw them approach out of the corner of his eye.

'Sir,' the older girl said to him, 'our youngest sister is locked in an inner chamber. Can you please get her out?' Pools filled her eyes as she pleaded, 'Please, sir, she needs help.'

'Do you know where the chamber is?' he asked.

'Yes, I think so. It's not far,' the girl told him.

Jared glanced at Ian. He responded with a nod, and they followed the girls into a nearby cell. Several other fighters fell in close behind. As Jared entered, he glanced around cautiously. The room was empty. The eldest girl crossed the room, going directly to a panel that hung along the far wall. She took hold of it and slid it over, exposing a concealed door behind the panel. Jared advanced to examine it. The door was covered in rust and secured with a shackle lock that hung on a thick, metal hasp. Jared broke the lock.

The Caelum fighters, standing ready, swept into the hidden room as soon as Jared swung the cell door open. When they emerged, Jared was stung by the sight. They carried a little girl, her young body severely withered and noticeably deformed even in the dimness. Whether from pain or fear, or some other cause, the girl shook violently as the soldiers brought her forth into the main corridor and set her gently down before the commander. Her two sisters, seeing the prince, immediately fell down before him, tearfully begging him to help their little sister.

Liam observed the broken mind and body of the small child, and compassion was in his eyes. He knelt and touched the girl gently; her trembling immediately ceased. Then resting his hands on the girl's legs, he spoke to her, 'Little girl,' he said, 'look at me.'

The girl lifted her face to Prince Liam, and as she looked, hope was kindled in the dark well of her soul. He spoke again in a low, gentle tone, 'The King has seen your suffering and has sent me to help you.'

'The King? He wants to help me?' the young girl's quavering voice asked in disbelief. Her eyes streamed at his words and wet her wasted cheeks. 'Why?'

'Because, child,' the prince told her, in a voice brimming with kindness, 'the King cares about you. He loves you. And he has sent me to set you free.'

A look of determination mounted in his keen eye, and, standing once again, he leaned toward her. 'Get up,' he said with authority, taking her by the hand.

Jared watched in wonder as the girl immediately obeyed. She stretched out her deformed and shriveled legs before her, and as she rose, they were immediately straightened and made whole beneath her. Jared stood dumbstruck, unable to grasp what he was seeing.

The girl's face reflected his own astonishment. She moved clumsily, like one who, though having the strength to walk, had not yet mastered the skill. She began to laugh—a welled-up, giddy, and joy-filled laugh—and the tear-streaked faces of her sisters joined in, their anguish melting into euphoric joy alongside her.

How is this possible? Where is this power coming from? Jared marveled, perplexed. For years, he had heard that the legends written in the Codex spoke of such acts—impossible acts—but, until now, Jared had never had the courage to fully believe them. He could scarcely fathom the far-reaching implications of what this could mean.

'We need to keep moving, Jared,' Ian spoke, coming up beside him. 'There are many more cells.' Observing his stunned expression, Ian continued with a smile, 'Truly, are you surprised? Did I not say rightly how little you understood of the power of Caelum?'

In amazement, Jared wordlessly followed behind Ian to the next door. His many, burning questions would have to wait. Ian was right; there was much work still to do.

As the night progressed, the fighters freed every slave therein: the King's men carrying out the injured and laying those with deep wounds at the commander's feet. Jared observed, with wonder, that none were found in the dark places that Liam could not heal; each was somehow made whole by the power of the prince.

After they had swept the premise to ensure every last one was freed from the accursed dungeon, the high commander gave the order for the university, along with all of its surrounding auxiliary buildings, to be razed.

The men speedily obeyed, lighting the inside furnishings on fire.

Then they stacked wood, refuse, and anything else that would ignite against the exterior, dousing it with fuel and setting the piles ablaze. Fire licked at the walls until they kindled and caught. Soon many long tongues of flame completely engulfed the buildings.

Turning their eyes, the King's men could see that behind them, beyond the market, the Tenebrae slave towers were also alight. The engulfing flames darted high and soared up against the dark cavern roof; they could be seen from the most distant corners of the city.

The people gave up a wild shout of victory at the sight of the imposing towers burning like colossal torches in the dark. They watched as the buildings were consumed before them. The captives joyfully claimed the gift of freedom granted to them. Wave upon wave of slaves joined the sea of freed people. They ecstatically celebrated their regained sovereignty, understanding now that they had become a powerful tide that could no longer be restrained by any domineering power.

Many songs of thankfulness rose in the streets, and as the blended voices of a multitude singing together mounted up, the ancient melody of the legend of Oan could now be heard:

For captives Oan sped to free
The lost ones from despair
Realm of death, he slaughtered fear
His deadly blade beware!

Son of battle, bright as dawn
Will of hardened steel
Perish the dark of haunted one
But Oan will surely heal!

Rising, Oan slayed the night
Will of steel prevailed
Reign in power prince of light
Evermore be hailed!

Watching the crowds pressed together in the thronged streets, Jared grinned at Ian in awe. The high commander had done it. They were all free.

'If only Stella was here to see this,' Jared shook his head wistfully.

'She would be pleased,' Ian agreed, leaning against a concrete pillar on the edge of the city square. After a pause, he continued, 'I've been told that you met Lady Estellah in Tenebrae.'

'Only a stone's throw from here,' Jared said and pointed to their left, 'on a bridge not far in that direction. It was five years ago.'

Thinking about Stella made his heart ache. He couldn't forget the commander's words regarding her; they still echoed in his ears.

He glanced at Ian, contemplating. Ian had known Prince Liam for many years, and Jared was aware that he had seen Stella and the commander together in Caelum. It was time Jared learned the whole truth. If Stella had chosen the prince, then so be it. He might as well know at once.

'Ian,' Jared said to him, 'I wonder if you can help me with something.'

'Anything for the King's glory, Jared,' Ian answered in his pleasant, lilting tone. 'Just name it.'

'There's something I'd like to know.'

'Now I'm curious,' Ian returned with a smile. 'What is it?'

'When you saw Stella in Caelum,' Jared said, taking a deep breath, 'how did she seem towards the commander?'

'She was comfortable in his presence and seemed to trust him,' said Ian, shooting him a surprised glance. 'Why do you ask?'

'Did she seem to care for him?' he asked pointedly.

'Yes, deeply. I believe she cares for him a great deal,' he answered honestly.

Jared's heart sunk at Ian's candid reply. He was silent for quite some time.

Ian observed Jared thoughtfully, arching an eyebrow. After a few minutes, he spoke, 'I think, perhaps, you may not have the complete picture, Jared.'

'Oh? What am I missing?'

'Well, for a start, her father,' Ian responded.

Jared blinked. 'Stella has a father?' he asked in disbelief. 'Where is he?'

'In Caelum,' Ian answered calmly.

'He lives in Caelum?' he asked bewildered. 'Who is he?'

Ian nodded and gave Jared a piercing look before replying. 'The King.'

Jared's mind worked in confusion. 'What are you saying, Ian? Is this a bad joke?' he demanded when he could finally speak.

'Jared, trust me, I would not joke about this. In truth, the King of Caelum is Stella's father. Lady Estellah is a royal princess of Caelum.'

Jared sat, stunned. Stella was the King's daughter? Impossible! He shook his head incredulously. She would have told him long ago if that was true.

After a moment of reflection, however, Jared hesitated. Stella remembered so little about her own past. If it was true, it was possible that she hadn't even known it herself. If that was the case, he wondered, why hadn't the commander said anything to him?

He thought back to what Prince Liam had said, and their conversation suddenly took on a new light. Jared inhaled a sharp breath as the revelation hit him. He was the greatest fool who ever lived! He had allowed his insecurity and jealousy to completely color his perception of what Liam had said. *The commander's deep concern for Stella makes perfect sense—through the lens of a brother!*

He remembered well everything that the commander had said, and Jared sighed heavily as it all became clear to him. Of course, any relationship between Jared and Stella would be impossible. If Stella, no—if *Lady Estellah* was truly the daughter of the King of Caelum, a princess in her own right, then she would be expected to marry within her own sphere one day, perhaps a great nobleman of Caelum or some other royal foreigner. Jared felt a deep pang at the thought.

There had been a time, not so long ago, when he was sure that he would spend his life with her. But that was before everything had drastically changed. He let out a slow breath.

Now, finally, he was beginning to understand why Liam had

asked, for the sake of Caelum, that he be willing to give her up. Estellah was not just nobility—she was royalty in one of the most powerful houses in all the realms—and Jared was just a common soldier. She was as far out of his reach now as she would have been if she were actually betrothed.

Ian interrupted his thoughts, 'The lady Estellah doesn't know any of this, Jared. Apparently, they did something in Tenebrae to erase her memory.'

'I thought as much. She couldn't remember her childhood— nothing before she was about thirteen.'

Ian continued, 'The King has chosen not to reveal all to her yet, not until she's ready. I believe they are concerned that the enemy may still have some kind of influence over her.'

Jared nodded. The King could be right. It seemed like the enemy had targeted Stella from the start, and the puzzle of why appeared to be coming together. He had seen what the enemy was capable of doing to her.

He silently pleaded with the Master to keep Stella free and safe from ever falling into the enemy's cruel grasp again.

* * *

The chancellor was late, uncharacteristically so. The councilmembers assembled in the council chambers and were waiting uneasily for their leader when the urgent dispatch came.

Our enemies are still advancing. The damage is catastrophic.

Councilman Nex, the most senior official next to the chancellor, angrily crushed the note in his fist and dropped it on the table before the council. Ruthlessness was the beginning and end of Councilman Nex's character; he was a man lacking all restraints of conscience. Morality, pity, love—to him, these were the vices of the weak. The sale of them had long ago purchased his wealth and greatness. His only creed was power, but the heart of that very power—the supreme authority of the council of Tenebrae—was now under siege.

'This High Commander of Caelum has been wreaking havoc on

our forces for weeks, and none have been effective in stopping him. The chancellor will not be pleased at this news,' Nex growled threateningly as the council shifted uncomfortably in their seats.

Councilman Malin, a regal-looking, grey-headed man, reached over, taking up the note. He had seen much during his long years of service to Tenebrae, but nothing came close to the threat that now faced them. He read it silently and then handed it to Councilman Jolon beside him. Grim set faces glanced at one another as the dispatch made its way around the table.

'Somehow their leader was able to move his men in and out of the tunnels of Tenebrae with the ease of mere shadows,' Councilman Jolon said in consternation. 'How? Could some of our men have been bought off?'

'The Caelum commander is as powerful and crafty as a fox, but there is something more going on here,' Councilman Malin agreed.

Nex stood, weighing the words of the councilmen. There was only one in the realms who had ever come close to besting them. *The Seer.* He narrowed his eyes and looked at the men seated before him, considering the possibility. It had been many years since any word had been heard of him, and according to their best intelligence, he was still away, journeying afar. But now the councilman wondered if he may have finally returned.

'There is one who could be helping the commander,' Nex said to the council. 'The one they call the Duke of Esen.'

A murmur rose in the council chambers and several councilmembers cursed under their breath.

'Regardless of who's helping him, things started to unravel when the girl was taken,' the councilman named Effroi spoke in exasperation. He was the newest and youngest of the council; fervent and idealistic still in his duties, he held firmly to the tenets of the ancient religion of their order and all that its dark nature demanded.

'We were so close to achieving our great objective,' Councilman Effroi reminded them. 'Now, the rebellion among the slaves has surged in the heart of the city, and despite our best efforts, it will not be squelched. Acting on the advice of Councilman Nex, our forces have gassed them, beat them, and starved them, but still the slaves are refusing to fall in line. There's too many of them. The call of "liberté" is heard throughout the streets, day and night, in every quarter of the city,' he said gravely. 'There is only one thing that can be done at this juncture. The gods must be appeased if we are to have any hope of success.'

The council buzzed once more with anxious discussion.

'That whole quarter of the city, as Effroi says, is now lost to us,' Councilman Malin concurred. 'The enemy's words and dangerous ideology have somehow even managed to infiltrate the ranks of some of the great houses, spreading like a virus throughout the whole city. Many are defecting. The knowledge of what is happening can't be contained much longer. People are asking too many questions and aren't believing our account of events any longer. They're seeing too many discrepancies with their own eyes.' He nodded towards the young councilman. 'An offering to appease the gods, as Effroi suggests, would shore up our authority and garner support from the great houses.'

'Perhaps, but it's not just the great houses and rebelling slave district that we must contend with,' Councilman Jolon interjected, continuing in the general feeling of gloom. 'We have many fronts. Vespera's General has sent disquieting news. Masses of escaped Tenebraean slaves have somehow made it to the surface and are being harbored by the group known as the Way. They have begun a campaign spreading the idea that the King of Caelum is the rightful ruler of Terra and Mare.

'Revolts and disobedience to the surface ruling system are rapidly spreading also. The authorities have employed similar tactics to quiet the rebels, but it has only seemed to add fuel to the fire. Where one is beaten and arrested, one hundred seem to spring up in their place, all spreading the treasonous idea of rejecting the surface government's supreme authority and pledging allegiance to the King of Caelum.'

'There has to be some way to turn the tide in our favor,' Councilman Nex said finally. 'The Caelum commander must be overcome.'

'Yes, but the question is how?' Councilman Malin added.

'By exploiting his weakness, gentlemen,' Chancellor Tallis suddenly interjected as he entered the room. Crossing it, he claimed his place at the table's center.

All those present bowed at his entrance. The eyes of the room turned inquiringly to the head of the council, the men noting that he looked pleased—indeed, almost jovial.

'You have new information, Chancellor?' Councilman Jolon asked, hopeful.

The head of the council laughed. 'More than that, Jolon! We have a plan. I have had news that will change the tide. While you have been wringing your hands like old women, I was in a meeting of upmost importance. But I see that hasn't stopped you from proceeding without me,' he said, eyeing his council. 'And what have my faithful councilors been discussing in my absence?' he inquired darkly.

'We were considering the wisdom of an appeasement offering, Chancellor,' Councilman Malin told him.

The chancellor turned to him. 'And who have you chosen?'

'No one, Chancellor. We would not discuss such a thing without your presence.'

The storm cloud seemed to pass at Malin's tactful words. Their leader surveyed them, and a strange eagerness set his gaze aflame.

'That is well, since an offering has already been selected.'

The men murmured in surprise.

He turned to Councilman Jolon. 'Tell me, Councilman, do we know the whereabouts of the escaped chasm jumper—the girl?'

'Yes, Chancellor,' he answered. 'She is reportedly on the surface—in the Midlands—being aided by military rebels and the insurgents that call themselves the Way.'

Chancellor Tallis nodded and turned to face the whole council. 'The enemy commander obviously cares for the girl. He sought her out and risked himself to rescue her,' he paused, his lip curling. 'She will be his undoing.'

'The girl would make an appropriate offering, Chancellor,' Councilman Effroi agreed.

The Chancellor turned his gaze to his youngest councilman. He knew well the young man's religious fervor. 'Yes, she would, Effroi,' he smiled knowingly. 'Your job will be to begin preparations in the ceremonial cavern immediately, *as if* we will offer up the girl.'

'As if? I don't understand, Chancellor. Will there be no appeasement, then?'

'The gods shall have their blood offering,' the head of the council told him, relishing the thought, 'but not the girl. She is nothing. She is only a means to a bigger prize.'

'I'm sorry, Chancellor, but I'm not following,' Councilman Malin interjected. 'If the girl is not to be offered, then what is the plan?'

The Chancellor turned to his council. 'It's simply this: the gods will be appeased with none other than the blood of the enemy commander himself. He will be our offering.'

The room exploded in exclamations. It took many minutes before the chancellor was able to quiet them.

'You know that I would love nothing more than to see his downfall, but you push too far, Chancellor! We cannot contend against the prince in battle, yet you want to somehow capture and kill him?' Councilman Nex questioned.

'The ancient writings all agree that he cannot be killed with any of the weapons that we can craft,' Effroi added.

Several others nodded in agreement.

'You are right, of course,' the head of the council said, gazing slowly around the table. 'We cannot kill him. Neither can our allies in the chasm form any weapon that will prosper against the King or his son.'

He paused, deep in thought, his eyes growing as black as night. Then slowly the corner of his mouth began to rise. 'But the King in his pride and folly has crafted the weapon for us. By the gods, I was blind not to see it before. Meant for the destruction of the great Leviathan, whom we serve, the sword, Iudicium, is a blade of terrible power—potent enough that it can pierce the King himself. Indeed, it is the only weapon powerful enough to do so. The King has unwittingly created the device on which he and his kingdom will fall. Whosoever takes and wields it, rules the realms without rival.'

'Perhaps, Chancellor, but the blade of bronze rests fully in the control of the enemy prince,' Councilman Malin reminded him. 'How can you possibly hope to claim it for your own?'

The chancellor smiled, his tight grin filled with malice. 'My delay to our council today was due to receiving a gift of unexpected and satisfying intelligence, Councilmen. I find that we have the most unlikely of allies. Erelong, the blade of Caelum will rest in my hands,' he said, his eyes gleaming in the shadows.

'But first, the girl must be captured and brought back to Tenebrae and contact with the chasm reestablished. And then the commander will play right into Tenebrae's hands. He will certainly attempt a rescue. And we will be waiting for him, ready to relieve him of his burden,' he said, a look of malicious hate darkening his aspect as he spoke.

'The accursed prince will be brought to his knees at last.'

**** *   ** ***   **** *   *** * * ***

This concludes the first installment of

The Assorted Archives and Histories of the Kingdom of Caelum

Compiled by Able S. Crux

**** *   ** ***   **** *   *** * * ***

*** **** *   ** ***   **** ** ***

Please look for his next chronicle

Leviathan Rises

June 2024

*** **** *   ** ***   **** ** ***

Made in the USA
Middletown, DE
26 June 2023

33743160R00136